Critical acclaim for

"Ludlumesque ... Talanov is a wonderful character!"
The Dallas Morning News

"Don't start this book in an airport. You'll miss your plane."
Samela Harris, News Ltd.

"Turner is King of the Cliffhanger."
Glenda Shaw, two-time Emmy Award nominee

"I love a great villain. Great villains demand great heroes and this book has both."
Adoni Maropis, AKA Abu Fayed, from the hit TV series, 24

"Jason Bourne meets The DaVinci Code meets Tom Clancy."
LAs the Place magazine

"Masterful."
Jessica Chapnik, Who Magazine (Time Inc)

"One of those searing cliffhanger books that simply defy you to put the thing down."
The Advertiser

"Turner's story-telling grabs the reader and never lets go."
Norm Goldman, BookPleasures

"Unputdownable!"
Peter Goers, The Sunday Mail

"Talanov: dark, sexy hero for the new millennium."
National bestselling author, Jordan Dane

"Talanov will be for James Houston Turner what Alex Cross has become for James Patterson."
Liz Terek, Charisma Media Network

Superb!"
San Francisco Book Review

James Houston Turner is the bestselling author of the Aleksandr Talanov thriller series, as well as numerous other books and articles. Talanov the fictional character was inspired by the actual KGB agent who leaked word out of Moscow back in the 1980s that James was on a KGB watchlist for his smuggling activities behind the old Iron Curtain. James Houston Turner's debut thriller, *Department Thirteen,* was voted the Best Thriller of 2011 by USA Book News, after which it won gold medals in the 2012 Independent Publisher ("IPPY") Book Awards and the Next Generation Indie Book Awards. A cancer survivor and former journalist in Los Angeles, he holds a Bachelor's Degree from Baker University and a Master's Degree from the University of Houston (Clear Lake). After living in South Australia for nearly twenty years, he and his wife, Wendy, a former triathlon winner, now live in Austin, Texas. Visit his website at www.talanov.info.

BY JAMES HOUSTON TURNER

FICTION

The Search for the Sword of St Peter
The Identity Factor
Department Thirteen
Greco's Game
November Echo
Dragon Head (2014)

NON-FICTION

The Spud Book
The Earth of Your Soul

JAMES HOUSTON TURNER

NOVEMBER ECHO

AN ALEKSANDR TALANOV NOVEL

REGIS

Published by Regis Books
Copyright © James Houston Turner 2013

First Edition

For more information about the author or Aleksandr Talanov, visit www.talanov.info.

To follow James, visit his Official Facebook page.

Aleksandr Talanov website design by Bogumil Widla

November Echo cover art by Frauke Spanuth of Croco Designs www.crocodesigns.com

Editing by Abigail Ortlieb

Proofreading by Wendy Turner

ISBN: 978-0958666428 (eBook)
ISBN: 978-0958666435 (paperback)

ACKNOWLEDGMENTS

I owe this book to you. Now before the cheese alerts start going off, allow me to explain. It has been a challenging two years since my *Greco's Game* tour, which is when many of you began asking for more background stories on Talanov. *November Echo* is the first of many such stories. The fact that you cared enough to ask is why I credit this book to you. But that's not where the story ends.

I had barely begun writing *November Echo* when Wendy and I were hit by a devastating family loss. The grief was unbearable and I cannot articulate how much it impacted us. It impacts us still. I then suffered a near-fatal accident where my life passed quite literally in front of my eyes. The first such experience like that for me was when I was diagnosed with cancer back in 1991. At the time, I was not expected to live eighteen months. But I did. This time, I survived again. The outcome was a decision to move from Australia back to the United States. In regards to that, may I simply say it is easy to underestimate the toll an international move can take. I certainly did. But we made it and we are here, in the great city of Austin, Texas. Thank you for standing with us with your many emails, prayers, phone calls and words of support.

One person deserves special mention: Nola Stover Beck, a longtime friend from my old hometown of Baldwin, Kansas, who welcomed us to Austin by opening her home. Nola, you are a true legend and we will always look back on our time with you and McDuff as wonderfully special and unique.

I also want to thank Bruce Kilpatrick and John Blamey of Lennar Homes. You worked overtime making our dream house come true. Thank you for everything you did. A very special thanks also to real estate agents Fran Weller and Joe Moreno, for your friendship and guidance.

Talanov's online presence received a huge boost when Bogumil Widla redesigned our website. Thank you, Bogumil, for the technical artistry you provided at www.talanov.info.

Many of you have remarked about the *November Echo*

cover and bookmarks. They are the work of graphic genius, Frauke Spanuth, of Croco Designs. Thank you *so* much, Frauke, for the brilliant work you did.

All authors need editors. Editors see what authors don't (or don't *want* to) see, and I had a great one: the glittering Abigail Ortlieb. Abigail, I cannot thank you enough for the wonderful job you did.

I've also had the enthusiastic support of some incredible people who have helped me get to this point: LL Cool J; Tara Grace, Steve Coito, Walker Hanson; Mark and Sharon Minkes; photographer Bill Rich; Jon Whelan; Mick and George O'Rourke; Thomas Miles; Stephanie Drouet-Rogers; Michael Forke; national bestselling author, Jordan Dane, for your special friendship and all the great hours of shoptalk we've enjoyed; Nick Blair and the great folks at Jacob's Creek wine. You add class to any occasion; Wally Mariani and the wonderful flight crews at Qantas Airways. Several new Talanov storylines have been born in Qantas Business, and you have enabled me to undertake numerous tours and G'day USA trips from our former home in Adelaide to the United States. Thank you for your many years of support.

Writing is solitary but exhilarating work, and no one understands this better than my gorgeous, dark-haired Aussie wife, Wendy. She endures the highs and lows of being married to this idealistic, determined day-dreamer of a writer with her unique brand of spunky Aussie humor. We have done this together, my love. Each day with you is a gift.

In closing, I again want to thank the actual KGB agent who inspired the creation of Aleksandr Talanov. You know who you are and what you did, and for that I give you thanks.

In Memory Of

JASON SCOTT KENNETT

1975-2012

Set Against Actual Events

1972 -- The Biological Weapons Convention becomes the first multi-national treaty prohibiting the production and use of an entire category of weapons. The United States and Soviet Union are among the original twenty-two signatories of this treaty. In compliance, the United States destroys its military stockpiles. The Soviet Union claims to destroy its stockpiles but in fact responds by creating *Biopreparat,* the largest biological weapons program in history. Over the next few years, forty-seven top-secret installations are built across Russia.

1979 -- "Anthrax 836" spores are accidentally released from military Compound 19 in Sverdlovsk, USSR. Nearly one hundred people die within days although thousands are believed to have perished. Sverdlovsk and the surrounding area is quarantined by the Soviet military. Decontamination trucks arrive. Reports of the incident surface in the West, and the Soviet Union is accused of violating the Biological Weapons Convention. The Soviet Union vigorously denies the accusations by insisting the outbreak was caused by tainted meat. All medical records relevant to the incident are immediately destroyed.

1982 -- Spain joins NATO and announces plans to join the European Economic Community, resulting in violent demonstrations and protests.

1983 -- U.S. President Reagan announces plans for his Strategic Defense Initiative ("Star Wars") missile defense system in space. Pershing II missiles are deployed in West Germany. Korean Airliner KAL 007 is shot down by the Soviet Air Force; all crew and passengers are killed. The Soviet leadership is convinced that KAL 007 had been an American intelligence mission. Cold War tensions between the United States and Soviet Union escalate to an all-time high. The Balashikha sabotage and terrorism complex near Moscow is now in full operation.

1985 -- Thousands are now demonstrating across Spain against NATO and the American presence. Violence is everywhere. The Soviet Union's manufacture of biological weapons reaches peak production. Except for the suspicions of a few individuals, the West has no clue.

CHAPTER 1

The Mediterranean Sea was the original information super-highway. For centuries, rulers have plied its waters carrying information to the remote corners of their empires. Legends were born here, as well as heroes, and tonight one more would be added to that list.

The headlights of the black Ferrari stabbed the darkness in a hillside village outside of Marbella, Spain. Located among the palm trees fifty miles northeast of Gibraltar, Marbella is part of a region in Andalusia known as the Costa del Sol -- literally, "Coast of the Sun" -- built as it was on the southern coast of Spain overlooking the Mediterranean Sea's turquoise waters. The area, with its winding roads and scenic white-washed villages, was custom made for a car like the Ferrari.

Except this driver, Sofia Dubinina, was not enjoying the scenery. She was focused on other matters.

"I do not question whether or not you *can* kill Gorev," Sofia remarked, downshifting the Ferrari into third, "but whether or not you *will.*"

"Why would I want to kill Gorev?" asked Colonel Aleksandr Talanov. Sitting in the darkened passenger seat, he heard the familiar click of gears and felt the Ferrari lean into the turn.

"To stop his defection," Sofia replied.

Their headlights illuminated an old man crossing the street near a small plaza. Sofia double-tapped the horn -- sharp reports, like pistol rounds -- and the man jumped out of the way.

"There are other ways to stop a defection," Talanov replied.

"So you keep telling me. But I have yet to hear what they are."

"Patience, my dear. You will."

"What exactly does that mean? This is Sunday, Sasha, *Sunday.* The night Gorev arrives. We cannot allow him to escape."

"He won't."

"Then how do you plan on catching him?"

"Did you make the reservation?"

"You're avoiding my question."

"So are you."

Sofia responded with an exasperated sigh. "Yes, I made the reservation."

"Which name did you use?"

"The one you told me to use. But I still do not understand what we are doing. We are here to catch a defector and you have me booking a suite in the name of a ballerina."

"Anna Pavlova is not just a ballerina."

"Stop it, Sasha. What is going on? How do we plan to catch *Gorev?"*

Talanov smiled. "Patience, my dear."

The assignment given to them last Tuesday in the office of KGB Deputy Chairman Walter Kravenko had been simple and clear: slip quietly into Spain and intercept Dr. Yefim Gorev, a scientist from the Soviet Union's weaponized anthrax facility at Sverdlovsk, in the foothills of the Ural Mountains eight hundred miles east of Moscow. But slipping quietly into Spain was not what they were doing. They were doing the exact opposite. And therein lay the problem.

Which would not be a problem if he delivered the goods -- in this case, Gorev -- and which *would* be a problem if he did not.

Silencing Kravenko's advisors had not been easy. Their argument: that Gorev had disappeared with his family in Leningrad. It therefore made no sense for him to cross all of Europe in a risky flight to Spain. Helsinki was the logical choice. Or London. Or some northern European city where sanctuary was obtainable at any of the American Consulates or military bases.

Talanov's counter-argument had been a chain of solid but circumstantial evidence pointing to Spain. Back and forth they argued, with neither side giving an inch.

It was a stalemate: a twenty-eight-year-old KGB colonel against five old-school gray-haired conservatives in cheap suits and polyester ties. Having come up through the army together, the five advisors viewed everyone with disdain and suspicion, especially progressives like Talanov and Gorbachev. The result was a group of individuals as antiquated and unimaginative as the clothes they wore.

The single exception to this dour group was a young woman Talanov did not recognize. Dressed in a gray wool uniform with red trim, she was sitting in the corner of Kravenko's office, her alert eyes toward the floor, listening to every word. No more than twenty-one or two, she looked to be Chinese, at least partially, with long hair the color of coal that had been pulled back in a severe bun. And although she was seated, Talanov could tell she was tall, perhaps as tall as he and he stood six-foot-one.

"The preponderance of opinion is against you, Colonel," Kravenko said.

"Then where is he?" asked Talanov. "Where's Gorev? He's been gone for more than two days."

"We are closing in," an advisor replied. "We have agents all over Helsinki. Gorev will not -- he *cannot* -- escape."

"Really?" said Talanov. "And if he is already in London?"

"We have agents there, too."

"Who no doubt are also closing in on him there just as they are no doubt closing in on him in Oslo, Copenhagen, Rotterdam and Hamburg."

"Be careful, Colonel," warned Kravenko.

"My apologies, Comrade Deputy Chairman," said Talanov with a slight bow of submission. "But if you wish Dr. Gorev returned to his post, then you must send me to Spain."

The outcry was exactly what Talanov knew it would be. Jabbing at him with angry fingers, the advisors accused him of being inexperienced, shortsighted, arrogant and impertinent, calling his evidence for "a fanciful vacation in Spain" wasteful, unsubstantiated and flimsy. Kravenko's chief advisor, the gravelly Kozloff, took it one step further. He said Talanov's flirtation with the whore of Western capitalism not only assured the certainty of Gorev's escape by stealing valuable manpower and squandering resources, but opened the way for Talanov to continue lining his own privileged pockets at the expense of the Soviet working class.

When Kravenko's advisors saw Talanov looking on with amusement, they intensified their protest, assuring Kravenko that progress *was* being made, that teams of experienced agents were on the verge of a breakthrough, that several sightings of Gorev and his family had been made, that informants were being interrogated and apprehension was expected any moment.

The jowly Kravenko, who sat like a scowling basset hound in his squeaky wooden chair, steepled his fingers thoughtfully in front of his face while Talanov stood before him in a long black woolen coat.

"Colonel, do you have a response?"

"Indeed I do. The reason Gorev has not been found in northern Europe is because he is not there. It's as simple as that. Spain is where you will find him."

"Why should I believe you?" asked Kravenko.

"Because I deliver results. It's why I'm a colonel in the field and not an advisor in an office. As for the suggestion that I am lining my pockets, may I remind this distinguished group that I am paid entirely by the State and scrutinized in all aspects of my life by three departments within the KGB. As you and others know, Comrade Deputy Chairman, I own no foreign bank accounts like Comrade Kozloff does, nor do I own a dacha -- like Comrade Kozloff -- nor do I have a mistress to go with it. Nor do I drive a luxury French sedan -- like Comrade Kozloff -- nor do I accept bonuses from the Russian mafia and various arms dealers seeking import and export privileges at our borders . . . like Comrade Kozloff. I realize I may be inexperienced and shortsighted, but it seems to me the whore of Western capitalism has already found a new pimp."

Over a storm of outrage, Talanov's proposed trip to Spain was approved.

After Kozloff was hauled from the room by guards and the other advisors dismissed, the young Chinese woman was called forward and introduced simply as his new partner, Agent Sofia Dubinina. Talanov objected, saying he preferred to choose his own team, but Kravenko told him the matter had been decided and that he and Agent Dubinina were to slip quietly into Spain, find Gorev and bring him back.

"But Comrade Deputy Chairman---" Talanov began.

"That is all, Colonel," Kravenko replied, busying himself with paperwork.

Out in the hall, Talanov stared thoughtfully at his new partner. Who was Agent Dubinina? What skills would she bring to this mission? Why had he never heard of her? The assignment to locate and apprehend Gorev was a critical one, so Agent Dubinina was either a deep cover operative whose background and qualifications were beyond scrutiny, or she was a rookie-in-training with no background aside from her looks, which would be useful if it weren't for that awful hair and a uniform that resembled a horse blanket.

"I am not sure that I appreciate this kind of inappropriate scrutiny," Sofia remarked curtly.

"Do you dress that way by choice?"

"What is wrong with the way I dress?"

"Everything," he said, taking her by the arm. "But there's nothing we can do about that now." He led her along the battered oak hallway and down a flight of stairs. "So this is what I need you to do: call Aeroflot and book a flight to Barcelona. I'll meet you there on Thursday."

"We were told to slip quietly into Spain."

"And we will be, depending on your definition of 'quietly.'"

"This is no joking matter, Colonel. Kravenko gave us an order."

"And we are left to interpret that order."

Sofia lowered her voice to a harsh whisper. "You do not *interpret* orders from the Deputy Chairman of the KGB. You obey them."

They reached the ground floor, crossed the foyer and stepped out into the noise and exhaust of the traffic circling the large roundabout in front of the seven-story Lubyanka building, which occupied an entire block and dominated the square where the roundabout was located. Other office buildings and businesses, none as prominent, were set back, as if timidly avoiding close proximity to the notorious Stalinist prison that now served as headquarters for the KGB.

Talanov squinted up at the yellow brick facade rising behind them. "I've never liked this building," he said, citing the old joke of how Lubyanka was known as the tallest building in Moscow because Siberia could be seen from its basement. "It's stuffy, it's old and it's cramped."

"Like those who inhabit its corridors, is that what you are going to tell me?"

With a smile, Talanov motioned for them to keep walking.

"I have heard about you, Colonel," she said, "and your legendary ability to see what others do not. You operate in multiple dimensions, which I admire and appreciate, even though you often offend people by pushing boundaries and taking unnecessary risks. Thus far, you have gotten away with it, which no doubt explains your reputation for achieving the impossible. Even so, I will not risk compromising the success of this assignment by flying into Barcelona aboard a commercial aircraft. Comrade Kravenko told us to slip quietly into Spain and I will not disobey that command."

"'Quietly' is such an ambiguous word, is it not?' What is quiet to one may be noisy to another. Who's to say which is right? Can it not be both?"

"Play word games all you wish, Colonel. I will not do it."

"I could order you to do it."

"Then I would respectfully decline. I will not disobey Comrade Kravenko. I will not have him yanking us from this assignment."

With a sigh of surrender, Talanov nodded. "Okay," he said. "Understood."

Sofia smiled appreciatively. "Thank you, Colonel. I meant no disrespect."

"None taken. I will inform the Deputy Chairman that you have chosen to remain behind."

Sofia grabbed Talanov by the arm and stepped in front of him. "But I am *not* choosing to remain behind. I insist only that we follow his orders."

"And it's up to me to decide how those orders are carried out."

"Kravenko's commands are not open to debate."

"Then quit arguing with me."

"I am sorry, Colonel. I will not do it."

Talanov grabbed Sofia by the elbow and led her around the corner, where he backed her against the rough gray stone of the Lubyanka building.

"Ow, you're hurting me!" she said as the jagged stones dug into her back.

Talanov got right in her face. "You may not like my methods, Agent Dubinina, and you may not even like me. Kravenko probably doesn't and I know his advisors don't. But let's get one thing clear. I'm not going to Spain because everybody likes me. I'm going to Spain because the Soviet Union has a problem and Kravenko needs me to solve that problem. So either you get on that airplane like I asked or it will be safer for you here at home."

"Safer for me here at home? What exactly do you mean?"

"Just what I said."

Sofia pushed Talanov back. "Spell it out for me, Colonel. I want to verify whether or not I'm hearing what I think I'm hearing."

"Fine," he said, "I'll spell it out. In the military, you've got the backs of your buddies and your buddies have yours. But on rare occasions, someone gets assigned to the unit who's lazy or afraid or doesn't want to do what they're told. And if they don't change -- and I mean fast -- they get shot. Whether it's an accident or because they stick their head up at the wrong moment and an enemy sharpshooter takes them out, they get shot and they get sent home, usually alive but sometimes dead, and nobody really minds because to have someone like that around jeopardizes the entire team."

"Are you threatening me?" she asked.

"You can't have it both ways, Agent Dubinina. So you'd better choose right here and now whether or not you're on my team. Because if you're not, you'll get shot. Take that however you like."

Stepping back, Talanov watched Sofia's eyes flash. She was both offended and furious. And yet as she looked away, he could see a mixture of emotion -- including fear -- crisscrossing her mind. He knew what she was feeling because he'd been there himself. Everyone gets told the same thing sooner or later.

He saw her run a hand across her mouth. Saw her take a deep breath. Saw her deliberating about what to do and whose orders to follow. Was it a threat? Did he mean it? *Was he right?* Even if he was, did she want to be partnered with such a man? Would she be safe? Should she report him?

The sudden exhale indicated she'd made her decision. She bit her lip and looked nervously around before turning to face him. "Do you realize what you're asking me to *do?"*

Talanov glanced toward the sound of grinding gears as a diesel truck sputtered past belching soot into the air. He saw the driver sitting behind the wheel, elbow out the window, cigarette dangling from his mouth while laughing at a remark made by his partner.

Looking back at Sofia, he said, "You want to catch a rat, you need to think like a rat and go where he goes but get there ahead of him. The old cats upstairs don't know how to do that. They've been in the house too long. They give their advice and meow when they're told and when everything falls to shit they blame it on somebody else. That's why I do things my way. I'm an alley cat. No one likes alley cats but alley cats know how to get the job done when it comes to rats."

"What if Gorev is not where you think? What if you're mistaken?"

"He will be. And I'm not."

"How do you know that, Colonel?"

"Because alley cats eat rats for breakfast."

Growling her frustration, Sofia stormed away a few steps before abruptly spinning around and storming back. "Do you know how insanely arrogant and *stupid* that sounds? You are asking me to risk everything on some wild metaphor about alley cats and rats -- which is *crazy* -- but even if you *are* right -- why alert him and everyone who is helping him -- in other words, the Americans -- by flying into Barcelona aboard a commercial aircraft? The only *possible* explanation is that we will be assuming different names. Is that what we will be doing?"

"No false documents. We travel as ourselves."

"Then you *are* crazy! Forget the problem of us getting visas at the very last minute, how can you *possibly* think traveling openly aboard a commercial aircraft qualifies as slipping quietly into Spain? Never mind any red flags associated with my name, you're a KGB colonel who's listed in every intelligence database on the face of the *planet*. They will *never* let us in!"

"Are you always this uptight?"

"Colonel!"

"Of course they'll let us in," said Talanov. "Who can resist a briefcase full of cash and the willingness to spend it?"

"Briefcase full of cash? From *whom?* Does Kravenko know about this?"

"Kravenko wants results. He is not interested in how we

obtain them."

"I do not *believe* this! Let us say by some unbelievable stretch that you are right, that Kravenko will miraculously look the other way regarding that money -- which I do not for a moment believe that he will, now that you have pissed everyone off -- but let us assume that you are right and we are allowed into Spain. What, then? Never mind, I do not want to hear another metaphor about rats. I will tell you what will happen. From the moment we board that plane to the moment we land -- everywhere we go, everything we do -- agents will be watching and following because we have told them exactly *who* we are and *where* we are. Which means it will be impossible for us to capture Gorev, much less get him out of the country. The odds are against us. *We cannot succeed.*"

"And therein lies the beauty of what we are doing. Question is: are you in or out?"

CHAPTER 2

In spite of Sofia's animated protest to such a ludicrous plan, Talanov knew her answer before she finally and reluctantly agreed. As promised, he was waiting for her in front of the Barcelona airport when she arrived on Thursday. He knew the polite gesture would have been to meet her at the gate. But what fun would there have been in that? So he waited in the loading zone so that he could see her face when she came out the door and saw him in the Ferrari.

As expected, she gave him the "Party scowl," as he liked to call the disapproving glare given by loyal Communists to flagrant examples of Western decadence.

So Talanov jumped out in his white tennis shorts, tank-top and canvas deck shoes, paused briefly to frown at her starched teal-colored worker's dress and clunky black shoes before giving her an effusive hug while pedestrian traffic flowed around them. When Sofia did not return the hug, he lifted her off the sidewalk and gave her a happy twirl, whispering that all of this affection was for the benefit of the two cars of *Guardia Civil* agents parked nearby, both in Peugeots, one at five o'clock and the other at two. When Talanov lowered Sofia gently back onto the sidewalk, she instinctively turned to look.

Talanov stopped her by taking her face in his hands and giving her a long deep kiss. The wide-eyed Sofia stiffened just as Talanov gave her another twirling hug in order to again whisper in her ear."Don't let them know that we know," he said.

"Of course, Colonel. I didn't think."

"And it's Sasha, not Colonel," he said, releasing her. With a sparkling smile, he sprang over to open her car door before ushering her down into the tan leather passenger seat. "By the way, that kiss was for them, not me," he said with a mischievous grin.

Sofia shook her head but could not help smiling.

A skycap approached carrying Sofia's brown leather suitcase. Scuffed from years of use, it had a tarnished clasp and worn straps in a contrasting color. When the skycap asked Talanov where he should put the bag, Talanov slipped the man fifty dollars and nodded discreetly toward a large trashcan.

Jumping behind the wheel, Talanov fired up the Ferrari and was peeling away from the curb before Sofia realized they did not have her bag.

"My suitcase, we've got to go back!"

"Too late," Talanov replied, glancing in the side mirror before accelerating quickly into the traffic.

"What are you *doing?*" she cried, craning around to see the skycap empty her belongings into one of the large receptacles in front of the terminal.

"Taking you shopping," he answered over the roar of jet engines from the runway.

"I *have* plenty of clothing."

"Not anymore."

Heading south along the highway, which curved west along the coast to become *Autovia de Castelldefels,* Talanov allowed Sofia to shout and pound on the dashboard while darting in and out of traffic, the wind blowing his aviator hairstyle -- long on top, parted and combed with short back and sides -- his laughing eyes constantly on the rearview mirror, where the two Peugeots soon faded from sight.

Once it was safe, Talanov downshifted in order to make a sharp turn off the highway, shot along a side street and through several roundabouts before speeding right up a short ramp onto another highway that took them northeast, toward the city. A range of hills paralleled them in the distance to their left. The hills were dotted with gleaming villages set among the trees. Far off to the right, beyond the red tile rooftops and palm trees, were the glistening waters of the Mediterranean, while directly ahead lay the eclectic geometry of downtown Barcelona, where the crafted spires, domes and ornate facades of the past competed with the more utilitarian emphasis of the present.

Leaving the highway, they passed the *Plaça Reial,* a large 19th Century plaza in the Gothic Quarter known for its nightclubs and restaurants. Turning down a narrow street, they cut through a residential area of flats before turning onto a wide boulevard, where they parked. Across the street was an expensive clothing store, and next to it a beauty salon.

The department store and salon were two of several businesses located in an ornate five-story building. A façade of arches fronted the street, and behind the arches was a covered walkway, where the stores could be accessed along a tiled sidewalk. A row of offices was situated on the floor above, with dozens of residential flats occupying the remaining three floors. The windows of the flats were decorated with tiny wrought iron balconies. Most of the balconies featured flower boxes spilling over with ferns or geraniums.

Sofia had settled into an angry pout by now, and after grabbing a stylish aluminum briefcase from behind the seat, Talanov had to virtually drag Sofia across the street, dashing with her at one point to avoid being hit by a car, which then slowed so the driver could whistle.

Pausing in front of the department store window, Sofia looked disapprovingly at the slender mannequins dressed in glittering party dresses. "Your plan is to -- what -- dress me up like an American Barbie doll? Is that it?"

"Communist Barbie had one dress and a uniform and thankfully we got rid of those. If it makes you feel any better, you can turn everything in to the State once this is over."

"You did not have the right to throw my suitcase away."

"Technically, the skycap threw it away."

With a roar of disgust, Sofia stormed away.

With a laugh, Talanov raced after her. "Will you please wait a minute?" he said, grabbing her by the hand.

Sofia yanked away.

Talanov grabbed her again, this time not letting go. "All right, I may have overstepped a bit back at the airport," he said.

Sofia whirled to face him. *"May* have? What if my passport had been in there?"

"No one carries a passport inside a suitcase. Besides, I saw how closely you guarded your purse. The way you wore the strap across your chest and clutched the bag itself with one hand, even inside the car. Everything of value is inside that purse."

"There could have been something else."

"But there wasn't. Look, I promise I'll make it up to you. In fact, that's why we're here."

Noticing several people looking their way, Sofia led Talanov by the hand to a quieter spot near a tiled stone bench. The bench was located near a planter containing flowers and a tree.

"It's not just the suitcase," she said.

"Then what?"

Sofia motioned for him to sit.

"Kravenko called me into his office before I left," she said, sitting beside him, "asking if I knew what you were doing. He said the KGB had intercepted several intelligence reports, saying you had been spotted in a number of casinos. Other reports said you had been seen in various expensive restaurants. You have already tested Kravenko's patience by insisting that we travel openly aboard a commercial aircraft. But this---" she gestured toward the Ferrari then at the department store "---this is beyond comprehension. Traveling publicly is one thing. Screaming for attention is another. You put *everything* at risk with this flamboyant behavior."

"That's being a little dramatic."

"We are in a *Ferrari,* Colonel. You are attracting more attention right now than the Rolling Stones. How did you manage to get hold of a Ferrari, anyway? And how the *hell* did you get the KGB to pay for it? I presume they are paying and that you didn't steal it?"

Talanov smiled and took Sofia by the hand. "Don't you see?" he said. "If this is how you are thinking -- how Kra-venko is thinking -- then this is how everyone is thinking, including the Americans. No one sees the design."

"I don't see the design. Neither does Kravenko. And even though you say this is a good thing,
the fact that he does not understand means he may well order us back home."

"He won't."

"He might."

"He won't."

"How do you *know?"*

"Because to pull us now means he will lose Gorev and all we've spent on this mission. He cannot afford to do that."

"What if he sends in replacements?"

"A handover like that not only takes time, it *wastes* time, and it's an admission that he was wrong. He can't afford that, either. Kravenko would rather lose Gorev and lay the blame squarely on us than admit he made a mistake. A scapegoat is better than a confession any day, and he can always send a team later to kill Gorev in America. We have agents there right now. Which means even though he may not understand or even like what I am doing, he will allow us the rope we need either to hang ourselves or bring Gorev back alive, one or the other."

"If you are trying to allay my fears you are doing a terrible job."

With a laugh, Talanov stood and offered his hand. "Come, we have shopping to do. It's already Thursday and Gorev will be here on Sunday."

"What do we do until then?"

"Have the time of our lives."

"You make me nervous talking like that."

"It's part of the smokescreen, my dear. It's what magicians do all the time. They distract you from what's happening on one hand with a dazzling display on the other. And that's precisely why we need you to dazzle."

CHAPTER 3

After striding into the salon and charming his way into an immediate appointment, Talanov and Sofia spent the next two hours with an ebullient stylist named Ramon, who fussed and fluffed over Sofia while cutting her long black hair in a trendy new wedge. A blue streak was then added to one of the wispy tails that hung to the side.

When finished, Ramon crouched behind Sofia while she sat in the chair, his face snuggled next to hers while they looked in the mirror.

"Darling, you do look *stunning,*" he gushed in Spanish.

"I feel . . . naked," she replied, remembering hair that hung nearly to her waist.

"I'm glad we banished that bun," remarked Talanov. "Your face had to hurt it was pulled so tight."

A reproving scowl was Sofia's reply.

Talanov tossed down his magazine and stood. "Ramon is right: you *do* look stunning."

"I wish I could believe you," she replied.

"You will by the end of the day."

Talanov paid the bill while Ramon made some final touches before whipping off the cape and offering Sofia his hand. When she stood, she was nearly a foot taller than the slender Ramon, who stood back to admire his work. Throughout the salon, the conversation fell noticeably quiet.

Sofia looked around and saw rows of women staring at her from beneath the plastic hoods of large hairdryers mounted on swivel-arms. Others were sitting in chairs.

Feeling suddenly self-conscious, Sofia withdrew slightly, shrinking back.

"Thank you, Ramon, brilliant work," Talanov said, slipping Ramon some extra cash before taking Sofia by the hand and leading her out the front door.

"I feel like a freak," she said, glancing in through the window at the women still watching. "Look at them in there, staring. And this new haircut makes them stare even more."

"We stare at beauty. It's just how people are. Especially spectacular beauty."

"I'm not sure I like the attention."

"I guess I could give you some spiel about embracing the beautiful woman within, but the fact is, you need to quit worrying about what people think. You're tall; use it. You're stunning; use it. If we don't learn to kick some serious ass, as the Americans love to say, somebody is going to kick ours."

With a sigh, Sofia nodded.

Wrapping an arm around Sofia's shoulder, Talanov angled his face near her ear. "Just to let you know," he whispered, "we're being watched by the same two cars of agents we left at the airport. They obviously put out a description about this gorgeous minx in a black Ferrari and figured out where we were."

With a smile, Sofia hooked her arms around Talanov's neck and whispered in his ear, "Did you just call me a minx?"

Talanov laughed and led Sofia into the department store next door, where he again introduced himself and told the sales staff how Ms. Dubinina and he were international travelers from the Soviet Union and that Ms. Dubinina was in need of a new wardrobe.

The manager was delighted to be of personal service and ordered his staff to immediately bring selections of whatever Colonel Talanov and Ms. Dubinina wished to see. He then ushered Talanov to a comfortable chair and ordered Champagne to be served.

After listening to Talanov's planned itinerary of casinos, restaurants and nightclubs, a staff of two young assistants selected dozens of outfits for Sofia to try on, which she did for the next three hours. They could have finished in an hour but decided to stretch it out for the benefit of the agents across the street.

Talanov made a point of occasionally strolling to the window with his Champagne while Sofia paraded in front of the angled mirrors, turning, craning, posing and evaluating while the assistants zipped and buttoned her into a steady supply of mini and micro party dresses of neon, geometric, striped, polka-dotted and plain fabrics. She tried on dresses that were padded, sequined, tasseled and feathered, as well as skirts of vinyl and spandex. Then came the tights and jeans, with sandals and shoes to match, including a variety of stiletto heels.

When there was a break, Sofia sat on Talanov's lap, wrapped her arms around his neck and again whispered in his ear, "Just how do you plan on paying for this?" She kissed him on his cheek, leaned back and smiled brightly.

"Oh ye of little faith."

Sofia chuckled and leaned close again. "I think they prefer hard currency." Another kiss on the cheek.

Talanov returned the kiss, then nodded toward a sales clerk approaching them with a selection of bikinis and lingerie. "Duty calls," he said, "and I really do think you should model them for me. I'm a highly trained professional with special skills, and I would *hate* to see you put one of those pieces of string on backwards. Something like that can have serious consequences."

"Perhaps you should give us a demonstration of how one is worn?"

Talanov removed his designer sunglasses and gave them a quick wipe with the bottom of his tank top. Showcased by the straps of his shirt, his shoulders were lean and tanned. "I would, of course," he said, "but people want Barbie, not Ken."

"Says who?"

"Ken's an accessory, an after-thought," answered Talanov. "Stick him in a tuxedo or a chicken suit, no one cares. It's Barbie that people want." He smiled and slipped on his glasses. "And it's Barbie they're going to get."

Eleven thousand dollars later, using cash from the aluminum briefcase, which Talanov counted out in hundreds to the dumbfounded manager, Talanov and Sofia stowed their purchases in the Ferrari's storage compartment. Talanov then slid behind the wheel and fired up the engine.

"Do I want to know where you got all that cash?" Sofia asked, slipping on her sunglasses.

"Casino de Barcelona," Talanov replied.

"How much of that was Kravenko's?"

"I spent his budget the first night on drinks."

"And the rest you won? Come on!"

"I got lucky."

"No one is that lucky."

"Apparently, some of us are."

In less than an hour, with two cars of agents in tow, they were heading southwest through vast stretches of orange groves toward Valencia.

Sofia slept most of the three hours it took to get to Valencia, where they checked into a resort that was built near one of the widest stretches of beach Talanov had ever seen. The beach was as level as a sports field and Talanov imagined himself driving a dune buggy and turning donuts, kicking up plumes of sand.

Their room was on the fourth and top floor of what looked like a fancy dormitory with arches and columns and palm trees around a tiled pool. Each of the rooms had its own balcony and faced the water. Talanov opened the sliding door leading out onto the balcony and allowed the afternoon sea breeze to freshen the room.

After changing into one of her new outfits, Sofia accompanied Talanov out onto the balcony, where she closed her eyes and lifted her face toward the sun. Talanov scanned the horizon. In the haze to the left was a range of hills that met the water. To the right was the Port of Valencia, where he could see numerous tower cranes and freighters. The masts of sailboats in a marina stood like a cluster of needles.

"Having a good time?" he asked.

Sofia did not reply.

Talanov turned to face her.

Sofia finally opened her eyes. "I want to believe you," she said. "I want to believe this fantastic and utterly frightening fairytale is actually true. That we can shop and party and dance until dawn and Moscow will not take notice."

With an understanding smile, Talanov rested his elbows on the balustrade and looked out to sea. "I wasn't always a colonel," he said, the light wind blowing his hair. "I wasn't born that way and no one handed it to me. I had to earn it. And you want to know how I did it? By doing what other people were unwilling to do. By taking risks others were afraid to take. Sure, you learn to follow orders and do what you're told. Everybody learns that. But if you want to climb out of the pack, you need to be creative. And you need to choose those moments carefully. This is one of those moments."

"But how do you *know* this is going to work?" Sofia asked just as a freighter bellowed in the distance. "How do you know this magician's act of yours will fool the Americans? How do you know we are not making a huge mistake? Please don't give me the rat speech again."

When Talanov laughed, she linked her arm through his.

"It's a collage," answered Talanov. "Information I've gleaned, deductions I've made, facts, intuitions, what I saw and even what I didn't see. Plus instinct, of course, and experience. In other words, I can't give you a clear-cut answer. But just so you know, I'm not asking you to follow me anyplace I'm not willing to go myself."

"You gave me the rat speech again," she said, giving him a token slap on the arm.

Talanov grinned.

"Then tell me how you figured out Spain is where Gorev

plans to defect."

"Another collage," explained Talanov.

"Meaning what?"

"Meaning it's another collage. Nothing that's really clear-cut."

"I get the feeling you are avoiding my question."

"It's not that . . ." he began.

Sofia folded her arms.

"Okay, I'm avoiding your question."

"Why?"

"Because the more you're concerned about Gorev -- is he really coming to Spain, will he get here on time, will he pull a switch at the last minute -- the more distracted and worried you'll be. Which means the less convincing you'll be in your role as my lover. And I need you to play that part to perfection. That's why I keep logistical matters like this to myself."

"If we were a squadron or a platoon, I could understand. We are not. There is only you and me."

"I can't keep having to defend every decision I make. That's not how I work."

"In other words, you don't trust me." Unlinking her arm, she stepped back.

"Come on, Sofia. Don't make this more than it is."

"You don't trust me. How am I supposed to not make this more than it is?"

"I didn't say I didn't trust you."

"You didn't not say it, either."

Talanov laughed. "So you're angry, not because I said something -- which I didn't -- but because I specifically didn't *not* say it?"

"You are twisting this around to make me look foolish."

"I am not."

"Yes, you are."

"Then I apologize. I did laugh -- I'll admit that -- but it wasn't because I was trying to make you look foolish for *not* saying something you wish I would have not said, but didn't. Or something like that."

"You are insufferable," she declared.

"Come on," he said, taking her by the hands. "How can I make this up to you?"

Sofia shrugged and turned away.

"Is there nothing I can do?" he asked, encircling her waist with his hands and drawing her to him, her back to his chest, nuzzling his face into her neck.

There was a long moment of silence.

*"May*be . . ." she finally said.

When Talanov stepped out of the shower two hours later, Sofia was still sprawled out on the bed, one arm dangling over the side, one folded behind her head, which was propped against two large square European pillows. Sofia's skin was flawless and white, like alabaster, except for the tattoo of a serpent that trailed up one arm and made a single coil over her shoulder, mouth open, ready to strike. The sheets and bedspread were a tangled mess on the floor.

Talanov stood naked in the doorway toweling his hair, dripping water on the floor. "Hungry?" he asked.

"That is the last thing on my mind," she said, looking at him with a lazy smile. "I am still floating and I do not want to get up because I do not want it to stop." She leaned up on her elbows. "I thought you said foot massage."

"I may have wandered a bit."

"A bit? There I am, relaxing, in heaven, when this tiny fire begins in an area that is, well, not my foot. But by then it is too late. The fire is spreading, taking over. At first I tried to get away. The next moment, I could not get enough -- of it -- of *you* -- and I was unable -- *unwilling* -- to stop as I was blinded by this raging inferno. And when I finally *was* able to move -- to *breathe* -- there you were, so near I could feel the heat of your breath. But I could not get away -- did not *want* to get away -- and the fire began again, this time faster, and I do not remember how long this went on, or how many times. I am still weak because of what happened. I have *never* . . . where did you learn that?"

"Learn what, a foot massage?"

Sofia flopped back on the bed, laughing.

Talanov enjoyed watching her laugh. She just laid there, completely naked, pounding on the edge of the bed, laughing. He said, "You learn it by thinking less about yourself and more about the other person."

"There has *got* to be more to it than that."

"Sex is a pleasure most men want to get, not a pleasure they want to give. They've got it all wrong. Now, come on, let's go, I'm hungry. We have a big night ahead of us tonight."

"I do not see how it can get any bigger."

Talanov smiled. "Believe me, it will. And we are just getting started."

Thursday night was indeed a whirlwind. Taking a taxi into the city, his aluminum briefcase in hand, they asked the driver where they should eat. He told them Valencia was the birthplace of paella and took them to one of the best restaurants in the city, where they ordered a mix of seafood and chorizo. Live music was playing so they danced. Talanov was dressed in his tuxedo and Sofia wore a sequined mini dress that reflected light like thousands of tiny prisms. From there it was a short walk to one of Valencia's Old World casinos, where Talanov led the way into the gaming salon and placed twenty thousand dollars on the felt of the roulette table. One bet. One color. One resounding win to cheers from the large crowd that had gathered around to watch.

Then came the Champagne: a round for everyone, including complimentary bottles for the two teams of agents skulking in the background. Leaving the casino, they went for cappuccinos and a dessert cart of everything chocolate at an intimate rooftop restaurant overlooking the Old City. Spread out before them was a vast jumble of red tile rooftops so ugly they were beautiful. In the distance was a floodlit rocky mount. Later, they walked barefoot on the beach. Talanov's tuxedo trousers were rolled up to his knees while Sofia carried her stiletto heels, her glittering mini dress in no danger from the mild splashes of surf lapping their feet.

On Friday, they were up early for the winding coastal drive to Torrevieja, just north of *Mar Menor,* a large, triangular-shaped salt water lake isolated from the Mediterranean by the Cape Palos peninsula and a narrow isthmus of land linking the cape with the mainland. The warm, shallow waters of *Mar Menor* made it ideal for sailing and diving, which is exactly how Talanov and Sofia spent the day.

Coming back to their hotel, they showered and dined before driving to the Torrevieja Casino, where Talanov made a commanding entrance with the striking Sofia, who turned heads the moment she stepped out of the Ferrari wearing a shimmering gold mini dress.

Entering the lobby, Talanov asked for the casino President who, after seeing the contents of the aluminum briefcase, effusively welcomed Colonel Talanov and Ms. Dubinina to Spain's 'Jewel of the Mediterranean.'

Talanov told the President he would be wagering a substantial sum of money but wished to place his bets in cash.

The President replied that it was against casino policy. Chips were the only currency allowed at the tables.

Talanov thanked the President and turned to go.

The President intercepted Talanov at the door and said he was happy to make an exception.

Talanov again thanked the President and strode with Sofia into the crowded casino, where they paused to get their bearings before making their way across the *fleur-de-lis* carpet to the brightly lit roulette table, where nearly thirty people were breathlessly watching a little white ball bounce across the frets of the spinning wooden wheel.

Standing on the perimeter of the group, Sofia glanced over her shoulder and saw four men trail into the casino. Their ties were loosened and their suit jackets were wrinkled. When they saw Sofia staring at them they dissipated quickly into the crowd.

"Our friends have arrived," she remarked.

"Then we should give them something to report."

"How much?" Sofia asked.

Talanov held up three fingers.

When the croupier called for bets, Sofia laid the briefcase on the table and took out three stacks of banded cash -- thirty thousand dollars -- and handed them to Talanov, who fanned through the bills and tossed them onto the felt while murmurs of the cash bet rippled through the casino and people hurriedly gathered around.

The croupier looked to his left and saw the President nod. He didn't look happy but had nonetheless given his approval.

One bet.

One color.

All or nothing.

After closing the table to further bets, the croupier spun the wheel in one direction before spinning the white ball in the opposite direction. And scores of onlookers -- including four agents -- held their breath when the white ball ran out of momentum and began its unpredictable bounce across the frets.

CHAPTER 4

Sofia heard Talanov chuckle. It was now Sunday night -- two days later -- and she glanced quizzically across the console of the darkened Ferrari. In the glow of the dashboard lights, she could see him sitting there, grinning, nestled comfortably in his seat, relaxed and amused, hands folded in his lap.

"What are you laughing at?" she asked, downshifting into third before making a squealing right turn onto *Avenida de Torreblanca,* a modest four-lane street bounded on both sides by blocks of highrise apartments.

"Torrevieja," he replied. "I still don't believe what happened."

They each thought about the strange hop the ball had taken once it settled onto the frets, where it kicked across the wheel before hitting another fret, which knocked it high in the air, spinning and hovering until it came back down and the motion of the wheel kicked it to the right, where it skipped like an Irish river dancer before settling on Talanov's thirty-thousand-dollar winning color.

"Why do you do it?" Sofia asked, her sangoire party dress glittering in the light of a passing streetlamp. "Why risk everything on a single bet?"

"I guess I could tell you it mirrors life," he replied over the muscular purr of the V-8 positioned transversely behind the seat. "That sometimes everything boils down to a single decision. Is this the right job? Is this the right person?"

"But?"

"Personality, simple as that. There are a lot of two-dollar personalities. They go to the races and that's what they bet because they're afraid to bet more. I'm not one of those."

"Easy to say when you're betting other people's money," Sofia replied, merging the Ferrari onto the busy Mediterranean Highway heading west toward Marbella.

"This isn't about money," he said.

"What's it about, then?" she asked.

"Who you are."

"Having a thirty-thousand-dollar personality can get you into a lot of trouble."

Talanov smiled eagerly. "That it can."

"And you love it, too. Beautiful women . . . fast cars . . ."

"Never met one I couldn't handle."

Sofia glanced sharply at Talanov.

"Car. Never met a *car* I couldn't handle."

"You *are* insufferable."

Talanov grinned.

Sofia said, "And definitely not the kind of man who sits for hours slipping coins into a machine. That much I know."

"What else do you know?" he asked.

"Plenty," she replied.

"Such as?"

"Well, let's see." She thought for a moment. "I know you are called the Ice Man because of your cold, impersonal nature, not that whoever gave you that name had his or her feet massaged."

Talanov laughed.

"I know that you were orphaned at seven," Sofia continued, "then reared by the State, and that you hold a black belt in Combat Sambo, which you first learned as a boy at the monastery of *Lóngshù,* in the foothills near Khan Tengri, in northern China."

"You read my file."

"Of course. I wasn't about to go to Spain with just anyone."

Talanov laughed again.

"I also know you are the youngest KGB colonel in history," she said, "and that you are an idealist with a strong sense of right and wrong, which -- I might add -- I was able to tempt wickedly on several occasions."

"That you did," Talanov admitted, recalling their afternoon together yesterday in a cliff-side resort in Nerja Capistrano where, after a lunch of local mango, oysters and Champagne at an outdoor bar by the pool, Sofia lured him back to their room and attacked him like a cat, scratching and biting and squeezing him with her legs until her sexual demands were met and she fell back on the bed, satisfied and content.

"So, what have you learned about me?" she asked.

"That you have no file."

"I prefer to be . . . discovered."

"A woman reveals a lot about herself in the bedroom."

"Even more by the way she handles a car."

"And even more by the way she handles a fork."

"Rubbish."

"Not at all. Take you and those oysters on the half-shell."

"I did not use a fork."

"Exactly. *Res ipsa loquitur.*"

"And how exactly does that speak for itself?"

"Well, for one thing, I've never seen a woman demonstrate such effortless skill shucking an oyster with a steak knife, only to turn around and brazenly eat off that knife in a flirtatious attempt to seduce me."

"But you would not be seduced. Why not?"

"Because you were toying with me."

"I was not."

"And you're manipulative -- seeing if you could make me jealous -- as evidenced by the way you treated the waiter, who was quite taken with you and you with him, which was obvious by the way you looked him over before dismissing him without a second thought."

"How was that manipulative?"

"You returned the mignonette sauce how many times?"

"It lacked pepper!"

Talanov smiled but did not reply.

"All right, so I toyed with him," she snapped. "And perhaps I *was* trying to make you jealous, to see if I mean more to you than a week in Spain. What harm was there in that?"

"Res ipsa loquitur."

"Quit saying that."

"I also learned," he continued, "that you are more interested in proving yourself than enjoying yourself. That is not to say you don't enjoy yourself, which your driving demonstrates -- but your clear priority is not enjoyment. It is proving yourself to be more than a garnish."

"Garnish?"

"Do not take offense. A woman's looks can be an effective weapon. Your stunning height, your Chinese heritage -- exotic eyes and flawless skin, inherited through your mother, I might add, since your Father's surname, Dubinina, is Russian -- only adds to your mystique. But you want to be more than your looks."

"And you think the reason I am here is to make you look good, is that it?"

"Every plate needs a garnish."

"What makes you think it is not the reverse?" she retorted. "That you are here to make *me* look good?"

Talanov rubbed his chin thoughtfully.

"Got you, didn't I?" she said.

"You did," he replied. "But now that you mention it, I do make you look good. Next exit, then a right. You may want to lower your landing gear before attempting the corner."

With a reluctant chuckle, Sofia accelerated into the right lane, passed a car, then slipped back into the left lane to pass three more cars before cutting across both lanes and down the exit ramp to the angry protests of several horns, where she applied the brakes, downshifted into third and hit the accelerator at the corner to make a squealing turn. She then hit the gas again, shot through a busy intersection, past two cars, around a corner and into a gravel parking lot, where she jammed on the brakes and spun the wheel to do a sliding one-hundred-and-eighty-degree stop.

With gravel dust drifting through the beams of the Ferrari's headlights, Sofia rotated in her seat and folded her arms.

"Okay, Sasha, talk," she said. "For three days we have been throwing money around as if the Soviet Union's entire national budget was at your disposal. At first I had my objections, fearing the Deputy Chairman would replace us, but as I came to understand what you were doing, I began to consent and cooperate."

"Consent and cooperate?"

"Okay, I began to enjoy it. My point is, I have been waiting for you to tell me how we plan to apprehend Gorev, which you have steadfastly refused to divulge. Perhaps you think this is need-to-know. Well, I need to know, because here we are -- on the night of his arrival -- going to yet another casino."

"The Gran Casino del Sol is not just another casino."

"Stop it. Sasha. You know what I am talking about."

Talanov smiled sympathetically. Sofia was right. It was time to read her into his plan. No, he did not entirely trust her, not that he specifically mistrusted her, either. It was simply the way he preferred to handle things with people he did not know. But her character arc over the last few days seemed natural and expected, so unless she was a brilliant actress who had completely conned him, he felt comfortable revealing his plan.

To provide her with some background, he outlined how the movements of all *Biopreparat* personnel were carefully monitored and recorded. The KGB knew when these people left home, when they arrived at work, when they left work and when they arrived back home. They also knew the names of all family members, what their movements were, and the names and movements of their friends.

Not so obvious were a number of more subtle indicators, such as how often people like Gorev laughed, what the audible level of his conversations were, who he sat with at lunch, how he spent his leisure time, what his normal expressions were throughout the day and to what degree those expressions changed when approached by an overseer. These and other statistics were then graphed and a baseline of normality established, so that if a significant change occurred in that pattern, it would be noticed.

Such a change occurred just over six months ago but was so slight it did not alarm his superiors. The good doctor was, after all, deliberately infecting labor camp prisoners with various strains of anthrax to determine which forms were the most lethal. He then set about purifying and concentrating those strains into a weaponized form that could wipe out an entire population. And while the subjects of these experiments were convicted enemies of the state, their constant cries of agony quite naturally took an immense emotional and psychological toll. Hence, certain behavioral fluctuations were to be regarded as normal.

"Which Gorev used against us," said Talanov. "He avoided setting off any alarms by working within those tolerable limits to organize and execute his defection. And not just for himself, but his wife, his daughter and his parents. That demonstrates premeditation, cunning and meticulous attention to detail, which is why the KGB in Leningrad failed to locate him. They had no idea who they were up against. So Leningrad called Moscow and Moscow called me."

"The Ice Man himself. The one who sees what others don't."

"There is nothing magical about it," responded Talanov. "I simply analyzed who I was dealing with, and in doing so, figured out where to look. In Gorev's case, inverse logic told me where he would *not* defect -- Helsinki, London or any of the northern European cities -- which would be too obvious for a man so methodical and cunning. But I needed specific information as to where he *would* defect. So I went to Sverdlovsk and questioned Gorev's colleagues and minders, from whom I gleaned the name of a political prisoner who had been assigned to clean Gorev's laboratory. That prisoner's name was Volkov and the date of his assignment to clean Gorev's lab coincided with the first recorded changes in Gorev's behavior. Based on that statistical correlation, I looked deeper to find that Volkov, a former history professor, was imprisoned because he had been quoting Thomas Jefferson in the classroom about all men being created equal. Not so bad, except that Volkov went on to say that all governments should be accountable to the people."

"So the prisoner, Volkov, infected Gorev with American ideology?"

"An interesting use of the word, but -- yes -- that's how it looks. Gorev was infected by Volkov's Jeffersonian philosophy. Records show the two men were often seen conversing quietly. So I kept digging and what did I discover? That Volkov had a cousin, an artist, who defected to the Costa del Sol in 1978."

"So Volkov has a cousin here in Spain?" Sofia asked.

"That's right."

"Do you know his name and where he lives?"

"Yes, I do."

"Then why not simply stake out the cousin's house and abduct Gorev when he arrives? Why drive around in a Ferrari drawing attention to ourselves?"

"Because he's not going to the cousin's house."

"Then, where?" asked Sofia. "Surely the Americans are not meeting him in a *casino?*"

"Inverse logic again told me someone as methodical as our good doctor would not choose such an obvious location, in case we were on to him. As to where he *would* defect -- well, we have the Americans to thank for that. It was not difficult to decipher their chatter, with their clumsy references to a special package being delivered to the office."

"With 'office' being a reference to their safe house?"

"Precisely."

"Do you know where their safe house is?"

"Yes, I do."

"Then we are back to my original question. Why the charade? Why not remain invisible so that we can take him by surprise?"

"On the surface that makes sense," said Talanov. "But I do not operate on the surface. I let them operate on the surface. I let them think they're tracking me when it's actually the other way around."

"I do not understand."

"The Americans know we'll come after Gorev. He's one of our top scientists and he'll be carrying information and possibly samples from our biological weapons program. So they know we cannot allow him to defect. But if they don't know where we are or what we're planning, they'll be on high alert, looking in all directions, taking extra precautions. We don't want that. We want them to be careless. And the best way to do that is let them know exactly where we are, in plain sight."

"I hope you are right," Sofia said, "because the Americans will kill Gorev if it looks like we are going to intercept him. They cannot allow us to return with him to Russia. Not now. Not ever. And certainly not alive."

Sofia suddenly hit the brakes. Ahead of them in the middle of the road, was a man waving his arms. Dressed in a white tank top and black pleated slacks, the man looked to be in his late twenties and had curly black hair. Sofia downshifted into second and brought the Ferrari to a stop.

The man approached and Sofia rolled down her window.

"¿Estás bien?" she asked.

The man drew a pistol from the rear of his slacks and pointed it directly at Sofia's face. *"Sal del coche!"* he yelled just as another man stepped into the wash of the headlights, his pistol aimed at Talanov, motioning him out.

"Ahora! Now!" he shouted.

CHAPTER 5

*"**No somos de** por aquí,"* pleaded Sofia, waving one hand out the window and fumbling for the handle with the other. Grabbing the keys, she finally managed to open the door and climb awkwardly out, one leg at a time. The man watched her short dress slide up her thighs while the other man circled to the side, keeping Talanov in his sights.

"No queremos problemas," said Talanov, opening his door and climbing out.

"You are not Spanish," the man covering Talanov said in broken English. *"Inglés?"*

"Russian," answered Talanov.

The two gunmen glanced at one another. *"Comunista?"* the first one asked.

"Sí." Talanov replied.

"My name is Paco," the man said just as three other men with guns appeared, "and I am the leader of the *Euskadi Ta Askatasuna* -- the ETA. We, too, are communist."

"It is good to meet a brother," responded Talanov.

"Perhaps," Paco replied, pacing the length of the Ferrari and looking it over carefully. "Where did you get this car?"

"It is part of our assignment," answered Talanov.

"What kind of assignment?"

"I cannot say."

"You *will* say!" Paco yelled, jabbing at Talanov with his gun.

"I would if I could, but I can't."

Paco returned to stand in front of Talanov for a long moment. "Juan!" he suddenly yelled.

The man nearest Sofia cocked his pistol, walked over and aimed it at her head.

"You *will* say," Paco repeated, tilting his head and looking Talanov in the eye.

"Or what, you'll kill us?" asked Talanov. "What kind of communist are you?"

"The kind with a gun," Paco replied, waving his pistol in front of Talanov's face. "So, you will tell me what this assignment is and why you are here."

"We're meeting someone."

"Who?"

"He is waiting at the casino."

"Who?"

"I've told you all that I can. We're on the same side. We believe the same things. We're working for the same goals."

"I work for myself," Paco said. "You have one minute to run before I kill you."

"Kill us? You can't be serious!"

"Kill *you*. The woman stays."

"What is *wrong* with you?"

Paco cocked his pistol.

"This is what is wrong with the system," Talanov said, turning away and gesturing angrily with his hands. "Nobody wants equality, not really. Somebody always wants to get ahead by taking what the next guy has." He returned to look Paco in the eyes. " Like you, right now. You're supposed to be my brother! A comrade in arms. And yet here you are, treating us like we're the enemy. How can you justify this?"

Paco and his men all laughed.

"You think this is funny?" asked Talanov.

"Yes, I do!" answered an amused Paco, whose smile then faded. "But not for long."

"I don't think you're a bad guy," Talanov said. "And I'm willing to let this slide. No harm has been done. *But we're not the enemy.* So tell Juan over there to lower his gun so that

Sofia and I can get back in our car and be on our way. Do that and no one gets hurt."

"Sofia. I like that name," Paco remarked, nodding pleasantly to the others before placing the barrel of his pistol directly against Talanov's forehead. "She stays. You run. One minute."

Talanov glared angrily at Paco, who began counting.

"Fifty-nine, fifty-eight . . ."

Walking away several steps, Talanov stopped and raked a hand through his hair.

Paco continued, "Thirty four, thirty three, thirty two . . ."

Talanov said, "We're *supposed* to be on the same side."

"Do something!" cried Sofia.

"Do what, exactly? Run? From someone who's supposed to be a brother? This is pathetic. If I thought it would do any good, I'd offer him the money."

"What money?" asked Paco, suddenly interested.

"Don't ask me, ask her," Talanov replied, nodding toward Sofia.

When Paco glanced at Sofia, Talanov's left hand shot up and grabbed him by the wrist, sweeping it left, away from his head. Talanov followed the direction of the sweep by pivoting into Paco while clamping his other hand around Paco's fingers and pulling the trigger three times as their arms swept left in a wide circle. The rounds dropped the gunman at his four o-clock position. Continuing the circular sweep, Talanov pulled off three more shots -- flat, shallow reports that seemed to dissipate into the night -- and dropped the gunman at his two o'clock position. Talanov then twisted the pistol out of Paco's hand while the man who had been holding Sofia -- Juan -- staggered backward holding his throat while Sofia looked on, his gun in her hand.

"Who's next?" asked Talanov, taking aim at the remaining gunman.

The gunman dropped his weapon and raised his hands.

"Please, *señor,* we meant you no harm," pleaded Paco, falling to his knees and clasping his hands, as if in prayer.

"I think you did," Talanov replied. "The question is, what do I do now? You see, I don't really have much time for people who gang up on others . . . who steal what they have. My partner and I came here on a peaceful mission and you just had to try and ruin it, didn't you? And we were having such a good time."

Talanov walked over and placed the pistol against the back of Paco's head.

"Please, *señor,* have mercy," sobbed Paco.

"You mean the kind of mercy you were going to give us?"

"I beg you, *señor.*"

Sofia said, "Get rid of them."

"Blood spatter from this distance would ruin my tuxedo," Talanov replied, noticing the glow of approaching headlights. "And that *would* ruin my evening." To Paco: "So I'll give you and your friend the same courtesy you were going to give me. One minute before I start shooting."

Paco looked over at his cousin, Juan, lying on the ground, gasping for air. "What about him?"

"Leave Juan to me," said Talanov, raising his wrist and looking at his watch. "Sixty seconds. Your time starts . . . now."

Climbing to his feet, Paco looked over at Juan, who reached out a hand.

"No me dejes," begged Juan, his voice raspy and weak.

Seeing Talanov in the Ferrari's headlights counting seconds on his watch, Paco and the remaining gunman fled away into the darkness. They ran in erratic zigzag patterns, heading for some shrubs in the distance.

Juan tried crawling away and Talanov grabbed him by the collar. When Juan took a wild swing, Talanov clubbed him on the side of the head, knocking him unconscious. Talanov then dragged Juan behind a bush and dropped him.

"What did you do to this guy?" asked Talanov, wiping the gun free of fingerprints and throwing it into the darkness. "One minute he's got us covered, the next he's on the ground."

"Men frequently underestimate women," Sofia replied, dragging the two dead bodies out of sight. *"Res ipsa loquitur."*

Talanov laughed as a car sped by without slowing. "Touché," he said. He held out his hand.

"What do you want?" she asked.

"The keys. I should probably drive. Once we get to the casino we may encounter real trouble, like you having to parallel park."

With a laugh, Sofia strode to the driver's side and again climbed behind the wheel. Seconds later, they were peeling away.

They came to an intersection and followed a sign to the left. Ten minutes later, a high rock wall appeared. Punctuated by occasional stands of floodlit palm trees, the wall paralleled the shoulder of the road as it curved to the northwest.

The road dipped and then crested a small hill. On the other side of the hill a lighted arch came into view. At the apex of the arch were the words, "Gran Casino del Sol," written in glowing pink neon.

Sofia slowed for a large group of protesters gathered beneath the arch. They were arguing with police officers. Filming the confrontation was a television crew. Waving anti-NATO placards, the protesters began banging on the top of the car when Sofia stopped. The officers pushed back the mob and allowed the Ferrari to pass.

"Protesters way out here?" asked Sofia, accelerating down the lane.

"Anything that threatens tourism brings out the police, which in turn brings out the cameras."

The lane curved along the bottom of a tree-lined *arroyo* and up the other side, which is where the majestic five-star Gran Casino del Sol came into view. The classic six-story resort looked like it belonged in another time and place, as if it had been transported from Renaissance Italy. And where the *vaqueros* of yesteryear used to wrangled cattle on horseback, golf carts now glided around small lakes and across verdant fairways landscaped with rows of Italian "pencil pine" cypress. Powerful floodlights accented the squared turrets on each corner of the resort, onto which adjacent wings had been added to house the expanded casino as well as additional rooms and banquet facilities. Sitting like an opulent island in the surrounding blanket of darkness, the hotel glowed with warmth. The grand entrance was jeweled with lights. The circular drive was lined with exotic cars.

Sofia slowed their speed to a crawl as they neared the brightly lit entrance. "I wonder who owns this place," she remarked, guiding the Ferrari into a space by the door.

"Countess Gabriella Herrera de la Peña."

Sofia turned off the ignition and stared at Talanov. "It was a rhetorical question. I didn't expect you to actually know."

"Women frequently underestimate men," he replied.

With a reluctant chuckle, Sofia touched a button and unlocked the door. A tuxedoed valet pulled open the door and offered his hand. Sofia looked up at him but did not accept. With a bow, the valet stepped back, allowing Sofia to swivel both legs out and gracefully stand. The doorman's eyes widened when the six-foot-tall Sofia rose above him several inches. Her tight party dress hugged a lean, athletic frame. Her stiletto heels added definition to her muscular calves.

Standing on opposite sides of the door, Sofia and the valet stared silently at one another for a long moment. When Sofia arched an eyebrow, the valet bowed and hurried away.

With Talanov still seated in the car, Sofia scanned the faces of people strolling in and out of the casino. Most of the men -- at least those with hair -- sported mullets with lots of gel, while a few of the younger ones were attempting various incarnations of the British rock star look, with sections that had been crimped, teased, colored and permed. The women were much the same: thin and sulky, with big hair made bigger by any means possible.

Satisfied everything appeared safe, Sofia tapped the top of the car twice, whereupon the passenger door swung open and Talanov stood, his short, aviator hairstyle appearing in sharp contrast to the sprayed hairstyles of the men strolling past.

Glancing toward the casino, Talanov signaled the valet.

" Sí, señor?" the valet responded, hurrying toward them.

"Our suitcases, if you please," Talanov said. "My driver will fetch them for you."

Suppressing a smile from the dirty look Sofia threw him, Talanov turned toward the entrance, unaware of the powerfully-built man in black getting out of a Peugeot van four cars away.

CHAPTER 6

The lobby of the Gran Casino del Sol was an opulent old-world atrium with a travertine marble floor. The spacious lobby was decorated with plants and furniture and statues that Michelangelo could have carved, they were so intricately detailed. To the right was the registration desk. It was clean and modern and staffed by smiling attendants. To the left was an arcade of shops, with a colorful stained glass ceiling that led to the casino. Ahead, through an arched hallway, was the outdoor pool, which glowed turquoise in the darkness.

Talanov paused inside the revolving brass door to absorb the echoes and sounds. The atrium rose five stories above him to an ornate dome. Walkways on each of the floors were visible through arched columns and balustrades. A lavish staircase led up to the mezzanine, where a happy bridal party of more than twenty young people were entering a nightclub. The bride was in a full-length wedding gown. Escorting her was the groom in his tuxedo. Lively flamenco music and the rhythmic clicking of castanets spilled out of the club. Everyone was in high spirits.

Hearing the sharp click of Sofia's stilettos, Talanov turned to see her coming toward him with his aluminum briefcase in hand. With her impressive height, glittering dress and confident stride, she cut a wide swath through the crowded lobby. Brushing past Talanov dismissively, she approached the registration desk with a radiant smile, where she was greeted by the young male attendant.

"Bienvenidos al Gran Casino del Sol, señorita," the attendant said, welcoming Sofia to the Gran Casino del Sol. "Do you have a reservation?"

"Colonel Akeksandr Talanov," Sofia replied, glancing sharply at Talanov, who was now beside her. To their right were several couples looking at brochures about local attractions.

"Ah, yes, here we are," the attendant said.

Sofia laid her briefcase on the counter, clicked it open and discreetly withdrew a red Soviet passport, which she laid on the counter. The attendant opened the passport, recorded the information in his computer, then smiled and handed it back.

"I'll have a bellboy escort you to your room," he said, dinging a bell and grabbing a key.

"Not necessary," Talanov replied. "If you'd be so kind to hold our key and luggage? I have an appointment with Lady Luck." And with a deliberate smile up at the CCTV camera mounted on the wall behind the counter, he offered his arm to Sofia before turning and strolling with her toward the entrance into the arcade.

Upstairs in the casino's darkened security center, agent Glenda Bixler and her team had been watching Talanov on a TV monitor. Bixler was the CIA's European Chief of Operations. With her was agent Donna Pilgrim and Spanish interpreter, Paul Franco. In front of them were other monitors connected to feeds from various cameras located in the foyer, corridors, and throughout the hotel and casino. The room was filled with the quiet hum of electronic equipment.

"Did you see the way he looked up at us just then?" Bixler said. "It's as if he knows we're watching."

A women's rowing champion from Dartmouth who majored in European history, the blond-haired Bixler was a competitive woman of twenty-nine who spoke fluent Russian and German. Her hair was cut in a classic bob and she was dressed in a dark blue slack suit and white shirt. An identification badge was clipped to her lapel.

"Impossible," said Pilgrim. "Most of the hotel staff don't

even know we're here."

Unlike her alpha-female counterpart, Pilgrim was much more reserved. Fluent in Russian with a background in medicine from the University of Houston, she had been assigned to Bixler's team to debrief Gorev. As far as hairstyles went, the brown-haired Pilgrim had likewise gone for the short bob, but because she liked the eighties trend for bigger hair, wore hers teased and full.

"He knows, all right," said Bixler. "I can tell by that cocky smirk."

"He does come across as a bit of a show pony," Pilgrim replied, "throwing money around the way he has. If he's supposed to be some super-secret top-notch spy, he's doing a lousy job. He even made reservations here at the hotel in his own name."

"Which is exactly the reason I'm worried," said Bixler.

"Who's the glam there with him?" asked Franco. "Man, she is one hot tamale. Definitely the *tallest* tamale I've ever seen, but totally bombdigity bitchin."

Bixler stared at Franco with incredulity. "Bombdigity bitchin?"

"What's wrong with that?"

"Nothing, if you happen to be fifteen years old."

The unfazed Franco rubbed his hands together eagerly. "So, who is she? What's her name?"

"Sofia Dubinina," answered Bixler, punching a button and calling up Talanov's reservation onto one of her monitors. "We know because he's been introducing her everywhere: Barcelona, Valencia, Torrevieja, Nerja. Other than that, we've got nothing on her, although Spanish immigration confirms her having entered the country two days after Talanov. Both of them used their Soviet passports."

"No attempt to conceal their identities?" inquired Pilgrim.

"None."

"Why isn't she listed on Talanov's reservation?" asked Pilgrim, reading the information showing on the monitor. "She came in with him just now -- has been traveling with him since her arrival -- and checked in using his Soviet passport. What about hers? Where is it?"

"The valet said he referred to her as his driver," said Bixler.

"Are you saying the Soviets sent an agent to act as Talanov's driver?" asked Franco.

"We don't know she's an agent," said Bixler, staring at the screen. She picked up the phone and called the front desk while other monitors showed Talanov and Sofia strolling around the lobby, admiring statues and art.

"Front desk," a voice said.

"This is Security," said Bixler. "Was only one passport presented with Colonel Talanov's reservation?"

"Yes, ma'am. Only his."

"Thank you," Bixler replied, hanging up.

"Do you think it's coincidence Talanov and Dubinina are here at the same time we're meeting a defecting Soviet scientist?" asked Franco.

Bixler again looked at Franco with disbelief. "Did you read *any* of the case notes I sent over?"

"Of course I did."

Bixler narrowed her eyes.

"Okay, so maybe not *entirely,*" admitted Franco. "But you said so yourself, I'm along mostly for my *español.* To set things up and keep everybody happy, especially here in the casino. If you recall, they didn't exactly welcome us with open arms when I told them we wanted to move in and set up shop. With all the NATO protests going on, America isn't exactly all that popular around here right now. And the casino did *not* want to be seen as sleeping with the enemy."

"We're not the enemy!" said Bixler. "We're the ones trying to help Gorev and his family escape."

"Which is exactly what I said to Countess de la Peña," replied Franco, "and you saw how far that got us. She was set to walk out of our meeting and would have if I hadn't told her the real reason we were here, which is to get proof from Dr. Gorev about the Soviet Union's biological weapons program."

"I could have strangled you for telling her that," said Bixler. "We have *no evidence* the Soviets are involved in the manufacture of biological weapons."

"Maybe not," said Pilgrim, "but we've all heard the rumors. Don't forget, Gorev *did* ask for a hematopathologist. Someone who studies the pathology of blood."

"Which proves nothing," Bixler replied.

"But *suggests* he has samples," said Pilgrim. "Dangerous samples. What else would they be if not bioweapons material?"

"I'm not in the business of guessing," said Bixler, "which is all we can do until we know otherwise. As far as I'm concerned, the Soviets are innocent until proven guilty."

"Then why didn't you tell that to the countess?" asked Franco. "Why let her think we're onto something?"

"All right, so maybe I *do* have suspicions," admitted Bixler. "But Washington is not interested in suspicions. Yours, mine or anyone's. Which is why we need to find out what Gorev knows, which is why we need to make sure Talanov does *not* stop this defection."

"What I still don't get," said Pilgrim, "is why he and Dubinina are living it up the way they are. Talanov flies into Spain ahead of Dubinina using his own passport, which of course triggers alarms all across Europe, then continues using his passport in hotels and casinos all along the Mediterranean coast. He then checks in here, and that's after he called ahead to make a reservation. In his own name!"

"He even called again to confirm it," added Bixler.

"Exactly," agreed Pilgrim. "And I'd like to know why he did that. I'd like to know why he wants everyone to know where he is and where he's going. I'd also like to know why he and Dubinina didn't slip into Spain undetected and hide in the shadows."

"When you figure that out, let me know," said Bixler.

"Whatever the reason, I am *so* glad they didn't," said Franco. "I mean, look at Dubinina. She is *hot,* man, and definitely no mall chick like you find back home. You can tell by the quiet, lethal way she moves: seeing yet ignoring everyone . . . moving against the tide with that totally awesome blue streak and that trendy new wedgie, or whatever it is you call those little-boy haircuts. Just look at those gorgeous long legs and the way she towers over everybody in that tight, tight---"

"We get the picture!" snapped Bixler. "And it's a *wedge,* not a wedgie. Do you honestly not know what a wedgie is?"

Bixler looked over, saw Franco grinning and growled with disgust. "Don't you have something to do?"

"Nothing this good," Franco replied.

"You do now. Put on your jacket, get down there and keep an eye on things. That's *him* -- Talanov -- not his girl. Don't let him out of your sight."

"Bangin," exclaimed Franco, punching the air. He grabbed his jacket off the back of a chair. "Nice perfume, by the way."

"Shut up," said Bixler.

Franco grinned and ran out of the darkened security center, letting the door cushion shut behind him.

"Why do you put up with him?" asked Pilgrim. "He's like this overgrown kid who clowns around all the time saying asinine stuff."

Bixler threw Pilgrim a sharp glance.

"Not about your perfume," Pilgrim added quickly. "I wasn't talking about that. I love it. We all do. Very chic."

"You're a terrible liar," observed Bixler.

Pilgrim smiled and did not reply.

"I don't mean to overdo it," said Bixler. "I just love fragrance. Fragrance represents happiness, *romance,* indulgence. God knows I need it since this job is anything but. Same with Franco. All day long I deal with terrorists and bad guys and people trying to harm our country, so having him around is like having an in-house sitcom. He's annoying, he's funny and he's obsessed with anything in a skirt. A welcome if at times irritating distraction from all the crap that comes with this job. I honestly couldn't manage without him. And if you repeat any of this -- and I mean *any* of it -- I will strangle you. With rope that's been dipped in perfume."

Pilgrim laughed. "Franco is definitely a charmer."

"He charmed Countess de la Peña," said Bixler. "If he hadn't, we wouldn't be here."

On one of the monitors, Bixler saw Franco dash out of a stairwell and immediately slow to a casual pace before threading his way across the busy foyer and into the arcade.

"I see them, they're entering the casino," he said, bringing his wrist to his mouth and speaking into a tiny microphone.

"Stay with him," Bixler replied.

Inside the casino, Talanov and Sofia paused on the paisley carpet and oriented themselves to the layout. More than a dozen security cameras were mounted on the ceiling at strategic positions above gaming tables. Slot machines, regarded as tawdry necessities by casino management, had been placed around the perimeter of the paneled room. In the center of "El Gran Salón," as the main gaming area was known, was a circular bar. Above it was a massive crystal chandelier. Positioned around the bar were the gaming tables -- craps, cards and roulette -- where customers were enticed as much by the cleavage of young waitresses as by the lure of breaking the bank.

Refusing the offer of Champagne from one of those young waitresses, Talanov glanced around to see Franco, who stopped abruptly in the arcade to look in the window of a women's lingerie shop. Talanov chuckled, then nodded to Sofia, who accompanied him across the carpet to where a crowd had gathered to watch a tiny white ball spinning in the opposite direction of the rotating roulette wheel. The ball finally slowed, hit a fret and bounced several times before settling on a number. Cheers and groans erupted from the crowd as croupiers began distributing and raking in chips.

The roulette wheel itself was at one end of what looked like a small pool table that was surfaced with green felt. Stenciled on the felt was a rectangular grid, with columns and rows of red or black numbers corresponding to numbers on the wheel. There were a total of four casino employees operating the table. Two croupiers managed the bets and the wheel, while two supervisors, one at each end of the table, made sure the game proceeded smoothly. All were men and all were attired in black slacks, white shirts, bow ties and vests of embroidered gold.

"Hagan sus apuestas," one of the croupiers called out, inviting gamers to place their bets.

While chips were being placed on the various numbers, columns and colors, Sofia laid the aluminum briefcase on the edge of the table and took out several stacks of banded one-hundred-dollar bills. Each stack was nearly two inches thick. Sofia handed them to Talanov while everyone openly stared.

"Imprisonment rules on a red-or-black bet?" asked Talanov.

"Si, señor, but I regret to say we do not accept cash at this table," the croupier politely replied.

"Of course you do," said Talanov. He laid the stacks of cash down onto the felt and nodded for the croupier to check with his supervisor. "Fifty thousand dollars, American."

The croupier looked nervously at the *Jefe del Grupo,* the "group chief" -- his supervisor -- who was standing beside him.

Wearing a thoughtful frown, the *Jefe del Grupo* scrutinized Talanov for a long moment then nodded for the croupier to accept his bet.

"Which color would you like, *señor?"* asked the croupier.

Talanov again smiled up at the camera.

Up in the security center, Bixler pointed angrily at the monitor. "The son of a bitch is *taunting us."*

"You may want to look at this," said Pilgrim, seated in front of another monitor.

"He just bet fifty thousand dollars!" railed Bixler. "I'll be lucky to see that in a *lifetime!* The cocky bastard's already won big in Barcelona, Valencia and Torrevieja, and now he's down there tossing money around like there's no tomorrow." She watched Talanov rub his chin thoughtfully before placing his bet.

"Glenda?" said Pilgrim just as the croupier called out, *"No más apuestas,"* telling people that the accepting of bets had now closed. A hush fell over the table as the croupier spun the wheel in one direction before sending the tiny white ball spinning in the opposite direction.

Bixler pulled her eyes away from the roulette table monitor and onto Pilgrim's. "What have you got?" she asked.

"Using our latest generation of facial recognition software, I've been keeping track of anyone who might be following Talanov or watching him beyond normal parameters."

"And?"

"Excluding casino employees, we've flagged this guy," said Pilgrim, pointing to a powerfully-built man in black. The man had short thinking hair and muscular arms.

"Built like a tree trunk. Who is he?"

"I ran his face through our database and got a hit. His name's Zakhar Babikov and he's a Soviet hitman."

"Are you sure he's following Talanov?"

"Positive. We have footage of him trailing Talanov into the hotel but turning away discreetly when Sofia entered, after which he maintained a safe distance but stayed focused on what Talanov was doing. On two occasions, when Talanov looked around, Babikov shielded his face, obviously not wanting Talanov to see him. When Talanov and Sofia left the registration desk for the casino, Babikov followed. When Talanov and Sofia stopped to admire a statue, he stopped as well."

"Why would the Soviets send a hitman to follow Talanov?"

"Isn't that what they do? Everyone spying on everyone else?"

"But why?"

"Talanov hasn't exactly been following protocol," said Pilgrim.

"Meaning he may have pissed off some of the permafrosts in Moscow with his extravagant living?"

"It's possible," answered Pilgrim. "We have to assume Talanov is here because of Gorev's defection, obviously to prevent it. We also have to assume the Soviets would send someone like Babikov to take out Gorev if it looks like Talanov can't stop the defection."

"What I don't get is Talanov's flamboyant behavior," said Bixler, looking back at the roulette monitor. "Look at him down there, living it up. Why would he be drawing attention to himself like that?"

Pilgrim scooted over in front of the roulette table monitor, where the white ball was starting to bounce on the frets while everyone looked eagerly on. "Maybe Talanov's a diversion? Maybe Moscow wants us to be watching him while Babikov slips in unnoticed?"

"To do what?" asked Bixler.

"Kill Gorev."

"If that were the case, Babikov wouldn't be following Talanov. He'd be honing in on Gorev. But according to what you just said, Babikov's following Talanov, right?"

"Affirmative."

"Could Talanov be the target?"

"Maybe," said Pilgrim. "Another scenario is that Moscow believes Talanov knows what he's doing and will eventually locate Gorev, so the hitman is tagging along to see what happens. One thing is certain: no way will the KGB allow Gorev to tell us what he knows. Nor will they allow his family to live, since they can't risk them telling us anything, either. They're walking dead people, all of them, and Babikov may well be their killer."

On the roulette table monitor, the white ball bounced several more times before settling into a slot.

A loud moan went up from the crowd.

"He lost, Talanov *lost!*" exclaimed Franco, his excitement broadcasting loud and clear over the speaker.

Upstairs, Bixler laughed and clapped her hands. On the monitor, people were patting Talanov consolingly on the back while the croupier raked in the two stacks of money.

"This guy is too much," continued Franco. "He bets a cool fifty grand, and with one bounce of the ball, loses all of that money. And he didn't even flinch. He simply shrugged like he'd just lost two bucks at the race track."

"How can he lose that much money and not throw a tantrum?" asked Bixler.

"Uh, because he's not you?" asked Franco.

"Shut up!" growled Bixler while Franco chuckled.

Bixler watched Talanov leave the casino.

Seconds later, Babikov followed.

CHAPTER 7

Unbuttoning his tuxedo jacket and loosening his bow tie, Talanov strode into the crowded lobby and paused amid the murmur of happy conversation to wait for Sofia. He looked up the wide staircase toward the nightclub located on the mezzanine floor, where he could hear a flamenco dancer stomping her feet in time to the staccato accompaniment of several guitars. He closed his eyes and listened to the rising intensity of the music.

His reverie was interrupted by the sharp sounds of Sofia's stiletto heels. Turning, he walked with Sofia to the reception counter.

"May I help you, Colonel Talanov?" the attendant asked pleasantly.

"Good evening," said Talanov. "May we place our brief-case in your safe?"

"Of course."

"We'll return for it after I've had something to cheer me up. Perhaps I'll fare better at the tango than I did at roulette."

The attendant nodded politely and accepted the aluminum briefcase.

"Shall we?" asked Talanov, offering Sofia his arm.

Appearing to be reading a tourist brochure in a stuffed chair across the lobby, Babikov discreetly watched Talanov and Sofia fall in with the stream of guests climbing the stairs. He folded the brochure back into its original shape, tossed it on the table and once they reached the top, followed after them.

Talanov paused inside the nightclub and surveyed the layout. Lighting was subdued except for a bright spotlight on a young woman in a fitted long red dress. She was on a stage at the far end of the club. Her thick brown hair was pulled back in a large bun. Her lips were bright red, her eyes seductive and dark.

The dancer held her torso erect and proud, her arms curving around her head, her castanets and feet keeping time with the passionate climax of the music. The bottom of her dress, which was ruffled and full, twirled with each of her movements. To one side of her were three guitarists seated on stools. In the darkened background were drums, a piano and other musicians holding instruments: a *bandoneón* -- similar to an accordion -- violins and a string bass.

The bar ran along one wall to their left. Every stool was occupied and people were standing two and three deep while vested bartenders -- mostly dark-haired young women -- glided expertly behind the bar mixing drinks. Tiers of mirrored shelves contained every imaginable liquor. Banks of waist-high refrigerators contained mugs, Champagne, wine, beer and mineral water.

Seating for patrons was to their right while at the center of the club was a wooden dance floor.

The wedding party Talanov had seen earlier had taken over the far corner of the club. The bride and groom were seated at the center of a table, surrounded by friends and family. Everybody was laughing and drinking and picking from large platters of flat bread, salmon, caviar, goat cheese, olives and grilled vegetables.

On stage, the young flamenco dancer twirled to the strumming guitar crescendo and finished in a flurry of castanets and stomping. When finished, the panting and perspiring dancer held her erect position for a long moment, back arched stiffly, arms poised high overhead before making several tumbling motions with her hands in a downward sweep that ended in a gracious curtsy, her front leg locked and extended, her arms in opposite directions, her head almost touching the floor.

She held that position for nearly ten seconds while Talanov glanced around the nightclub at the people chatting among themselves, not paying attention.

"Bravo!" he called out. "Magnificent!"

When Talanov began clapping, the club grew momentarily quiet. When he stepped forward and continued to clap, people around him joined in.

The dancer straightened and curtsied again, hands extended to her sides -- a gracious bow of appreciation -- and after straightening a final time, she blew Talanov a kiss before dashing through the crowd and leaving by way of a service door located at the end of the bar, near the restrooms.

By now the guitarists had regrouped with other members of the combo, and after a dramatic, pounding introduction on the piano, the *bandoneón* began playing a tense, smoldering, sexual tango, with swirling upper notes by the violins and a deep, lustful moan by the string bass, all of it building slowly, aggressively, like a mating ritual between predators circling one another.

Talanov again glanced around the nightclub at people chatting, not paying attention. A group of seven girls got up and began dancing in place, arms and hips swaying wildly, laughing, enjoying themselves. Several were nursing drinks in stem glasses while they danced. The young bride and groom then took to the floor and began shuffling around in a clumsy box-step, watching their feet, giggling at their clumsiness. They were soon joined by three other couples from their wedding party, who began doing the same box step, having obviously taken dance lessons in preparation for this night.

"Come on," said Talanov, taking Sofia by the hand. "We can't allow a good tango to go to waste."

Sofia resisted.

"What's wrong?"

"I *can't,*" she whispered over the intensifying waves of

music.

"Why not?"

"Because . . . I *can't.* I don't know how."

"Then it's time you learned."

Talanov led Sofia onto the dance floor and spun her to face him. "Hands here and here," he said, showing her where they belonged then pulling her to him so they were but inches apart, their thighs and abdomens touching. He moved his hand to the small of her back and pulled her tightly against him, holding her there, staring into her eyes with the hint of a smile.

"How long do we stand here like this?" she asked.

"Fifteen minutes should do it."

Sofia raised a skeptical eyebrow.

Talanov grinned, lifted his elbow and moved his hand up to the middle of her back. "Think of the tango as walking -- I lead, you follow -- like mirrors."

"You have got to be joking."

"I never joke when it comes to the tango. Are you ready?"

"No!"

"Relax, you'll be fine. I'll be stepping forward and you'll be stepping backward -- mirroring -- legs brushing against one another, bodies close, never losing that connection. We then keep walking -- one, two, three -- then step to the side, bring our feet together and stamp, then continue in a new direction, or maybe the same, who knows?"

"Who knows? What do you mean by that? How am I supposed to know what you'll do next?"

"It doesn't matter. I lead, you follow. Are you ready?"

"No! I have to know what we're doing."

"And that is precisely why no one out here is doing the tango," Talanov replied. "Those girls are too busy doing their own thing. Everybody else is worrying about the wrong things. This dance is about us, not our feet."

By now Talanov and Sofia had been standing together in the center of the dance floor for several minutes while the wedding party continued to shuffle around them and the girls continued to jump and laugh. On stage, the musicians continued to play in the red glow of the stage lights.

Sofia noticed the bride and groom looking at them curiously. "People are staring," she whispered nervously.

"Let them. You're worth it," said Talanov.

From his position near the end of the bar, Babikov stood watching, sipping from a glass of mineral water, one elbow on the bar, his back to the wall, his jacket sleeves stretched by the size of his arms.

Entering the nightclub, Franco moved to one side of the door, his eyes on Talanov, his wrist to his mouth, speaking quietly into his microphone. "Are you watching this?" he asked.

Up in the security center, Bixler had positioned herself beside Pilgrim in front of the nightclub monitor. "What the hell are they *doing?*"

"Looks like he's giving her a dance lesson," Franco replied.

"Or trying to, anyway," added Pilgrim. "By the way, we're all set in Talanov's room."

"Audio and video, both?" asked Bixler.

"The whole place is wired. To the hilt."

On the dance floor, Sofia pulled away and tried to leave. "I can't do this," she said.

Talanov grabbed her and pulled her back. "Yes, you can."

"No, I can't!"

Talanov saw the young flamenco dancer enter the club and join a group of friends at the bar. She was no longer in costume but was dressed in boots, a mini-skirt and a ruffled blouse.

Motioning for the musicians to keep playing, Talanov told Sofia to stay where she was. Squeezing and sidling between tables, he reached the bar, excused himself for the intrusion, grabbed the flamenco dancer by the hand and led her onto the dance floor, where he glanced pointedly at Sofia before spinning the dancer into his arms and pulling her tightly against him.

Talanov and the dancer stared into one another's eyes for a long moment before the dancer arched her back and looked away. Moving slowly forward while the dancer moved backward, each step sexual and deliberate, Talanov began steering the dancer in a tight circle around Sofia.

Twirling the dancer away like a yo-yo until their arms were fully extended, they glanced at one another briefly before Talanov twirled her back. He slid her from side to side, trying as part of the ritual to get her to look at him while she steadfastly refused, avoiding his demanding eyes with darting quick-step reverses, taking tiny steps back and forth while making exaggerated movements with her knees and hips. Then a dismissive glance before throwing her head back, avoiding eye contact until the next compelling, dismissive glance.

Standing in the epicenter of this spectacle, Sofia grew increasingly embarrassed as more and more people stopped talking to watch. The wedding party had stopped dancing and moved to the perimeter of the floor to observe, as had the group of girls, who were holding on to one another's arms, pointing and whispering about Talanov while scrutinizing Sofia.

Near the door, Franco stood watching.

Babikov was at the end of the bar.

Upstairs were Bixler and Pilgrim.

Everyone was watching.

Scanning the faces of everyone staring back at them, Sofia shuffled awkwardly in place. "All right, you've made your point," she whispered harshly.

The tempo of the tango intensified and Sofia looked at the musicians, who were lost in their music, eyes closed, feeling the notes. With folded arms, she glared at Talanov, who was lost in the dance. Rivulets of perspiration trickled down his face.

Talanov paused and threw her a sharp glance, then twirled the dancer away and back, yanking her close before moving his nose slowly down and up her neck, not quite touching her skin while the group of seven girls stared open-mouthed at the sensual scene.

Muttering a curse, Sofia brushed past Talanov stormed away.

Talanov grabbed her by the hand and pulled her back.

Sofia tried breaking free but Talanov released the dancer and spun Sofia into his arms. He bent her backward and kept her off balance, as if over a barrel while staring down into her eyes. He then pulled her upright, snapped her to him and began moving with her about the floor, advancing while she retreated, mirroring, in step, legs brushing, abdomens pressed tightly together.

"This is the tango," he said in a husky voice. "It is passion. It is *jealousy.* It is desire."

She stared into his eyes while the music swelled to a climax.

And with a twinkle in his eye at the final crescendo, he added, "It's also a great way to work up a thirst."

Twirling Sofia away in grandiose style, Talanov presented her to the musicians, who stood and began clapping. He then glanced at the flamenco dancer, who blew him another kiss. With a nod and a smile, he blew her one in return before sweeping Sofia off the floor.

"For the record, I was not jealous," Sofia remarked in a low voice.

"Whatever you say," said Talanov with a grin as they left the club.

Seconds later, the man in black followed.

CHAPTER 8

They reached the bottom of the stairs and crossed the lobby to the reception counter.

"Good evening, Colonel Talanov," the receptionist said, handing him his aluminum briefcase.

"Indeed it is," he replied. "So good I'd like to upgrade to the Presidential Suite."

The receptionist checked her computer and suddenly grew nervous. "Please excuse me for a moment," she said, stepping over to her supervisor.

After a brief exchange, the supervisor, a man of forty, approached Talanov.

"I am very sorry," the supervisor said, "but the Presidential Suite is occupied."

"Are you certain?" asked Talanov.

The supervisor smiled. "I'm afraid so."

"Have they checked in?"

The manager's smile remained fixed in place.

"Perhaps you could place them elsewhere?" tried Talanov. "I would be *most* appreciative."

"The hotel is full. There are no other rooms."

"Are you absolutely sure?"

The supervisor cleared his throat discreetly.

Talanov turned to Sofia. "Did you hear that? The hotel is full."

Sofia placed her briefcase on the counter, opened it and took out a dark gray "brick" cell phone, which she handed to

Talanov, who peeked over the counter at the number listed on the hotel phone and began punching those numbers into the phone's keypad.

"Are you seeing what I'm seeing?" Franco said into his wrist mike from across the foyer.

"*Yes,* dammit!" shouted Bixler, who was watching on the security monitor. "Where the *hell* did he get a DynaTAC 8000? *We* hardly have cell phone technology like that, and here he is, pulling one out of a briefcase *in full view of the camera.*"

"Who's he calling?" asked Franco.

"How the hell should I know?" yelled Bixler.

Talanov handed the phone to Sofia. Seconds later, the hotel desk phone began ringing.

"Gran Casino del Sol, *buenas noches,*" the receptionist said.

"Good evening," Sofia replied from ten feet away. "My name is Anna Pavlova and I would like to transfer my reservation for the Presidential Suite to Colonel Aleksandr Talanov, who is standing in front of you."

The receptionist had been staring wide-eyed at Sofia during the conversation, and once Sofia had finished, slowly hung up before lowering her eyes and sheepishly telling her supervisor what had just happened. Talanov watched the man's face turn ashen. The supervisor stood there for the longest moment, not able to look Talanov in the eye.

"Our key, now, if you please," said Talanov.

The receptionist looked over at her supervisor, who reluctantly nodded.

"While you're at it," said Talanov, "please have room service bring up a bottle of vodka, a bucket of ice, some limes, smoked salmon, *two dozen oysters,* cream cheese, capers, gourmet crackers, a wedge of brie and some dark chocolate. Have you got all that?"

Talanov looked pointedly at the supervisor.

"Of course, sir. As you wish," the supervisor replied, still avoiding Talanov's eyes.

"Excellent," chirped Talanov. He reached into his pocket and took out a casino chip. "Next time, be careful who you're betting against," he said, placing the chip on the counter.

Upstairs in the security center, Bixler pounded her fist on the counter. "Did you see what he just *did?* We go to all the trouble of bugging his room -- and I mean *trouble,* because the countess did *not* want us installing video and audio surveillance in one of their rooms -- and he up and pulls this cute little stunt and ends up in the *Presidential Suite,* where we've got *nothing!"*

"We can improvise and get audio," a technician said.

"What about video?" she asked.

The technician shook his head.

Bixler shouted an expletive and began pacing the floor in front of the monitors, one hand rubbing her forehead. "How soon on the audio?" she asked.

"Once room service has been there and gone."

"Want me to stay close to him?" asked Franco.

"Like stink on shit. Report back when they get to their room, then get down to housekeeping and change into a waiter's uniform. I want you delivering that cart to make sure it's *them* in that suite."

"Talanov may know who I am."

"What do you mean, he may know who you are?"

"When they entered the casino, Talanov paused and looked back. I pretended to be window shopping but may have been spotted. If I show up in a waiter's uniform, he'll know we're onto him."

"As if he doesn't already. All right, I'll figure something out. In the meantime, *stay with him."*

Talanov and Sofia took the elevator to the top floor and were soon in their suite. Twenty minutes later, the elevator doors opened and a waiter emerged with a fully laden service cart. Pilgrim intercepted the waiter, took the cart and wheeled it to the housekeeping closet, where she finished getting dressed in a white shirt, bowtie, black vest and black slacks.

"I don't see why *I* have to do this," she complained to Bixler, who was standing beside her. "I look like an emperor penguin."

"You're doing it because no one else possesses your level of technical skill."

"I'm pushing a service cart into a room. What kind of technical skill does that require?"

"All right, you're doing it because I'm your boss and I'm ordering you to do it."

Pilgrim scowled and Bixler smiled.

"Problem is, I don't speak Spanish," said Pilgrim.

"Your point?"

"You do, which means you're the ideal choice for this job, not me. He'll peg me in no time if I have to read a menu or answer a question."

"You'll think of something," Bixler replied. "The big hair has to go, too."

"Come on, Glenda! I spent a lot of money on this hair."

"Which looks great in DC. This is Spain and you're supposed to be working for a hotel."

While Pilgrim growled her discontent, Bixler combed the volume out of Pilgrim's hair.

"Sometimes, I hate this job," grumbled Pilgrim.

"Good thing you've got such an understanding boss," chirped Bixler. "Okay, off you go. Any gratuity, by the way, becomes government property and must be surrendered."

Pilgrim replied with an exaggerated smile and in less than a minute was knocking on Talanov's door. Seconds later, Sofia opened the door and Pilgrim pushed the cart into the suite.

To her left was a massive fireplace with a flat granite mantle and a stack of cut logs in an alcove to one side. Along the wall, beneath a framed painting of the rolling Spanish countryside, was a pedestal holding a glazed blue urn. Straight ahead were two large, open, curtained windows with small balconies overlooking the golf course. A summery breeze was wafting the curtains. To her right, beside a tall, carved wooden armoire, was a door leading into the bedroom, where a king size bed and a polished walnut writing desk could be seen.

"Por ahí va a estar bien," said Talanov, seated on one of three cream-colored sofas positioned around a glass coffee table. Using the remote control, he pointed to a small round table near one of the opened windows.

"Mne ochen' zhal', ya ne govoryu po-ispanski," Pilgrim answered in Russian.

Talanov nodded with approval. "Very considerate, speaking Russian."

"We have a range of translators here at Gran Casino del Sol," Pilgrim replied, pushing the cart across the travertine floor to a table by the window.

Talanov watched her remove the silver dome and place it on a lower shelf of the cart.

"May I serve you a drink?" Pilgrim asked.

"No, thank you," Talanov replied, aiming the remote at the TV and clicking on a soccer game.

Sofia handed Pilgrim a hundred dollar bill and gestured her toward the door. With a slight bow, Pilgrim thanked Talanov and Sofia and left the room. Before closing and locking the door, Sofia hung a do-not-disturb placard on the handle.

With a quick glance at the placard rocking back and forth on the handle, Pilgrim hurried down the corridor to the housekeeping closet, where she was motioned inside by Bixler. Beside Bixler was surveillance technician, Tom Miles. Miles stood six-feet-two and had a receding hairline of shaggy black hair that was pulled back in a ponytail.

"Well?" Bixler asked Pilgrim.

"It's definitely them," she said. "Looks like they're in for the night."

Bixler gave Miles the nod. "Okay, big guy, you're up."

"Why didn't we just put a listening device on the cart?" Pilgrim asked Miles.

"I didn't want to take the risk of Talanov finding it," he replied. "There aren't a lot of hiding places on those carts."

"Let's get this done," said Bixler.

With a nod, Miles picked up his kit and moved quietly

down the carpeted corridor, staying close to the wall. When he neared the door of the Presidential Suite, he knelt, opened his kit and placed a rubber replica of some vomit on the floor. He then took out some paper towels, so that if a hotel guest walked by, he would pretend to be cleaning up the mess.

Miles took out a filament listening pod. At one end of the pod was an adhesive strip. Miles peeled off the protective cellophane, slipped the pod under the door and pressed the adhesive strip into place, near the hinge. He then plugged a thin wire into the pod and ran it along the edge of the carpet to a small transmitter. At that moment, Pilgrim walked by and handed him a platter of dirty dishes and leftover food. Miles concealed the transmitter among the dishes and covered it with an inverted plate and some crumpled up napkins. No guest would stop to investigate a mess like that, and the hotel staff had been instructed to leave it alone. Miles then picked up the vomit and returned to the housekeeping closet.

"Are we up and running?" Bixler spoke into her wrist mike.

"Loud and clear," a voice came back.

"Okay, we're done. Let's go," she said.

Inside the darkened security center minutes later, Bixler and other members of her team gathered around an operator wearing a headset. Seated at a reel-to-reel console, the operator unplugged the headset and the conversation could be heard by everyone over the speaker.

"I've already established a baseline of their voices," the operator said.

"And you're certain this is a live conversation and not a prerecorded tape?" asked Bixler.

"Positive," the operator replied. "You can tell by specific remarks imbedded in the narrative."

"Such as?"

"Comments about Donna speaking Russian."

"And he bought it?" asked Bixler.

"Absolutely. Talanov was impressed."

"I told him it was a service the hotel provided," offered Pilgrim.

"Good thinking," said Bixler. "Did Talanov give you a tip?"

"Nothing. Can you believe it?" Pilgrim replied, gesturing with indignation.

"Asshole," Bixler snarled.

"Whoa, did you see *that?*" a man's voice exclaimed in Russian over the speaker just as a cheering crowd could be heard on the television in the background. "Look at the way Ireland kicked that ball wide right, across the field, then brought it back into the middle for a score!"

"Are we really watching soccer all night?" a woman's voice asked.

"Are you kidding? This is a World Cup Qualifier! Not too much ice, by the way."

"Do I look like your waitress?"

"Let me know if anything changes," said Bixler, motioning for the operator to plug his earphones back in. "If Talanov tries to go out, I want him tackled and stuffed in a closet."

"You're not serious?" said the operator.

"You're damned right I'm serious. All we need are four more hours, so if Talanov decides to leave that room -- for *any* reason -- I want him taken into custody. We'll apologize later. Say it was a case of mistaken identity. But he is *not* to step out of that room during the next four hours. I'll post Doug and Tim at each end of the hall and Gary outside on the grounds."

"And the man in black. What about him?"

"He's following Talanov, not us, so if Talanov stays in, so does he. Where is he, by the way?"

"No idea. With all the focus on Talanov, we lost track of him."

"Find him. See if there's any video footage of him checking in."

"On it," the operator replied.

Bixler checked her watch. "Okay, let's go. It's time to welcome Gorev and his family to freedom."

They left the security room and took the stairwell down to the main floor, where they paused to check for anyone following. Hearing no one, they pushed open the door and slipped out of the building by way of the swimming pool, where they skirted the luminescent turquoise water. Making their way around the outside of the casino and across a putting green, they followed a line of pencil pines to the circular drive, where they quietly piled in their van. Franco slid behind the wheel, Bixler into the passenger seat and Pilgrim directly behind. Within minutes, they had passed through the mob of protestors gathered at the entrance and turned onto the darkened highway.

They drove in silence for just over a mile. Franco had his elbow out the open window, enjoying the warm night air, which was scented with lemon balm and lavender.

Bixler finally broke the silence with a question. "Have we ever done this much for a man we know so little about?"

Pilgrim and Franco looked at Bixler.

"I mean, what do we know about Gorev?" she asked.

It was a rhetorical question and Bixler went on to elaborate how she understood why Gorev was so guarded about revealing any details about his defection. He was, after all, fleeing a totalitarian country that exiled defectors to Siberia. Barring execution, of course, which also was possible should they be caught. Small wonder Gorev was so frightened and cautious. Those fears also explained why he elected to use his teenage daughter, Noya, to initiate contact with Sharon Williams, a translator working undercover as the temporary CIA Chief of Station in the American Consulate in Leningrad, when she returned home from work one night. Noya spoke English, and a polite teenage girl in a stairwell was far less threatening to a woman than an older man would be. Plus, Gorev knew he could not risk being seen, especially with an American in a city where Americans were carefully watched.

Sharon's report, which Bixler had read several times, detailed the encounter and how Noya said her father was a Soviet medical scientist who wanted to defect, but because he feared Sharon's apartment had been bugged -- which Sharon knew that it had -- was asking to meet with her in a nearby location. Ordinarily, Sharon would have ignored the request and continued up to her apartment. Typically, meetings like that were either a scam or a set-up for a robbery.

But there was something in Noya's sad eyes that let her know the girl was telling the truth. However, street scammers were seasoned actors, so she needed to be sure.

"Who is your father?" asked Sharon.

"He said he would tell you if you agreed to meet with him."

"Where is he now?"

"He said I should bring you to him."

"Where is that?"

"I will take you."

"You're not telling me very much."

Noya did not reply.

"Why should I trust you?" asked Sharon.

Noya replied by asking her the same question. "Why should I trust *you?* My father said I should bring you, but I am not so sure. I do not trust so easily."

Sharon smiled. "Do you trust your father?"

"Of course."

"If your father trusts me enough to send you here, shouldn't you trust me, too?"

Noya replied with a thoughtful frown.

Sharon said, "I need to know who your father is and what he does."

"My father said he would tell you if you agreed to meet with him."

"Okay. I get that. I know your father needs to be careful. But I need to be careful, too. People have tried this before and not everyone tells the truth. That's why I'm asking you these questions. I want to help, but like you, I need to be careful. Do you understand?"

Noya nodded.

"Okay," said Sharon. "What kind of a scientist is he?"

"He is a medical doctor but he does not speak about it very much. Speaking about it makes him anxious."

"But you don't know what he does?"

Noya shook her head.

"Does he see patients, like doctors do?"

Noya shook her head again. "He works in a laboratory, in Sverdlovsk, with other scientists."

"Why did your father pick me?"

"I do not know. He told me what you looked like and said I should wait here in the stairwell for you to come home."

Sharon nodded. "Why America?"

"My father said people can become whatever they want in America."

"They can. But America's a long way from home. Are you sure you would like it there?"

"My father talks to me about Disneyland, thinking I am still eleven or that I believe America is a happy place."

"But?"

"It may be happier than Soviet Union but it is still a place where you can be unhappy as well. In school, we hear only bad things. At home, I hear only good." She shrugged. "I do not know who to believe."

Sharon smiled with understanding. "Then we'd better do something about that. Come on, let's meet your father."

CHAPTER 9

Noya led Sharon to a neighboring block of highrise apartments, where they climbed the stairs up to the floor above, hurried to the far end of the building and back down the other stairs and out the door, where they ran across an empty lot, between four more blocks of apartments and into another block, where Gorev was waiting in a basement corridor beneath the harsh glare of an overhead bulb. The corridor led to a furnace room and was sooty with coal dust.

With Noya translating, Gorev introduced himself, thanked Sharon for coming, then introduced his wife, Anna, and his parents, saying they were being pursued by the KGB and wanted to defect if the Americans would grant them asylum. Speaking fluent Russian -- to the surprise of Gorev and his family -- Sharon asked what Gorev's medical specialty was. Gathering his family together in front of him, Gorev replied that it was too dangerous to speak of in such informal surroundings. Sharon nodded pleasantly, indicating that she understood his not wanting to communicate details about what he did in front of the others.

Nevertheless, if Gorev wanted asylum, Sharon needed more than a few vague hints. "We grant asylum to people whose lives are in danger in their own countries. Is this the case for you and your family?"

Gorev nodded.

"Why is that?" asked Sharon.

Gorev rubbed his forehead anxiously. How much should

he reveal? From what he'd heard, the Americans did not know about the secret laboratories of *Biopreparat.*

He thought about the laboratory where he worked and how it had been constructed beneath a compound of mustard-colored hospital buildings. And because it was underground, it was impossible to detect by satellite or ground surveillance. Built four blocks from the edge of a depressing downtown district, the complex was surrounded by wooded parklands and a concrete parking lot full of cars. Beyond was a river and the residential sprawl of the city. Ambulances came and went to the hospital, and a nearby factory spewed soot into the air. By all appearances, it was a functioning medical facility in a medium-sized polluted Russian city.

Protected by a garrison of armed troops, the underground complex was accessed through blast-proof steel doors. Comprised of laboratories, clinics, surgical theaters and more than a dozen observation and experimentation rooms connected by a network of reinforced concrete tunnels, the complex employed over one hundred medical and scientific personnel in rotating twelve-hour shifts. Unlike the deteriorated appearance of the hospital above, the underground complex was outfitted with the latest computers, equipment and supplies. There were miles of electrical wiring for communications, lighting, air filtration, heating, incubators and refrigerators -- rows and rows of them -- plus freezers capable of holding dozens of cadavers. There was a cafeteria and sleeping quarters, and the complex maintained its own generators and sanitation. Prisoners were brought in for experimentation through a separate tunnel accessed from a parking garage two blocks away. Bodies were removed the same way and burned in the nearby factory.

He knew biological weapons was one of those murky areas you didn't really let yourself think much about, because if you did, you would crack under the pressure. A genetically engineered strain of bacteria in a Petri dish was one thing. Injecting that strain into the arm of an inmate to see how quickly he died was another. The screams . . . the cries of desperation for something -- anything -- to end the suffering had eventually become unbearable.

His supervisors considered the Nazis barbarians, doing what they did to the Jews. What they failed to see -- or saw but did not want to admit -- was how little difference there was between what the Nazis did and what they were doing.

His last group of prisoners had been the worst. After unknowingly being fed a powerful laxative in the food line one day, the five targets -- three men and two women between the ages of twenty-six and sixty -- had been brought into his clinic for treatment, having been told they were being inoculated against dysentery, after which they would be kept for observation. The inmates were actually excited to be sick, thinking they would be given decent food, some clean clothes and a comfortable bed. He then had the assigned task of recording the progression of their symptoms while watching their initial optimism turn to uncontrollable shivers and raging fever within hours of being injected. Several hours later, terror set in when each of the inmates started coughing up blood. Within twenty-two hours, every one of them was dead.

And all because of a virulent new strain of bacteria that he himself had engineered.

His supervisors and department heads -- all five of them -- were ecstatic. He could still see them laughing and dancing behind the window when he went home that night.

Something had to change. Someone had to speak up.

Ordinarily, he would not have had the strength to carry out a defection. But over the last year, he had seen the light fade from Noya's eyes. She never laughed. She seldom smiled. She didn't eat. The same with his wife, Anna. They were slowly dying under the constant surveillance, being followed wherever they went, eyes watching them everywhere.

Thus, he set about planning their defection, knowing if they were caught trying to escape, or if anyone got so much as a hint that he was planning something like this, his family would be exiled or executed. Their only hope was reaching the West.

And so, here he was, in Leningrad, on the border of freedom, meeting with a woman he hoped would help them escape. But now was not the time to explain what the Soviet Union was doing.

Gorev glanced at his daughter, who was looking around at the spider webs and dirt of the corridor. Here they were, on the run, fearing for their lives, hoping beyond hope they didn't starve or get caught. Noya deserved a future, which he could not give her so long as he did what he did.

"Dr. Gorev?" asked Sharon in the absence of a reply.

"I cannot say, not here."

"I sympathize, Dr. Gorev," Sharon replied. "Unfortunately, before we can talk about whether or not you qualify for asylum, I need to know why your lives are in danger."

"My government does not want me to explain to you the nature of my research."

"Which is?"

"I cannot say."

"But this has placed your lives in danger?"

Gorev nodded.

"I've heard rumors that some of your laboratories are researching germs that make people sick," Sharon continued, speaking in Russian and choosing her words carefully since Gorev's family could understand every word. "Can you speak to those rumors?"

Clearly nervous at the question, Gorev repeated that he was unable to answer any specific questions right now, adding that a hematopathologist would be able to verify everything he had to show them once he and his family were safe.

"Are you saying you have something to show us? As in samples that would speak to those rumors?"

Gorev nodded.

Sharon said, "All right, then, based on what you're telling me, the United States can grant you and your family asylum. Unfortunately, we have a big problem and that's my inability to get you out of Leningrad without some advance planning. As you know, Cold War tensions have never been greater between our two countries. Thus, to risk an escalation with anything less than a well-planned strategy is out of the question."

"I do not require you to help us escape," Gorev replied. "I will take care of that myself. I ask only that you grant us asylum once we arrive."

"That can be arranged."

"I mean no disrespect, Miss Williams, but you are a secretary. Do you have the authority to make such a guarantee?"

Sharon smiled. "Yes, I do."

"Can your people receive us in a city of my choosing?"

"Where might that be?"

"With respect, I do not wish to state right now where that is."

"That's fine. When you're ready, let me know when and where and we'll work something out."

And for the first time that night, Gorev smiled.

"Thank you very much," he replied, shaking Sharon's hand vigorously. "Noya speaks very good English. I will have her phone you at your Consulate in three days with the information that you require."

"I'll wait for her call. When she phones, have her ask for Walt Disney so I'll know who it is."

And for the first time that night, Noya smiled.

Bixler rode along silently in the darkened van thinking about Sharon's report. Sharon knew how to read people and said Gorev had been difficult to judge. He had dropped all the right hints but in fact had said very little of substance. She had encountered people like that before and most of them had been fakes.

For Sharon, it was Noya's fatalistic honesty that let her know Gorev was probably legit. Sharon went on to say she had done a lot of reading between the lines, but thought with a high degree of certainty that Gorev was probably part of a top-secret biological weapons program. "We've got no evidence such a program even exists," Sharon concluded, "but I think Gorev may well be that evidence. I recommend we grant him asylum."

"You're awfully quiet up there," said Pilgrim, breaking Bixler's reverie.

"I was thinking about Sharon's report," Bixler replied.

"Gorev does know to expect long lines at Disneyland, doesn't he?" asked Franco.

Bixler and Pilgrim both laughed.

Picking up her phone, Bixler entered a number and put the phone to her ear. After some static and a series of clicks, a connection was made to Ricardo Valerdi, the operator in the security room. Bixler asked if everything was secure.

"Talanov and Dubinina are still bickering over soccer," Valerdi replied, "and their conversation matches exactly what's happening in the game."

"So we know they're still in the room?"

"Affirmative. When Ireland scored, Talanov cheered and made glowing remarks about Ireland's genetic superiority. Dubinina responded by saying how pretty Swatch watches were and did Ireland have anything that could top that. 'You mean aside from a winning soccer team?' Talanov replied." Valerdi laughed. "Great response."

"Great response? He's deadlier than a snake, Valerdi. Don't ever forget that."

"Affirmative. But you should have heard what Talanov said next. He told Dubinina it was no surprise the Irish were winning. He said, 'Those bonny Swiss lads grow up on milk chocolate, the Irish on whisky.'" He laughed again.

"Snap out of it, Valerdi, and stay alert. This guy is slippery as an eel."

"You got it, Boss."

Bixler clicked off and sat with the brick phone in her lap, drumming her fingers thoughtfully while staring out the windshield at the passing lights.

"Slippery as an eel?" asked Franco. "Deadlier than a snake?"

"Clichés are clichés for a reason," Bixler replied.

"Well, I'm no rocket scientist," quipped Franco, "but

where's the line in the sand?"

"Cute."

"You're barking up the wrong tree, Paul," chided Pilgrim. "Better quit while you're ahead."

"Oh, you two are a barrel of laughs."

"Sorry, Boss," said Franco with a grin. "I know we're skating on thin ice."

"Go ahead, give me your best shot," said Bixler, swiveling in her seat to look at them. "Tonight, it's water off a duck's back. And you want to know why? It's because we did it. We gave Talanov the slip. So while he and Dubinina are up in their room living it up, we're about to steal a top scientist right out from under their noses. Man, I would *not* want to be in Talanov's shoes come morning. His Irish lads may have won at soccer, but his head is definitely going to *roll* for letting Gorev slip through his fingers. And I cannot *wait* to see how this wipes that cocky smile off his face once and for all."

CHAPTER 10

Bixler allowed herself the indulgence of recounting how she had done it. The key was not that she had kept communications coded, but that she had used a code she knew the Russians had already broken, which contained a thinly veiled stream of disinformation about their scheduled meeting with Gorev. The real communications about when and where the CIA would be meeting the scientist and his family were buried much deeper, and the fact that Talanov and Dubinina were living it up back in their hotel room proved they had taken the bait.

The plan for tonight's actual meeting at their safe house in Marbella was to arrive an hour early and park in an adjacent neighborhood to make sure no one had followed. Once satisfied, they would drive to the safe house and park up the street, where they could monitor any and all activity occurring on the street. Once Gorev and his family arrived, Bixler and her team would take them into the house for a quick debriefing and some food before loading them into the van for the short ride to the Málaga airport, where a chartered flight would take them to the U.S. Naval Station at Rota, on the Atlantic side of Gibraltar, where a C-130 would fly them to the United States.

"The Navy won't be stocking any booze," said Bixler, "so I've asked Alejandro to buy us a bottle of tequila, which we'll crack open for a celebration once we're on board."

"Not before I debrief Gorev," said Pilgrim.

"Let's save the heavy stuff for Washington," said Bixler. "I'd rather you spend time building rapport. Make Gorev and his family feel comfortable and secure."

"That's all well and good," said Pilgrim, "but if Gorev is carrying blood samples -- he did say a hematopathologist could verify his claims -- then we need to know what we're dealing with. And that means asking some very specific questions so that I can determine whether or not quarantine measures need to be put in place."

"What kind of quarantine measures?"

"That depends on what Gorev is carrying. Which is why I need to debrief him in order to ascertain what those samples are."

"All right," conceded Bixler. "Do what you need to do. But I don't want to scare them with a lot of heavy questioning. They're going to be scared as it is. We're the first friendly faces they're going to meet, so I want them to feel welcome."

Pilgrim nodded just as Bixler's brick phone rang.

"Bixler," she said into the instrument.

Speaking in Russian, Gorev politely asked if he had the correct number. Bixler replied by identifying herself as Walt Disney, the codeword Sharon had given her. Gorev replied with a sigh of relief.

Bixler asked where Gorev was calling from. Gorev replied that he was phoning from the train station, where the last of his family had just arrived. Bixler gave him the name of their street and told him to take a taxi, that everything was set and she looked forward to meeting him soon. After hanging up, Bixler dialed the security center at the casino for a final check on Talanov. Valerdi said Ireland was winning three-to-nothing and that Talanov was in high spirits cheering the Irish and maligning the Swiss. Sofia, by the sound of it, had fallen asleep.

"Are you're certain she didn't slip out?" asked Bixler.

"No one has left the room. The guys report in every fifteen minutes and each of them says the same thing: no movement . . . everything quiet."

"What about the man in black?"

"We still haven't managed to locate which room he's in or if he's in one at all. I've got Alexis and Montana reviewing video footage now, but so far we've found nothing."

"Maybe he has a confederate? Someone he's staying with?"

"The hotel doesn't have cameras in all the corridors, but we're checking the passport numbers of all guests to see if any red flags pop up."

"Stay on that and let me know when you find him."

"Copy that," Valerdi replied.

Bixler ended the call and checked her watch just as Franco parked the van four blocks from the safe house and turned off the ignition.

"Now we wait," Bixler said, glancing again at her watch.

The time passed quickly, due in large part to the string of crass jokes told by Franco. Bixler kept feigning disgust, but in truth she enjoyed how Franco diverted her mind from the stresses of her job. Laughter tended to do that and she had had few reasons to laugh these days apart from Franco's obsession with beautiful women and locker-room humor. Time driven, uptight and focused like her alpha-male counterparts, Bixler was convinced she would die of a heart attack while the happy-go-lucky Franco would outlive her by half a century. The consequences of climbing the ladder.

"Okay, let's head over to the safe house," she said, checking her watch.

"Are you sure, I mean, *really* sure?" asked Franco. "You've only checked your watch, like, a hundred times during the last forty minutes. Are you positive you don't want to check it again?"

"Shut up and start the engine."

The grinning Franco fired up the van.

The safe house was located on a narrow street called *Calle del Bergantín*. The houses along *Calle del Bergantín* were set behind hedges and clusters of palm trees and plastered walls with red tile caps. At the corner leading into the street, the van was stopped by two police officers waving flashlights. Nearby, a squad car was parked diagonally across one lane, its lights flashing. In the distance, a large group of protestors was being controlled by other officers. The group was shouting about NATO, police corruption and the presence of Russian spies.

The two officers at the corner approached the van, one on each side. One of the officers was accompanied by a man wearing a white tank top and black pleated slacks. On the man's forehead was a large red welt.

Franco rolled down his window. *"¿Qué tiene de malo?"* he said, asking what was wrong.

The policeman aimed his flashlight at Franco's face, then Pilgrim's. The other officer told Bixler to roll down her window. When she did, he directed his flashlight into her face. Everyone inside the van squinted and turned their heads.

"What's going on?" asked Franco, shielding his eyes with a hand. He could see the man in the tank top looking inside the van. The man finally stepped back and shook his head. The officers switched off their flashlights and waved them past without explanation.

"What was that about?" asked Bixler as Franco shifted into gear and eased the van forward.

"No idea," Franco replied, looking in his rearview mirror. He could see the man in the white tank top shouting at the policemen.

Up ahead was the safe house, which was a whitewashed two-story structure with an upstairs verandah and bars covering the windows. Other houses along the street looked much the same: mostly white or pastel, some with round turrets, most with red tile roofs, all with bars on the windows. The safe house was fronted by a low brick wall with intermittent high pillars of plastered brick. Between the pillars were panels of bars, and growing through the bars were thickets of trimmed bougainvillea. Behind the wall were several palm trees. The silhouettes of their tops could be seen against the night sky. Above the front gate was an awning of red tile, with an old-style square lantern illuminating the entrance.

The residence was occupied by a young Spanish couple named Alejandro and Carmen, who worked as English teachers in a local school. The downstairs lights of the house were on and cast a warm glow through the foliage. A summer sea breeze carried the faint drift of someone grilling meat.

Backing into a parking space three cars away from the lighted front gate, Franco switched off the engine but kept an uneasy eye on the activity behind them. Several protesters had broken away from the police barricade and were coming toward them, whooping it up.

"Possible trouble, six o'clock," he said.

Bixler and Pilgrim rotated in their seats and saw the approaching group.

"Sit low and keep still," said Bixler, rotating back around and sinking low in her seat. "With luck, they'll pass us by."

"Do you think that roadblock was for Gorev and his family?" asked Pilgrim.

"No way to know for certain," said Bixler. "The cops weren't exactly forthcoming."

"Perhaps we should tell Gorev to meet us elsewhere?"

"There's no way to get hold of him," answered Bixler, "so all we can do is wait and hope for the best."

The protesters coming toward them were all male. There were seven of them, all young -- in their twenties -- and full of bravado and crude humor from the local sangria they had been drinking. When they passed by, one of them saw Bixler sitting low in her seat.

"*¿Qué tenemos aquí?*" he called out, skipping over to the van and banging his hand on the window. The others soon joined him and began peering in.

"What are we going to do?" asked Pilgrim, instinctively scooting to the middle.

"Get out of here! Get lost!" shouted Bixler, waving them away.

"*Americanos!*" shouted several members of the group,

pumping their fists in the air.

"Bad move," mumbled Franco as the emboldened group fanned out around the front of the van and began pounding on the windows. Two of the protestors ran around the van and began trying the handles, to see if any of the doors were unlocked.

"I don't like this," mumbled Bixler.

"Slap me," said Franco in a low voice.

"Una rubia! Hemos nosotros de una rubia!" the protester shouted, pointing at Bixler's blonde hair, then placing his face against the window and making an exaggerated licking motion.

"What?" said Bixler, glancing at Franco then recoiling from her window.

"Slap me," mumbled Franco again as the protesters began rocking the van.

Bixler looked over at Franco, alarmed and confused.

"Hit me!" shouted Franco.

"Abra la puerta!" shouted the protesters while continuing to pound on the windows.

Franco saw the flash of fear in Bixler's eyes. Saw her hand drift down toward her weapon.   "I ask you to do one simple little thing!" shouted Franco, startling Bixler. *"One simple thing!* But you obviously don't have the brains of a *duck's ass* if you can't manage something as simple as that."

Bixler snapped her head toward Franco.

"You heard me," he said. "A *duck's ass!* Duck's a-s-s. Now, are you going to hit me or *not?"*

Bixler stared open-mouthed at Franco, her expression one of anger and disbelief.

"Man, you are *too much!"* Franco shouted, throwing up his hands. "How you ever managed to get yourself hired by our company is beyond me. So I'll take my chances out there."

Franco was just opening his door when Bixler's fist knocked him out of the van and down onto the ground."

"¡Maldita perra!" Franco shouted, climbing unsteadily to

his feet. He pointed an accusing finger at Bixler and began a wild, rambling sentence in Spanish while the protesters gathered around to watch, surprised and amused.

Suddenly, with a loud anguished cry, Franco grimaced and doubled over, as if struck by a crippling pain. He then began writhing and clawing at his groin before grabbing a protester by the arm and pleading with him. The protester twisted out of Franco's grip and shoved him away. When Franco reached out for him again, the entire group turned and ran. Franco fell to his knees and allowed his excruciating wails to trail off slowly and plaintively. After a few seconds, he hopped up and climbed back in the van.

"What the *hell* was that about?" asked Bixler. "And what's with all the . . . scratching?"

"What's with the *fist?* I told you to slap me, not deck me."

"After calling me a duck's ass, I guess it got lost in translation. Now, what the hell did you tell those guys?"

Looking in his rearview mirror, Franco saw a taxi stop at the police barricade. "I told them you and I were through," he replied, his eyes fixed on the mirror. "That you'd slept with a goat farmer who loved goats a little too much. That you ended up giving me some kind of contagious parasitic worm -- which I couldn't get rid of -- after which I begged them to take you with them."

"You said *what?*"

"Hey, it's not that you're going to be seeing those guys again," he said, looking at her. "I had to think of something to keep you from drawing your gun. Now, come on, they're almost here."

"Who's almost here?"

"Gorev. The police just let them through."

Bixler and Pilgrim turned to see a taxi creep past the police barricade and drive slowly toward them. When they turned back around, Franco had already leaped out of the van.

"I swear I'm going to strangle him," said Bixler, reaching for the handle.

"You have to admit, he did send them packing," remarked Pilgrim with a grin.

"Yeah, well, he didn't have to enjoy it so much," said Bixler, throwing Pilgrim a sharp glance. "So wipe that smirk off your face and go ring the bell. The code is two-five-three-two. That'll let Alejandro and Carmen know it's us."

Still grinning, Pilgrim opened her door, slid out with her medical bag and went to the front gate, where she entered the code on the touchpad. Seconds later, the light over the front gate was extinguished.

Crossing to the other side of the street, Bixler waited with Franco. When the cab stopped in front of them, Bixler opened the passenger door.

"Is this the correct address?" Gorev asked in Russian. The question was pre-arranged and the correct response was the same codeword Bixler had used on the phone. Any other response was a signal to leave immediately and call an emergency telephone number he had been given.

"Walt Disney. Welcome to Spain," Bixler replied.

Gorev smiled at the correct response then looked warily at Franco.

Reading his expression, Bixler grabbed Franco by the elbow. "It's all right, Dr. Gorev. I'm Agent Bixler and this is my colleague, Donald Duck."

"Your government prefers codenames from Disneyland?" asked Gorev.

"When it suits the occasion," replied Bixler.

"Who's going to pay?" asked the driver in Spanish.

"That would be me," Franco replied, bowing politely to Gorev before rounding the front of the car and stopping beside the driver's window, asking how much.

The driver, a hairy Spaniard in a t-shirt that was way too snug for the size of his belly, glanced at the illuminated meter and told Franco an amount. Franco pulled out his wallet and paid the man. Gorev watched the exchange between the bored driver and the American agent. When Franco handed the driver a generous tip, he saw the driver's apathy become a wide grin.

"Muchas gracias!" the driver exclaimed.

"De nada," Franco replied.

After watching the grateful driver make the sign of the cross over his chest, Gorev looked back up at Bixler. When she extended her hand, he accepted it and climbed out of the cab.

"I am sorry for all of the precautions," he said, helping his family out of the backseat while the driver retrieved their suitcases from the trunk. "You must think me excessive."

"Not at all," Bixler replied. "My world runs on precaution."

Once the cab had driven away, the five-foot-six-inch Gorev found himself looking directly into the eyes of the five-foot-six-inch Bixler, who was not at all what he expected. Although Gorev could tell he and Agent Bixler were the same height, she somehow seemed taller, no doubt because Americans carried themselves erect and confident. And while the finer details of her face were not visible in the darkness, the ambient light from the houses showed her to be beautiful and alert, with a warm and genuine smile that was also impatient, which was not surprising, given her position.

Bixler's impressions of Gorev were much different. Although Bixler could tell she was the same height as Gorev, the man somehow seemed shorter, no doubt because of the emotional weight he had been carrying as well as the oppressive conditions in his homeland. Slender but not skinny, Gorev looked to be approximately one-hundred-and-forty pounds, with a thin moustache, mousy brown hair and a broad forehead and receding hairline, like a professor.

"They're expecting us inside," Pilgrim said, joining them.

Bixler introduced Pilgrim while Franco grabbed the suitcases.

"Agent Pilgrim is our medical expert," Bixler explained, gesturing them toward the gate. "She'll be assisting with your transition. You and your family will get to know her very well in the coming months."

While they walked, Gorev introduced his family. First was his wife, Anna, whom Bixler could see she was pretty but plain. Next was their fourteen year-old daughter, Noya, who had alert, penetrating eyes and thick brown hair. And finally there were Gorev's gray-haired parents, Albert and Irina. Both were short and heavy.

"Did you and your family travel separately?" asked Bixler.

"I traveled alone," answered Gorev, "with my wife traveling with Noya and my parents together."

"Smart thinking, dividing yourselves into groups like that."

"I thought it prudent," Gorev replied.

"Mrs. Gorev, how was your trip?" asked Bixler.

"My wife is tired," Gorev responded while Anna walked beside him, eyes lowered, hands folded in front of her.

"Some coffee, perhaps?" inquired Bixler.

"My wife seldom drinks coffee," Gorev replied.

Bixler glanced at Gorev, then back at Anna, who had still not looked at her.

They arrived at the gate.

"Here we are," Bixler said. "We'll let you freshen up and have a bite to eat before leaving on a short flight to the U.S. Naval Base at Rota, where a military aircraft will take you and your family to America."

"Will you be traveling with us?" asked Gorev.

"All the way," Bixler replied. She pressed the coded sequence on the lighted keypad. The heavy wooden gate buzzed. Bixler pushed the gate all the way open and stepped inside to hold it. Gorev looked anxiously around at the high walls enclosing the yard, which extended away into the darkness.

"It's okay," Bixler said gently. "You're safe now. I just entered a code that let the residents of the house know who we are. No one can get inside that house without the code. If someone tries, an alarm goes off and the police show up. We also extinguished the front light so that no one can see your face or the faces of your family. We've taken every precaution, Dr. Gorev."

Gorev stared at Bixler for a long moment before stepping tentatively inside. "In the taxi, we were frightened when we saw the police," he explained. "We thought they were looking for us."

"Like I said, we've taken every precaution."

"There were many people shouting at the police," added Noya in English. "What were they angry about?"

"Spain joining NATO," replied Bixler, surprised. "Your English is very good."

Gorev asked Noya what Bixler had said and she told him.

"Noya has been studying your American language for many months," Gorev told Bixler in Russian.

"How do you like it?" Bixler asked Noya in English.

Gorev again asked Noya what Bixler had said and Noya told him.

"She is quite proficient," Gorev replied, "and very studious."

Bixler smiled at Gorev then looked back at Noya, waiting for a reply.

"I like it very much," Noya explained while Gorev scowled his disapproval. "I speak English with my girlfriend from school, in secret, when we are alone. We read magazines and newspapers and Bibles that are smuggled into our country."

"Well, you're doing an excellent job," said Bixler. "You should be very proud."

Gorev again asked Noya what Bixler had said and Noya told him.

"Yes, I am very proud," said Gorev in Russian, wrapping an arm around Noya's shoulder, drawing her close while Noya lowered her eyes.

Bixler got the message and ushered Gorev and his family into the yard just as a police car raced past with its lights flashing. Bixler watched it screech to a stop at the end of the street before shutting the gate behind them.

Gorev and his family followed Bixler and Pilgrim along the darkened path toward the house. On their right was a high wall separating them from the neighboring home. A thicket of jasmine topped the wall and spilled down in curling tendrils. On their left was a patch of tartly-scented lemon balm, a hearty plant similar to mint that is used across Europe as a medicinal herb and groundcover. Beyond the lemon balm was a thicket of shrubs and beyond these were a stand of palm trees. The walled-in front yard was a collage of fragrant deep shadows.

In the street out front, another police car sped by. Gorev reacted nervously when he saw the reflection of its lights flashing briefly through the bougainvillea.

"It's okay," said Bixler in Russian. "There are lots of NATO protests going on around town."

"Our driver spoke with the policemen when they stopped us," said Gorev while Bixler pressed the same coded sequence of numbers into the lighted touchpad mounted near the front door, "but they spoke in Spanish and I did not understand. I did recognize one word -- *espías* -- which is like our Russian word, *shpiony* -- spies -- so I began to worry that there would be trouble for us. But the policemen and another man, they looked inside the taxi with flashlights and waved us past."

"Espías?" asked Franco, catching the reference. To Bixler: "Did Gorev say spies?"

"Yeah, why?" she asked in return.

"I heard the protesters yelling something about Russian spies when we came through," he said just as the front door was opened by Alejandro and Carmen. "If they weren't looking for Gorev, then who?"

"I believe I can answer that question," said Talanov, stepping from the shadows.

CHAPTER 11

Bixler instinctively went for her pistol but froze with her fingertip just touching the butt when she saw the long, thick silencer of Talanov's Makarov 9mm aimed directly at her chest. With him was Sofia, who stepped in front of the open door and aimed her Makarov at Carmen and Alejandro.

Bixler slowly raised her hands. "But you you're supposed to be---" she began just as another police car raced past out front.

"Inside," commanded Talanov, who was dressed in black fatigues and rubber-soled boots.

Bixler noticed several scuff marks and rips on Talanov's fatigues, as if he had been in a fight.

After herding everyone into the house, Talanov shut the door and motioned for Sofia to search the rest of the house. Sofia placed her aluminum briefcase on the floor and crept quickly down the hallway, leading with her pistol, moving silently from room to room.

Talanov directed everyone into the living room and told them to sit in front of the fireplace. On each side of the fireplace were built-in bookcases and cabinets. Couches and stuffed chairs were positioned against the walls, with a colorful, mosaic-tiled coffee table in between.

When she sat, Bixler saw Talanov using the back of his hand to blot a cut on the side of his forehead.

There had been no cut there before, she thought, recalling the CCTV footage.

Talanov saw Bixler studying him.

"For the record," he said, his eyes combing the group, "we are not here to hurt anyone, so I hope none of you attempts to interfere. If you do, these Makarovs are loaded with cartridges that can penetrate 4mm titanium body armor, which none of you is wearing. In other words, you would not survive. Nor would anyone hear the shots. Our suppressors would reduce the muzzle noise to roughly that of a hair-dryer."

Talanov looked each person directly in the eye to make sure they understood. He then directed his attention back to Gorev. "Dr. Gorev, my name is Colonel Aleksandr Talanov of the KGB. I am here to escort you and your family back to the Soviet Union. If you cooperate, I will make sure your family is not executed. Everything hinges on your good behavior. Do I make myself clear?"

A terrified Gorev looked over at Bixler.

"Agent Bixler will be unable to assist you," Talanov continued. "In fact, Agent Bixler is now your enemy as her orders will be to kill you and your family now that we are stopping your defection."

"That's a lie!" yelled Bixler. *"You've* been sent here to kill him."

"I've been sent here to bring him home."

"And if he refuses, what then? Does he have any say in the matter?"

"Dr. Gorev does not realize the consequences of what he has done, as you no doubt have neglected to inform him about crime in America and how his daughter is one hundred times more likely to be raped or shot there than she is in the Soviet Union."

Talanov glanced at Noya and saw her deep brown eyes staring up at him. Her long brown hair was hanging loose about her face and she was sitting between her mother and father. Her eyes seemed to hold his, not letting go, so he shifted his focus back to Gorev.

"Do you realize, Doctor," he said, "that you will be discarded like an empty wrapper once the Americans have stolen what they want?"

Said Bixler, "Then why don't you tell us why everybody in the world wants to live in the United States. Why is that, Colonel? Why is it no one's all that eager to defect to the Soviet Union?"

"Do you see Americans helping poor people defect?" replied Talanov, his eyes still on Gorev. "Or do they only help people like you from whom they can steal information? Ever wonder where their so-called humanitarian aid goes? It goes to oil-rich countries they can then plunder in return. That is how they work, doctor, and you and your family will be discarded once they are finished."

When a worried look appeared on Gorev's face, Talanov shifted his attention to Bixler.

"You do not take care of your citizens," he said. "Look at your slums. At the gangs who fight and kill over pairs of shoes. At the homeless people living under bridges and in cardboard boxes."

"And you think imprisoning them behind an Iron Curtain is better? Sure, we've got problems. Freedom is messy. But it sure beats the hell out of tyranny."

"Messy? Is that what you call living every day in fear of violence?"

"I wonder which of us Dr. Gorev is afraid of right now? Why don't you ask him, Colonel? Hear what *he* has to say. Unless, of course, you're afraid of what you might learn."

"I am not here to debate the matter," said Talanov. "Dr. Gorev is an important person in our medical research programs."

"What kind of research might that be?"

"Stand up and get ready to leave," commanded Talanov, motioning Gorev and his family to their feet.

After a tense moment of hesitation, Gorev and his family reluctantly stood. They were starting for the door when Sofia entered the room.

"Remain where you are!" she commanded, waving them

back.

Gorev and his family stopped.

"What's going on?" asked Talanov.

"Change of plans," she replied.

Talanov took Sofia aside. "What are you talking about?" he said in a lowered voice.

"Your aluminum briefcase, pocket on the left. There you will find the letter I placed there from Walter Kravenko, who has of this moment placed me in charge."

Talanov stared hard at Sofia.

"The letter explains everything," she said, stepping around him and keeping the group covered with her pistol, her eyes roaming from face to face, reading every expression.

"I am not interested in reading a letter," he replied, turning to face her. "I'm interested in you telling me what the hell is going on."

Sofia glanced over at Talanov and smiled. It was a soft, tranquil expression that lasted a brief moment before she aimed her Makarov and pulled the trigger, the pistol spitting four quick rounds into the heads of Gorev's mother and father. With her smile still in place, Sofia watched them collapse to the floor before turning to see Talanov pointing his Makarov at her head.

"Perhaps now you will read the letter," Sofia remarked.

When Talanov lowered his gun she stepped over and smashed the butt of her pistol against Gorev's forehead when he began to wail at the sight of his dead parents lying in two bloody heaps on the floor. Anna tried catching her husband, to keep him from falling, but toppled with him to the floor, where she did her best not to cry while working her way out from under him. She then scrambled around and lifted his head into her lap, where she used the bottom of her dress to gently blot the gash on his head.

"If any of the rest of you makes even the *slightest* noise, I will kill you," Sofia remarked, glaring first at Bixler and Pilgrim, then Franco, then Alejandro and Carmen as they looked up at her with terrified expressions.

Terrified expressions were good, thought Sofia. *They kept people in line.*

Talanov grabbed his briefcase but paused when he saw Noya sitting calmly beside her father, looking vacantly at the bodies of her dead grandparents. She noticed him staring at her before looking dispassionately at the pool of blood spreading across the tiles.

What kind of a kid just sits there like that? Adults are the ones who are supposed to be the realists and pessimists. The ones burdened by life. Not kids. When they're not giggling and squirming, kids are supposed to be up and down, all over the place with their emotions: afraid, angry, shocked. Some kind of imposed control on all that natural energy and immaturity. They're supposed to be . . . something. Not nothing. What kind of a kid shows nothing?

The kind of kid who knows her fate has been sealed and accepted it.

With pinched lips, Talanov clicked open his briefcase, found the letter and in less than a minute had read how Sofia Dubinina was now the agent in charge of returning Gorev and his family to the Soviet Union. She was further commissioned to use any means necessary, including Department Thirteen protocols, to assist her with those duties.

Department Thirteen protocols.

Wet work.

Assassination.

No wonder Sofia had no file. She wasn't a novice. She was an assassin with Department Thirteen, which meant she was beyond scrutiny by everyone except the highest echelons within the KGB.

Talanov stared at the letter for nearly as long as it had taken him to read it.

"Let a man think he is in charge and you can lead him like a dog on a leash until it is time to reveal what is *really* going on," Sofia remarked, looking at Talanov with a drilling stare until Talanov averted his eyes, a sign of submission to the new orders he had just received. Addressing the group, she said, "For the benefit of those who do not understand what has taken place, Colonel Talanov is no longer in charge. I am. Are there any questions?"

Talanov stuffed the letter in his pocket. Said, "What is the plan?"

"Need-to-know," Sofia replied. She stared directly at Talanov to drive home her point.

"How did you find us?" asked Bixler.

"You have Colonel Talanov to thank for that," answered Sofia. "He was the one who figured out where Gorev would defect."

"And now that he's done his job, you're taking over, is that it?"

"Colonel Talanov's role in this mission is finished."

"Judging by the look on his face, I don't reckon he saw this coming," said Bixler with a laugh. "In fact, I'd say you managed to yank the rug right out from under him. So, how'd you give us the slip? Since you two are here, who's back in your hotel room?" She looked at Talanov standing off by himself, lips pinched, seething.

Using her Makarov, Sofia pointed to Alejandro and Carmen. "You and you: drag those bodies into one of the bedrooms and shut the door. Then get back here and clean up this mess."

"I can't believe Moscow ordered these murders," said Bixler, watching Sofia glare at Carmen, who was squeamish at having to pick up a bloody body.

"Move!" Sofia told Carmen, who tearfully took the arm of Gorev's mother, apologized to Gorev and began dragging her out of the living room.

"We may be adversaries," said Bixler, "but we've never gone around executing innocent people."

Sofia told Carmen to hurry up or her husband would be hauling another corpse to the bedroom: hers.

Bixler said, "What gives you the right to do something like this?"

"This gun does," answered Sofia, aiming her Makarov at

Bixler's head.

Bixler closed her eyes an instant before Talanov grabbed Sofia's hand.

"We are not here to start a bloodbath with the Americans," he said.

Sofia tried wrenching free but Talanov's grip was too strong.

"Challenging my authority would be a very big mistake," she said.

They continued glaring at one another, their eyes clashing, neither one backing down.

Finally, Sofia said, "All right, the American lives. Unless she provokes me again."

Talanov looked hard at Bixler -- a warning -- just as Sofia tugged again and Talanov let go.

"Sit down and get out of my way," commanded Sofia.

Talanov did not move.

"Would you like to read Kravenko's letter again?" Sofia asked with a sneer. "Sit *down,* Colonel!"

Bixler watched Talanov lower his eyes and walk into the dining room, where he sat at the table and began rubbing the bridge of his nose. *How quickly things can change,* she thought. *Back in the casino, Talanov was in charge. Now he's a dog on a leash. How quickly things can change.*

CHAPTER 12

How did I not see this coming? Talanov thought, unable to accept -- unable to *deny* -- what had happened. *I am trained for this. It's what I do.*

The betrayal had obviously been planned from the outset, as evidenced by Kravenko's letter granting Sofia control, which she had conveniently withheld until Gorev had been located.

But a betrayal planned by whom? Sofia? Kravenko? Someone else?

In thinking back, Sofia's objections after their initial meeting in Kravenko's office appeared sincere, no doubt because she genuinely feared being pulled from the assignment, which implied Kravenko's innocence. Sofia would have no reason to fear something she knew would never happen. Unless of course Kravenko *was* involved and Sofia was simply that good of an actress.

Whatever the case, he had still missed two very obvious signs. The first was the speed and seamlessness of her conversion from being adversarial and argumentative to openly embracing her role as his lover and partner. It had all happened a little too easily, but because he was enjoying the challenge of showing her how clever and witty he could be, he had missed it. He had fallen for his own magician's distraction by focusing in one direction and missed what was going on elsewhere. The second sign he had overlooked: her constant stream of questions and temptations.

How did I not see this coming?

Talanov knew the answer. The deadliest lies are half-truths and the greatest stealth is openness. All agents at Balashikha learn this. Do them well and your enemy will not see you coming.

And he had not.

He remembered being taught this principle when he was sixteen and had been sent to a remote training center in the foothills of the Ural Mountains, where he and twenty-nine other young men were being groomed for various roles by Spetsnaz instructors. After an eighteen-hour day in the classroom, each of the thirty trainees -- the gray team -- had been tasked with a simple assignment: reach the finish line and don't get caught by the red team of twelve Spetsnaz commandos. Whoever got caught -- and everyone always did -- would be put through an unimaginable week of misery.

The first ten to be apprehended would be immediately dismissed from the program, with the final three competing in a hand-to-hand combat tournament for the ultimate prize: a weekend on the nude beaches of Berdyans'k, a Ukrainian spit of sand on the shallow Sea of Azov, just north of the Black Sea. It would be a weekend of pleasure the victor would not soon forget.

After being deposited in the heart of a vast forest by one of the huge Mi-26 heavy-lift cargo helicopters used by the Soviet Air Force, the gray team was given an hour's head start while the Spetsnaz commandos set up camp. The gray team was given no food and enough water for only one day. The finish line was three days away, to the southwest, so the ability to survive off the land -- food, water and shelter -- was critical.

The gray team began running as fast as their feet would take them. However, at a point just out of sight, Talanov changed direction and circled left a hundred meters, where he dug himself into the base of a pyramid-shaped fir tree, with a tangle of branches growing close to the ground. There he scooped out a shallow burrow, covered himself with needles and settled in to let the red team pass him by, which they did at full cantor just over an hour later. Talanov waited for their tail gunners to pass, as those trailing team members were called who held back purposely to protect the team's rear flank, and once they were gone, crawled out from his burrow and circled around behind the massive Mi-26, which had been left in the care of two guards, the pilot and a captain, who were taking it easy in the command tent with glasses of vodka. Talanov crawled aboard the chopper, located the group's food and beverage supply and settled in behind one of the bulkheads to eat, sleep and drink his way through the next three days.

Throughout the third and fourth days, Talanov listened to his commanders use the helicopter's radio to offer headquarters a wide range of excuses about why they had not been able to locate the thirtieth member of the gray team. Justifications ranged from his having defected to the West, to being eaten by wolves or bears, to having been abducted by aliens, to his having been kidnapped by American Special Forces. The generals at headquarters, however, were growing impatient and the Spetsnaz commandos were looking increasingly inept.

Embarrassed and furious, the commandos organized a full-scale campaign for 0400 the next morning using infrared and thermal imaging scanners. One way or another, Talanov would be found in the forest.

Thus, at 0200, Talanov crept from behind the bulkhead with a half dozen bottles of vodka and some chocolate, which he distributed to his teammates before leading them in a raid with buckets of ice water, which they dumped on the sleeping commandos, who stumbled and slipped and cursed while chasing them out of the tents into the darkness, where other members of the gray team were waiting with more buckets.

At dawn the next morning, Talanov was brought before the commander for disciplinary action. When asked if he had anything to say, Talanov replied, "You said not to get caught and I did not. And if it displeases you that I do not play by your rules, then consider this: instead of sleeping behind the bulkhead, I could have slipped out during the night and killed each and every one of you. Enemies do not play by rules. Neither do I. If you do not wish me to win, then keep me out of the game."

When told he was not being punished for his rather unorthodox achievement but the ice water, he smirked and said, "If that is what makes our great Spetsnaz commandos whimper and whine, then perhaps they should be put through this training and the gray team placed in charge." Drawing himself to attention, he then added, "I stand ready to accept any punishment as a badge of honor."

The commander was caught between a rock and a hard place and he knew it. So while he and his advisors deliberated and glared, Talanov stood ramrod straight, eyes ahead, arms at his side.

There could only be one decision and Talanov knew what it would be long before they had the courage to announce it.

And he was ready.

When told that he would receive the weekend away in Berdyans'k, he replied crisply that he should be disqualified. When asked why, he replied, "You said the winner would be decided from the final three *who were caught.* I was never caught, so I do not qualify. Let the others fight it out. I will stay with my comrades, the gray team, and together we will accept whatever hardship you give us."

Later that morning, Talanov was taken aside by one of the commandos. "This way," he said, nodding for Talanov to follow. Dressed in fatigues of mottled greens and grays, with wide smears of black camouflage paint on his face, the commando was a powerfully-built man about three inches shorter than the six-foot-one Talanov.

They walked through the forest in silence along a narrow path. The trees around them, mostly spruce and fir, were tall and straight and provided a thick blanket of needles. Smaller conifers, struggling for survival, competed with bushes and bracken. The cool air was damp and clean.

"In Spetsnaz, an individual may quit at anytime," the commando said as they walked along, pushing branches out of the way. Slashes of early morning sunlight penetrated the forest through wisps of drifting fog. "Pain is our existence, and we do not accept anyone who does not embrace it."

"I understand," Talanov replied.

"Don't talk, just listen," the commando barked, glancing sharply at the slender sixteen year-old trailing behind him in green cargo pants and an olive green t-shirt.

They reached a small clearing and the commando stopped. "If you were in Spetsnaz, my job would be to break you," he said, turning to face Talanov. "To make you suffer and bleed. But you have been selected for other duties and I have been assigned to guard you . . . to train you and offer counsel. But this arrangement is between you and me. No one can know. Do you understand?"

Talanov nodded.

"Good," the commando said. "And the first advice I will give you is this: never let them see how good you are."

"Why not?"

The commando backfisted Talanov across the face, splitting his lip and knocking him to the ground, where he lay dazed for a moment before rolling up onto one elbow and wiping his mouth.

"Speak when I say, not before," the commando advised, motioning him to his feet.

Talanov hesitated for a moment then stood.

"You are skilled but not yet wise," the commando said. "You must learn to control your punches."

Talanov opened his mouth to reply but stopped. The commando smiled and nodded for him to speak.

"I have been trained in Combat Sambo," Talanov said. "I know how to pull a punch."

"You miss what I am saying," the commando replied. "I do not speak of combat technique. I speak about knowing what kind of force to use and how much. Reveal only as much as required, so that no one but you knows the full limits of your capability and strength. In our world -- and you must listen carefully to what I am saying and what I am not -- friends become enemies when ineptitude or corruption is exposed. Today you made fools of the fools, and this can be dangerous. From this day, I will have your back, but I will not always be with you, so you must learn to control your punches, like this . . ."

The commando let fly two lightning backfists to the head, one below the eye -- for the classic bruise known as a black eye -- and the other just above, slicing open the skin and again knocking Talanov to the ground.

Seeing Talanov sprawled out on the grass with a black eye and blood running down his face, the commando laughed and offered his hand.

Talanov took it and the commando pulled him easily to his feet.

"They expect you to return beaten and bleeding," the commando explained, "and by trailing me into camp streaked with blood, they will be satisfied. Do you understand what I am saying and what I am not?"

Talanov reached down, grabbed some dirt and smeared it with his blood across the side of his face.

The commando grinned.

"How should I address you?" asked Talanov, seeing the arrangement of four captain's stars positioned like an upside-down "Y" on his shoulder.

"Around others, by rank. In private, by name."

"Which is?"

"Zakhar Babikov. You may call me Zak."

Refocusing on the present, Talanov thought about Gorev and Zak and their magician's trick with the CIA, which was a simple bait-and-switch that took place earlier in the Presidential suite, where Zak and a curvaceous Russian call girl named Aurelia had been waiting. Because Sofia had already made an advance reservation for the Presidential suite, Zak knew in advance where to wait. Thus, by the time the CIA had planted listening devices on the door, Talanov and Sofia had already rappelled down the outside of the hotel and were hurrying across the darkened golf course toward Zak's Peugeot van, where duffel packs containing changes of clothes, water, food, maps and weapons were waiting, including sturdy Soviet "black knives" and ankle sheaths.

Hence, the first voices heard and recorded by the CIA were those of Zak and Aurelia. All Aurelia knew was that she was to play the role of someone named Sofia, which she was happy to do for the thousand dollars promised her by Zak, half of which he had already paid. Her duties included little more than voicing protests against having to watch soccer, which was not difficult since she considered it such a boring game. Thankfully, the food and beverage were first class and she had only to follow a few simple rules, which were to eat, drink and be merry while referring to the man in black as Alex.

Once Talanov and Sofia left the casino, Sofia brought up the subject again.

"So, do you think you can kill him?" she asked, slipping out of her party dress. "I know you said there were other ways to stop a defection, but you would if you had to, yes?" She tossed the dress into the back of the van, where the floorboard had been padded with a gymnastics mat and some blankets. She then pulled a pair of black cotton fatigues out of her duffel pack.

"We want him alive, not dead," answered Talanov.

"As do the Americans," replied Sofia, swiveling to face Talanov. The dashboard lights cast a faint glow across her naked breasts. "But we cannot allow him to defect any more than the Americans can allow him to be caught. So unless you really are a magician, the man will die."

"It's why we are here. To keep that from happening."

"But you would kill him if you had to, yes?"

"If I had to, of course."

"And his family? What about them? They'll slow us down."

"We'll be driving them to a freighter in Málaga, not hiking

with them through the mountains."

"And the daughter? What about her?" asked Sofia.

"What about her?"

"She is, I must say, very pretty."

"Meaning?"

"That she is a tool to be used, if required," answered Sofia. "Gorev will no doubt resort to any means necessary to avoid recapture. If he decides to do something drastic, then the girl can be used as leverage. Hold a knife to her throat and he will do as we say."

"If Gorev were unpredictable and volatile, then perhaps. But he is not. He's intelligent and methodical . . . a scientist. There is no reason to harm the girl."

"And if he refuses? If your profile is wrong?"

"I'm not."

"But if required, you would kill her, yes?"

"Why do you keep asking me this?"

Sofia leaned over and bit Talanov on the ear. "Because it turns me on," she whispered.

When Talanov jerked the steering wheel left, the van swerved into the path of an oncoming car. Talanov yanked the wheel right, avoiding a collision but sending the van onto the shoulder, where they bounced along for a short distance before Talanov was able to ease it back onto the pavement. In his rearview mirror, he saw the car they had just passed slow down, make a sweeping U-turn and speed after them. His rearview mirror then lit up with flashing blue lights.

"Damn, the *police!*" he said.

Sofia reached into her duffel kit and withdrew her pistol. "Pull over. I'll handle this," she said, screwing a silencer on the barrel.

"*I'll* handle it," said Talanov, switching on his blinker and guiding the van onto the shoulder. Once they had rolled to a stop, he stuck his pistol in his waistband and covered it with his jacket. "Stay here. This won't take long."

The police car pulled up behind them, its headlights on high beam, its flashing lights bathing the area in strobes of blue.

Talanov got out and held both hands up in a friendly wave to greet the two officers getting out of their patrol car.

"¿Has estado bebiendo alcohol?" asked the uniformed officer in charge. In the bright wash of their headlights, he and his partner strode toward Talanov, their hands on their pistols.

"No, I have not been drinking," replied Talanov in Spanish. "Something flew in the window and caused me to swerve."

"Your accent is not Spanish," said the officer in charge, "so we will need to see your passport and license."

"Is that necessary?" asked Talanov. "I'm a visitor to your beautiful country, have just come from the casino and am running late to an important function. Please, I really am late."

"Foreigners who commit traffic offenses are normally taken into custody," the officer said. "Unless of course they post a bond."

"I am happy to comply with the bond," said Talanov, reaching into his pocket and taking out some cash. "Is three hundred dollars enough?"

"There is also the matter of speeding, as well as swerving into an oncoming lane."

Talanov counted out another two hundred dollars.

The officers smiled.

Sofia suddenly threw open her door and stumbled out of the van in her party dress, where she staggered a few wobbly steps and bent over to make a heaving sound, as if throwing up. The officers watched her catch her breath before bracing herself against the side of the van and looking their way. She then began giggling while weaving unsteadily toward them in a clumsy side-shuffle.

The policeman in charge jabbed a finger at Talanov. "You said you had not been drinking."

"And I haven't."

"She has. And you almost caused a collision! You lied to

officers of the law."

"Sir, I have *not* been drinking," insisted Talanov. "Smell my breath, if you like. It may stink but it won't be from your sangria."

Talanov regretted the quip the moment he said it.

The officer snatched the handcuffs off his belt. "We are done talking, *señor.* You and the woman are coming with us."

CHAPTER 13

Sofia had been careful to keep her right hand concealed behind her while moving toward them. When she was within ten feet, she lifted her Makarov in a smooth quick motion and fired four times in rapid succession, two shots in the forehead of each startled officer, spaced evenly above the bridge of the nose, like giant snakebites that exploded huge chunks of bone out the back of their heads. The muffled reports dissipated quickly as the two dead officers crumpled to the pavement.

Sofia strode casually past Talanov. "You had a problem and I fixed it," she said.

"You don't fix problems by creating bigger ones," Talanov replied.

"Ice Man would have done the same thing."

"Not this time. Some bribe money would have done the trick."

Sofia laughed. "Then I just saved you some money."

Talanov shook his head and began dragging the first officer off the pavement.

"It is how we were trained, Sasha," Sofia said. "To strike preemptively. To eliminate potential threats before they become threats."

Talanov stopped in his tracks. *How we were trained? There was only one place where agents received training like that.*

Sofia laughed at Talanov's stunned expression. "Yes, Sasha, I, too, was at Balashikha."

Talanov looked hard at Sofia. Admission into Balashikha was reserved for two types of individuals: elite Soviet agents and extremists interested in learning the latest techniques in assassination and terrorism.

Which one of those types was Sofia?

"I knew what I did would shock you," she said, dragging the other body off the pavement, "and although it may not have been necessary to kill them, I wanted you to see how good I am. That my skills match yours. That you can depend on me."

"Depend on you? I told you to remain in the van!" He finished dragging the first policeman's body into the scrub, where he laid it behind a tangle of prickly pear.

"Do not be angry," she said.

"You *killed* two men!"

Sofia waved that away. "You are offended that I did not do what I was told. I understand this, just as you must understand why I chose to kill them: to show you that I can be as cold and calculating as you. It is why we make a good team."

"We are nothing alike."

"Oh, but we are. You are the Ice Man! I read, for instance, how you refused to visit your uncle when he was in the hospital dying with cancer. Vov, I think was his name, a foolish man -- superstitious -- wishing you would forgive him for killing Olaf. You must tell me this story sometime. I read also how as a foster child you were passed around like an unwanted party gift. They called you headstrong and eager but difficult to manage, always thinking your way was best. A rule breaker," she laughed, "like me."

They saw headlights coming toward them. Sofia ran to the squad car and pulled it forward over the blood pool until the cars had passed. She then switched off the flashing lights and drove the squad car into the scrub, out of sight.

A solemn Talanov was waiting behind the wheel when Sofia climbed back in the van. He did not look at her when she got in but simply shifted into gear and drove away.

"I ended up at Balashikha by a much different path than

you," Sofia said as if nothing had happened. She slipped out of her party dress and again pulled on her fatigues before strapping the black knife onto her ankle. "And all because I made the mistake of outrunning the boys."

She glanced over for some kind of a response but Talanov kept his eyes on the road.

"It was a dreary Moscow morning," she continued, "and I was eight. It was wet and gray and I was playing in a neighborhood park, which was not much more than a few pipes in the ground and some trees. I was tall and skinny and I remember this boy, Ivan, telling us the Beatles had disbanded. I didn't know who the Beatles were, and when I said so, the kids all laughed, especially Ivan. He began calling me stupid stick and giraffe. So I kicked him in the nuts and it dropped him like he had been, well, kicked in the nuts. I stood there watching him roll around on the ground screaming. A couple of the bigger boys grabbed me so I kicked them, too, and punched one of them in the throat. Then I started running. They gave chase -- probably half a dozen of them -- some of them teenagers, all of them boys -- and I outran them all. I ran for maybe six or seven blocks until they gave up and I got away.

"But not for long, because a man from the KGB named Grigory -- he was short and fat, and had hairy ears and a veined nose -- had seen it all and found out where I lived. So he came to my boarding school -- my parents were both dead from overdoses -- and Grigory made the boarding school an offer they couldn't refuse. I don't know how much he paid them, but Grigory took me away and began making me do things I will not speak of here. I hated him, and I kept hating him more and more every day. So one night, when Grigory was asleep -- I was fifteen by then and he was making me sleep with him -- I got up and crushed his head with a heavy bronze statue of Lenin that he kept on his desk. I was accused of murder, of course, and thrown in jail to await trial. That's when I met the stern woman in the gray uniform. She had oily black hair that was cropped short and full of dandruff. I was taken in to her, and I remember her being seated behind a wooden desk in a windowless concrete room. I was shivering and she did nothing for the longest time. Finally, she got up and came over to me. She was short and she just stood there, not saying anything, staring up at me. Finally, without warning, she slapped me in the face. I started to punch her but stopped. That's when I saw the hint of a cold smile crease her lips, She walked back over to her desk, sat down and said, 'You belong to me now, and the first piece of advice I give you is this: the next time a man abuses you the way Grigory did, do not wait seven years to kill him.' The following day, I was sent to Balashikha, where I was given a set of clean clothes and a juicy steak dinner. And thus my training began."

After a long moment of silence, Talanov said, "If you're trying to prove that you're more than your looks, you have done so. You have proved you're a terrible liar because most of that story was a lie. Not everything, but certainly most."

He glanced over and saw the hint of a smile on Sofia's face.

"They said you were good," she replied. "How could you tell when you were not able to see my face?"

"Is there a point to this?" he asked.

"I have money, Sasha. Lots of it. If you doubt what I am saying, look into my eyes. You will see that I am telling the truth."

"Again, what's your point?"

"The Soviet Union is disintegrating. It is collapsing from within. But you and I, we need not be casualties of this collapse." She placed her hands on his thigh and squeezed it affectionately. "Come with me!" she said.

"Come with you? Where? To do what?"

"Everything. There is a market for people like us. People with specialized skills."

"As in mercenaries, you mean? Hired guns?"

"I wouldn't put it so crudely."

"Then what would you call it? And where exactly would

your loyalties lie? With whomever pays you the most, no matter what other commitments you've made?"

With a deep sigh, Sofia returned to her side of the seat, where she looked out the window for a long moment. "This is why Moscow favors you," she finally said, her attention on the lights of some passing houses, "and why you are allowed certain indulgences." She looked at him again. "Have you ever thought about that? Why you lead such a privileged life when we as a nation can barely feed ourselves?"

Talanov did not reply.

"It is for the ideals that you hold," she said, answering her own question. "Your belief in equality and fairness and the faith you place in our system. And so you do their bidding and follow their orders because you believe the end will one day justify the means. It is how you were trained, by instructors you admired and respected. Idealists, like yourself. That is why Moscow needs people like you. People they can trust to follow orders while they line their pockets with the fruits of *your* labor. People like Kozloff. Communism is profitable only for those who run it, Sasha, and the people running it are getting rich."

"I've seen no evidence to support such a claim."

"Why do you think that is? Why have you -- a KGB colonel who sees *everything* -- not seen that?"

Talanov did not reply.

Sofia said, "Because those at the top do not want you to see. And the reason is simple. It is because you frighten them. Honesty in the face of corruption. *That* is why you have been excluded."

"If what you say is true---"

"It is."

"Again, if what you say is true, how is it that you know? How did you come by this information?"

"When the target is a lion, the mouse is ignored," she replied. "I hear the whispers. The careless remarks."

Talanov pursed his lips thoughtfully. The headlights of oncoming cars were like strobes across their faces.

"Come with me," she said again. "Why should others be the only ones profiting from our labor?"

"How long have you been planning this?" he asked, stopping for a red light.

"Does it matter?"

"If it didn't, I wouldn't be asking."

"What I need to know is whether or not you will join me. That is the question."

Talanov did not reply.

"Allow me to put it this way," Sofia said. "Moscow is full of trained operatives. Men as deadly as you. But I want *you,* Sasha, and do you want to know why? It is because we are so much alike. Because we have skills. Because we have *chemistry,* especially in bed. You took me to the edge. Made me scream like no one else. Believe me, many have tried."

"Our role as lovers was scripted for a purpose," he said as the light changed to green. "We were actors on a stage, playing parts."

"At the beginning, yes, that was true. But along the way, things changed."

"Nothing has changed."

"Everything has changed. We became more than actors."

"Then you got the wrong impression."

"Acting in public is one thing," Sofia replied. "But no one -- not even you -- can fake the kind of intimacy we had. Making love is much more than a technical skill learned by an actor."

"If love had actually been part of the equation, then, yes, it would have been more than a technical skill. Having sex is different. That is why satisfying a man in the bedroom is easy. It's a physical release. Satisfying a woman is different. I simply learned how to do it."

"I know what we experienced."

"It was a performance," Talanov replied.

"No one is that good."

Talanov shrugged.

"You *had* to feel something. I *know* it."

"Why do you fight me on this?"

"Because I do not believe you!" Sofia declared. "Everyone has feelings."

"Feelings, yes -- anger, laughter, sadness -- but feelings *for* someone: no. Those I do not permit. If I am called the Ice Man, this is the reason. Not because I am a cold-blooded killer."

"But you ignited desires within me. Desires I did not know I had. How is that possible if you do not feel anything more than . . . nothing?"

"You said you wanted to know about Olaf. Well let me tell you that story. Olaf was my great uncle Vov's dog, a big, galloping Caucasian Shepherd who lived with Uncle Vov on his farm in the pine country east of Nizhny Novgorod, which was about two-hundred miles east of Moscow. One winter morning in December -- the snow was deep by then -- Uncle Vov took me into the forest on a hunting expedition. I was eleven. On the second day a snowstorm set in. We found shelter -- an old cabin -- but the blizzard lasted for days and our food soon ran out, and there was no chance of going outside to shoot anything because of the snow. On the fifth day we were seriously hungry -- Uncle Vov, me and Olaf -- all of us. That night, the wolves came and Olaf began howling with them. Uncle Vov told him to shut up but Olaf became agitated and restless. So Uncle Vov killed him. Shot him right there on the floor in front of me. I remember crying and Uncle Vov told me to stop crying and build a fire, that dogs were dogs and we needed food, and that if he hadn't done what he did, the dog would have turned on us. Animal eating animal. The strong eating the weak.

"When I wouldn't quit crying, Uncle Vov said I needed to learn a lesson. So he locked me outside until I heard the wolves again and began pounding on the door. He let me back in and I hid in a corner and watched him skin Olaf and begin roasting him over the fire. When the meat was done, he told me to eat. I shook my head. He just shrugged, tore off a hind leg and sat down in front of the fire. Finally, later, after he had fallen asleep, I tiptoed across the floor and took a few bites. I hated what I was doing, but I was so hungry and the meat tasted so good. After a few mouthfuls I looked over and saw Uncle Vov looking at me, so I ran back to my corner.

"'Do you think me cruel?' he asked in that deep, gruff voice of his. I nodded. 'Have you ever seen a starving dog turn on a man?' he then asked. I shook my head. 'Well, I have,' he said, 'and Olaf was ready to turn. Not on me, but you, the smallest and the weakest.' 'But Olaf was my friend,' I replied. 'Any dog will be your friend until he gets hungry enough to eat you. And people are not much different. They'll just turn on you a lot quicker. And the more you care for them, like you did for Olaf, the harder it is to see the truth and the easier it will be for them to kill you. Feeling nothing will keep you alive. Remember that, boy. It's the best piece of advice I'll ever give you.'"

"Why do you tell me this story?"

"Because part of me died that day, and it was not until Uncle Vov was gone that I saw the value in what he had said. Because when he died, I wasn't sad. I wasn't . . . anything. And I haven't felt anything since."

CHAPTER 14

Talanov and Sofia rode in silence for a while, each lost in thought. They were heading in a southerly direction, toward the Mediterranean Highway, which ran east-west and paralleled the Mediterranean coast. They stopped for another red light. On their left was a small downtown precinct. Talanov could see cafés, shops and some modest office buildings. The area was landscaped and pretty. A few structures were concrete and glass but most were classic Spanish, with white-washed exteriors, red tile roofs, angled stairways and upstairs passageways.

The light changed to green and they began moving forward again. Traffic was getting heavy. At the next intersection, Talanov looked left. Midway along the block, a phalanx of police cars had cordoned off the street. There were officers in riot gear. Beyond them was a crowd of angry protesters. Some were throwing rocks and bottles. Others were thrusting placards into the air.

At the next intersection, Talanov saw more of the same: flashing lights and policemen in riot gear holding back protesters.

By the time they turned left onto the Mediterranean Highway a mile later, the pace of traffic had picked up again. A balmy crosswind carried the smells of fast food and the ocean. Cafés and restaurants were full. Long lines of partygoers stretched in front of nightclubs.

Within minutes, they had taken an exit off of the Mediterranean Highway and turned left over a bridge spanning the highway. Before long, they were parked in a quiet neighborhood three doors from the safe house. There had been a number of parking spaces along the narrow street but Talanov chose the one in a dark gap between two vintage streetlamps.

Talanov turned off the ignition and sat quietly for several minutes, the windows down, listening to the sounds of the night in order to formulate a baseline of what was normal and what was not. Aroused animals posed the greatest threat, in particular dogs, who could smell a person's approach as acutely as they could hear it. And a barking dog almost always brought an owner to investigate.

Other sounds, however, afforded them cover: the hum of traffic; the faint drift of Spanish guitar; the rustling of palm fronds and several dogs already barking at the distant clamor of the protests.

"I'll change clothes and then we'll go," Talanov said, unbuckling his seatbelt and stepping into the rear of the van.

"By the way, I saw through that little act," Sofia said.

"What act was that?" asked Talanov, undoing his tie.

"About your Uncle Vov eating his dog."

Sitting on a fender well inside the darkened van, Talanov laughed.

"And you are laughing because I caught you," she said.

"I'm laughing because you know every word of that story was true," he replied, unbuttoning his shirt in the dim light from a street lamp shining in through the rear window.

"Says who?"

"Says you."

Sitting in front with her elbow resting on the back of the seat, Sofia stared at Talanov for several seconds. "How could you possibly know that?"

"What I want to know is why you insist on playing these games," he replied, removing his trousers and tossing them aside. "You knew the story was true and yet you tried to convince me otherwise. Why?"

Sofia saw the contours of his shoulders in the dim light.

"How did you know I was faking it?" she asked.

Talanov pulled on his fatigues and zipped them up. After buckling on his utility belt, he slipped on his boots, took out his 9mm Makarov and checked that it was loaded.

"Tell me," she said. "How did you know I was faking it?"

With his elbows resting on his knees, Talanov looked at the dark shape that was Sofia. Something was not right about her but he was not sure what it was. First it was her story about killing Grigory. Then it was her schoolgirl talk about chemistry and taking her to the edge. Then it was that wild tale about Moscow fearing him and how she wanted him to join her in some vague project or venture, specifically what she would not say. Was all of this a trap? *Did* Moscow fear him? Had they sent her to test his loyalty . . . to see if he could be bought?

"Tell me," she said again, looking at him from the front seat. "Tell me how you knew I was testing you."

"It wasn't hard," he replied, sticking the Makarov in his belt. "You're a twenty-two year-old kid. You're inexperienced, immature and way too obvious."

Even though Talanov could not see the features of Sofia's face in the darkness, in the ensuing moment of silence, he could sense her rising anger.

And it was time to provoke that anger. To find out who she really was.

"You're a garnish -- a Barbie -- that's all," he said. "So quit trying to prove yourself to be something more."

It was an insult to say this. He knew that. He also knew Sofia was a lot more than a Barbie. The question was how much more. Who was she, really?

There was only one way to find out and that was crack open her façade as an actor. To push her beyond tolerable limits.

"Stick to what you do best," he added, "and that's look pretty. It's a lot safer, too. For everybody."

"Fuck you, Sasha. I can shoot -- I can *kill* -- as good as anyone, including you. I think I have demonstrated that adequately."

"A chimpanzee can pull a trigger. Pulling a trigger proves nothing other than how much of a liability you've become. I need assets on my team. People who are more than just a pretty face. Which you are not. Stay here. I'll handle Gorev myself."

When Talanov turned toward the rear of the van, Sofia vaulted the seat in one quick motion, like a gymnast, knees drawn to her chest until she cleared the headrest and extended both feet to the floor, bounding for his back, her hands like claws.

Talanov ducked left, came up behind Sofia and clamped a hand across the back of her neck, slamming her face-down onto the padded floorboard of the van. Sofia tried to kick free but Talanov's knee in the middle of her back prevented her from moving.

"I forgot to add, gullible," he said. "So, Miss-whoever-you-are, why don't you tell me why you're really here."

"You're hurting me!" Sofia cried out in a muffled voice, her face pressed into the mat.

"I'll hurt you more unless you start talking."

"Why are you *doing* this?"

Talanov pressed harder with his knee.

"All right! Can you at least let me up so I can breathe?"

Talanov thought about it for a moment then let her up. She maneuvered into a sitting position on the other side of the van.

"Who sent you? Why are you here?" he asked, sitting on the fender well opposite her.

"I cannot believe you did that!"

Talanov responded with an impatient sigh.

"You provoked me!" she said. "You *made* me lash out."

Talanov grabbed his duffel kit, rifled through it and took out a roll of duct tape.

"What are you doing?" she asked.

"Making sure you stay put," he replied. He peeled off a long strip and it made a coarse ripping sound.

"You can't *do* this!" she declared.

"Hard way or easy way?" he said.

Sofia scooted into the corner of the van, trying to get away.

Talanov followed.

"First it was the chemistry you claimed we had," he said, pausing on one knee, the tape ready. "Then it was an offer of money, advising me that Moscow has betrayed me, that others were growing rich from my labor, that we made such a good team and that you wanted me to join you in some vague enterprise that you would not divulge."

Talanov heard voices and laughter outside but did not divert his eyes.

"Did Moscow send you to test me?" he demanded to the distant sound of hissing and cracking glass. "Is that what this is about?"

"No, Moscow did not send me to test you," Sofia explained, "but, yes, I have been testing you with lies and stories."

"Why?"

"To see if you were as good as your reputation."

"Why?"

Sofia maneuvered up onto her knees. "Because I *do* want you to come with me," she said. "I know you cannot see my face, but you can hear the truth in my voice. I want you to come with me because there *is* money to be made -- lots of it -- for people like us. It is also true that Moscow has excluded you. The old ways are being questioned, Sasha, and the elite of Moscow know this. It is why they are lining their pockets. Kravenko's advisor, Kozloff, is but one example and you know what he was like. But the time to act is now, before they know that we know . . . before they blame us for their failures."

Kneeling in the rear of the empty van with the strip of duct tape in hand, Talanov had to admit Sofia made sense. The old ways *were* being questioned and men like Kozloff *were* lining their pockets. He may not agree with her solution

-- to become a mercenary -- but her explanations at least mandated further investigation as to whether or not he had, in fact, been betrayed . . . and by whom.

"Once Gorev and his family have been returned to Sverdlovsk, I will look into this," he said. "To determine how much corruption there is and how far it has spread."

Sofia eased the duct tape aside and placed her hands on Talanov's knees. "We need to act now. Tonight. You required me to trust you about Gorev, without revealing any details about where he was or how you planned to apprehend him. Even now, I still do not know the location of the American safe house. I could have gone behind your back and tried to locate it. But I did not. Why? Because I trusted you, and I still do. All I am asking right now is that you grant me the same consideration. That you place the same faith in me that I placed in you."

Talanov did not reply.

"We *are* good together, Sasha," Sofia continued. "Even if you do not permit yourself personal feelings -- and I am still not sure that I believe you when you say this -- you have to admit the efficiency of our partnership."

With a sigh, Talanov wadded the strip of tape into a small ball and tossed it aside. "Three houses down," he said, giving her the address and a description of the safe house just as a woman outside their van began shouting for a group of *vándalos* -- hooligans -- to leave her car alone.

Talanov looked out the rear window. In the faint light from a distant streetlamp, he could see an old woman scolding what looked to be a dozen young men. Short and squat and dressed in a plain black dress, the woman appeared to be in her sixties. The young men were in their twenties. One against twelve. An old woman against a mob carrying ball bats and knives.

"You mean, this piece of shit?" asked Paco. He rested his ball bat on his shoulder and patted the fender of an old car before stepping back to smash in the windshield. It collapsed inward onto the seat. A blanket of broken glass.

Talanov hated people ganging up on others. He always had. Even as a boy, he would stick up for the one being picked on. Maybe it was because he had never had anyone stand up for him when he was growing up. Whatever the explanation, something within him bristled when he saw the kind of harassment he was seeing now. And he sometimes suffered the consequences. He remembered getting kicked and beaten when he tried defending a girl whose name he never knew. Some older boys were pushing her around. So he stepped in and they beat the stuffing out of him instead. Three against one. He didn't stand a chance.

And it didn't matter. Some things were just not right.

Talanov reached for the door handle.

Sofia stopped him.

"Do not jeopardize our mission for an old woman," Sofia said.

"It's one against twelve."

"And we have our orders. The woman is useless. Of no importance."

Talanov stared at Sofia for a long moment, then looked out the window again when he heard Paco smashing in the side windows of the woman's car.

"Why do you do this?" the old woman cried.

"Because I can," Paco replied.

"Please, I am a pensioner. A *widow."*

"You are a leech. A rich capitalist leech who deserves to be taught a lesson."

The others whooped their agreement.

The old woman tried to run but Paco grabbed her. The woman begged to be left alone.

Paco said, "And allow the leech to suck blood from others?" He shoved her into the arms of one of his friends, who began grappling for her buttons. The terrified woman tried fighting him off.

"Feisty for an old cow!" the man yelled with a laugh.

Talanov swung his hand like a hatchet and caught the man behind the ear. The man flapped his arms like a beheaded chicken. A nerve reaction of some kind even though the man was out cold. Talanov scooped the old woman to safety before twisting the bat out of Paco's hand and smashing it into the forehead of the man beside him.

"You!" Paco shouted as another of his friends hit the pavement. To the others: "Get him! He's that Russian spy!"

The man across from Paco aimed his bat for Talanov's head. Full swing, like he was practicing T-ball for Little League. People usually went for the head. Very few went for the knees. Going for the head, however, means the other guy can duck.

And Talanov did.

The bat smashed into the man's face beside Paco, knocking out his front teeth and shattering his jaw. The man staggered backward, cursing and spitting before tripping over the curb and falling. The man swung again but Talanov responded with an uppercut swing of his own, his bat knocking the other man's bat high into the air. It clubbed him in the chin on its way out into the darkness.

There were bats flying everywhere now and the man across from Talanov reared back with his. Talanov flung his bat underhanded into the man's crotch. The man made a gagging sound and dropped to his knees before toppling facedown onto the street.

Grabbing Paco by the throat, Talanov slammed him against the side of the old woman's car, where he jammed his Makarov between his eyes. In the light of the streetlamp, Talanov could see Paco's eyes focused on the ominous black silencer pressed hard against his forehead.

Paco's hand crawled slowly toward his pocket.

"Reach for that knife and I'll break every one of your fingers," Talanov said in fluent Spanish.

Paco moved his hand away.

"You really should find something better to do with your time," Talanov growled. He twisted the gun back and forth. The tip of the silencer made an imprint on Paco's forehead.

Sofia appeared at Talanov's side. *"My dolzhny idti,"* she

said quietly in Russian, telling him they needed to go while keeping a careful eye on the others. Some were moaning on the ground. Some had climbed to their feet. All were eyeing him angrily.

Talanov knew she was right. Gorev would be arriving soon and he now had another problem: leading this mob away from their van and the safe house.

His impulsive decision to save an old woman had just put everything at risk.

CHAPTER 15

Talanov did a quick scan of his surroundings. They were near the corner, where *Calle del Bergantín* met a cross street. Several blocks to the left was the busy Mediterranean Highway. To the right was a quiet residential section of apartments. Talanov could see lighted walkways and windows beyond a high wall bordering the street. Vines spilled over the top of the wall and floodlights illuminated the tops of trees.

He had no idea where the old woman lived, but right now that didn't matter. What mattered was leading this mob away from the safe house.

He looked back at Paco and said, "Well, Paco, I guess this is your lucky night. You get to live. For the second time. So why don't you and your playmates run along home before one of you *really* gets hurt?"

Taking the old woman by the hand, Talanov and Sofia ran with her to the corner, where they turned right and hurried along the sidewalk. Thankfully, the street was dark. Roaming bands of hooligans had smashed out the streetlights.

A car came toward them and they ducked through an arched doorway that opened into a secluded courtyard. Lighted staircases and passageways overlooked the area, which contained deep pockets of shadow among the palm trees and shrubs. A lighted path meandered among the foliage to the other side. Bordering the path were flower beds of colorful impatiens.

Talanov told the old woman to stay hidden in the shadows. "We'll lead them up the street," he said, unscrewing the silencer from his Makarov. He placed it with his pistol in the gun pockets near the small of his back. "Once it's clear, hurry home and lock your door. I'm sorry about your car."

"They will not go home, *señor,* not after the way you insulted them."

Talanov smiled. "I know. Stay here. You'll be safe."

Leaving the courtyard, Talanov and Sofia turned right and jogged along the base of the courtyard wall, which soon became a series of garage doors for the whitewashed apartments above. Balconies overlooked a row of carports across the street. The parking spaces beneath the carports were filled with cars. A few spots were empty, but not many. Beyond the cars was a high wall topped with terra cotta tiles. On the other side lay more apartments.

Running silently in boots with soles of hardened rubber, Talanov knew his insults would provoke the mob into coming after them. The key was running slowly enough for them to maintain pursuit until they fatigued and collapsed. Not only was it important to lure them away from the safe house, but drive them to the point of exhaustion. That part was essential.

"Hurry, this way!" Talanov shouted in Spanish, cupping his hand near his mouth so his voice would carry.

Seconds later, he heard excited shouts and the clapping of footsteps. The mob had taken the bait and were coming after them.

Keeping pace beside him, Sofia said nothing. Talanov could tell she wanted to but was holding back.

Talanov knew he was not an impulsive person, nor was he reckless, although what he had done -- helping the old woman -- was both impulsive and reckless. Sofia therefore had a right to be angry. He would be angry, too, if the situation were reversed. And he was sure he would hear about it sooner or later.

His nickname, the Ice Man, had been given to him many

years ago by his *dǎoshī* -- literally, "mentor" -- in the ancient monastery of *Lóngshù,* set among the peach trees high in the foothills near the colossal mountain of Khan Tengri. Known also as "blood mountain," Khan Tengri was located in the remote Tian Shan range, where Soviet Kazakhstan met Soviet Kyrgyzstan at the northern tip of China, near the ancient Silk Road that skirted the perimeter of the forbidding Taklimakan Desert. The *dǎoshī* were a group of Chinese martial arts philosophers who trained elite Soviet youth in the various disciplines of survival, combat and fitness.

Lóngshù was a compound of eleven wooden buildings -- some open and spacious, others tiny and confined -- all austere and devoid of furnishings -- all with tile roofs and open windows and wooden floors. The *dǎoshī* slept on bamboo mats and required neophytes to do the same.

The goal of their training was fitness and self-sufficiency, which was why survival and self-defense skills were emphasized. The neophytes trained barefooted on gravel and in snow. They did knuckle push-ups on stone. Building up calluses in training prevented injury in combat.

It was the same with people. A callused attitude toward others prevented injury from those people, or because of them, which was why friendships among the neophytes were strictly forbidden. Indeed, neophytes were forbidden even from speaking with one another, and those violating this directive were punished and sent home.

Young Alex not only embraced his training, he excelled, and his *dǎoshī* saw in him a combination of drive and determination that was unmatched by anyone else. However many push-ups young Alex was given, he did more. However many miles he was required to run, he ran more. He smirked at deprivation. He endured hardship without complaint. His mentor kept looking for a weakness but could find none. He even pitted young Alex against a Chinese girl brought in as a sparring partner for the Soviet youth. The girl beat Alex every time. Young boys were usually filled with ego and resented being beaten by a girl. Not Alex. He took it in stride and trained even harder.

Then an incident occurred. The girl beat an older Chinese boy in a sparring match that took place among the trees beyond the vegetable garden. Blossoms were still on the branches and when the wind blew it caused a flurry of soft petals. The older Chinese boy had also been brought in as a sparring partner for the Soviet boys but had made the mistake of challenging the girl. And got beaten. So the older boy brought two of his friends and cornered the girl out in the peach grove. They would teach the girl a lesson.

Watching from his upstairs balcony, the *dǎoshī* saw Alex come to the defense of the girl. He saw the smaller Alex push the boys away from her. Saw young Alex fight a valiant but losing battle. Saw him take their kicks and punches and finally go down. Saw the older boys leave him bleeding on the grass, sobbing silently, in pain.

The *dǎoshī* called the Chinese boys to his room. The boys stood trembling before him, fearing his wrath. Instead, he commanded them to attack the girl again. And he watched while Alex was beaten defending her again.

The *dǎoshī* smiled. He had finally found a way to break young Alex Talanov.

And he did.

Completely.

The incident at *Lóngshù* flashed through Talanov's mind as he and Sofia ran along the darkened street. His compulsion then for a girl whose name he never knew had cost him dearly -- several times -- just as his compulsion tonight was costing them again.

Exactly how much remained to be seen.

They came to a Y-shaped fork in the street. To the right, two cars were parked in the middle of the street, engines idling, their drivers talking. One car faced toward them and the other faced away. The street was lit up with headlights in both directions. That much light was bad, so they ran left.

This section of the street was dark. On one side were more garage doors. The lights above the garage doors had been smashed out. Chunks of broken glass littered the pavement. On the other side was a high wall. Tangles of jasmine hung over the wall, which was punctuated with several arched doorways and gates of wrought iron. Beyond were the lighted windows of apartments.

Talanov spun around and ran backward. "Hide in here!" he shouted. He could hear the quickening of footsteps behind them. His plan was working. Time now to ditch their pursuers.

The canyon of garage doors and walls turned left and terminated abruptly at a high chain-link fence preventing access into some new blocks of apartments that were being constructed. Talanov and Sofia reversed direction only to see the darkened silhouettes of their pursuers racing toward them.

Talanov ran over to a wrought iron gate and tried the handle. It was locked. A locked gate on one side. Garage doors on the other. A chain link fence behind.

The footsteps grew louder.

They were trapped.

CHAPTER 16

Paco had positioned himself in the middle of the loose semi-circle of men that slowed to a stop roughly twenty feet away from Talanov and Sofia. In the faint ambient light from the lighted windows of some upstairs apartments, Talanov saw the shapes of six men.

Paco held up his *navaja* and snapped open the blade. The others did the same.

Hearing the *click-clack* of four distinct blades locking into place, Talanov pulled out his Makarov. There was no time to screw on the silencer, which meant if he had to fire, it would make a lot of noise. And in a quiet street like this, surrounded by hundreds of apartments, the sound of a Makarov would echo for blocks. One shot, much less seven or eight, plus any associated cries and screams, would bring the police, who were already out in force controlling the protests. No police or this mission was over.

He held up his gun. "I don't want to shoot. But I will."

"Really?" Paco said. He pointed to a parked car and one of his men used his bat to bash in the rear windshield, setting off its alarm. "We will see what the police have to say when they arrive to find the two Russian spies who killed my friends."

"An excellent idea," said Talanov. "We'll see whose fingerprints they find on the gun used to shoot your friends. I guarantee they won't be mine. So we'll see who the police want to believe. Us or a mob of extremists who have already been causing a lot of trouble. And when they *do* identify those fingerprints as yours, you and all of your friends here with you right now will be implicated. That means jail. I'll also be interested in seeing who that old woman picks out of a lineup when she's called to identify the men who assaulted her."

The car alarm continued to wail. Porch lights began to click on. A few people emerged onto their balconies to see what was happening.

Paco's men began to grow nervous at the prospect of getting caught. Even in the darkness, Talanov could see them glancing at one another.

Talanov knew they did not have a lot of time. A car alarm *would* bring the police. But not as quickly as gunshots would. A fast negotiation was the best way out of this crisis.

"What's it going to be, Paco?" asked Talanov. "I'll kill you if I have to. But I don't want to. We all walk away. We live to fight another day. See, I'm lowering my gun. I mean you no harm unless you force me."

Talanov lowered his Makarov.

A tense silence ensued between the two men while the alarm continued to wail. Talanov kept his eyes on Paco. Paco kept his on Talanov. It was dark but the two men were keenly aware of one another. To the exclusion of everything else, each ready to spring into action the instant aggression was sensed. Talanov with his gun. Paco and his men with their *navajas*.

Which is why neither of them were paying any attention to Sofia. Had either of them been able to see her, they would have known what was about to happen. Talanov in particular would have seen the angry glare that said her patience had run out. It was not that Sofia was not patient. Soviets was trained to outlast any enemy, to lay in wait until just the right moment. Sofia was trained to wait.

Her problem was duress. Duress changes everything. And it did with Sofia. She was agitated by the way Talanov had manhandled her in the van. She was agitated by his smug attitude about Gorev, he being the only one who knew for sure where Gorev was going to defect. No one else had been able to figure that out. And she was agitated by his reckless compulsion to rescue that worthless old woman, which had now jeopardized *everything*. And here he was, trying to *talk* his way out of a situation that should have been handled differently.

Which is just what she was going to do.

Moving left to right, Sofia slid quickly behind Talanov and with a twirling pirouette, used her momentum to snatch the Makarov from his hand, rack a cartridge into the chamber and emerge an arm's length away to lift the weapon effortlessly and take aim.

"Enough talk," she said, pulling the trigger.

Click.

Talanov lunged right and grabbed Sofia's hand, lifting it upward in an arc above his head before pivoting beneath it and yanking downward to pry the Makarov out of her hand with the same ease she had taken it from him.

Turning in time to see the glint of steel, Talanov front-kicked the *navaja* out of Paco's hand. He then used the butt of the Makarov to smash Paco in the forehead. Paco made a brief gargling sound and fell to his knees just as Talanov leaped to his right and used the pistol to backhand the man standing next to him. The man staggered awkwardly into a parked car and collapsed.

Another man flew at Talanov with his bat. When the man swung, Talanov did a tumbling roll to one side and came up to catch the man in the back of the head with a spinning roundhouse kick. When the man stumbled forward, Talanov deflected a clumsy swing that caught him in the face, grabbed the man by the scruff of the neck and hammered a knee up into his chin.

While Paco crawled to safety, Talanov squared off against the others.

Paco scooted up into a sitting position against a wall. "Kill him!" he shouted in a raspy voice. *"Vuelo Navajas."*

Talanov's heart sank. *Vuelo Navajas,* or "flying knives," meant three knives were about to come flying toward him. And while his reflexes and the darkness afforded him a measure of protection, they were no guarantees that at least one of the knives would not hit its mark.

In moments of shifting strategy there is a instant of time -- almost like a vacuum -- when momentum is paused and power is refocused. An instant for new information to be processed, old courses of aggression to be suspended and new courses of aggression to be commenced. An instant for Paco's men to receive their orders, suck in sharp breaths, plant their feet and loop their *navajas* back and around in tight figure-eights before snapping them forward and releasing them as spinning, razor-sharp blades.

Which gave Talanov even less time to rack another cartridge into his gun.

Paco's men planted their feet and drew back their knives just as Talanov fired.

Three shots. Three grunts. Three casings tinkling on the pavement.

Talanov grabbed Sofia by the wrist and began running. He would take this up with her later. Right now, they needed to escape. Right now, he needed to cool down.

It was not that he was against shooting an adversary. He had done so on other occasions. These killings, however, could and should have been avoided. They were unnecessary and would intensify the police search to find them, especially with witnesses alive to identify them.

At the corner, Talanov glanced back to see people streaming out of an arched gateway. Several rushed over and helped Paco to his feet. Others rushed over to the dead bodies. Seconds later, they started to scream.

Sofia said, "See? In the end, Ice Man did what needed to be done although I do not understand why your Makarov misfired. Such things never occur, not to us. We clean our weapons more often than our teeth. What happened, Sasha? That first shot was a dud."

Talanov kept running and did not reply.

"As you wish, it does not matter," she continued. "We can talk about it later. What matters now is following orders. You following yours and I following mine."

Talanov glanced guardedly at Sofia.

"Yes, Sasha," she said, running beside him. "We have a defector to catch and we must put aside our differences for the sake of that purpose. But no more stepping out of line. For either of us. We must now set our sights on Gorev."

CHAPTER 17

What matters now is following orders. You following yours and I following mine.

Sitting at the dining room table in the safe house, Talanov snorted bitterly at the irony. Sofia had ended their little escapade with that remark because she knew what was about to happen and wanted to remind him about his obligation to follow orders.

Kravenko's orders.

How could he have not seen this coming? How could he have missed all the signs?

He had missed them because for the last few days he had been focused on showing Sofia and the Americans how clever and witty he was.

Learn to pull your punches, Zak had told him. Don't ever let them see your full capability.

Talanov rubbed the bridge of his nose. What would Zak say if he could see him sitting here now, marginalized and powerless? What would he say if he knew how careless and egotistical he had been?

What Sofia was planning to do with Gorev, he had no idea. Was she planning on selling his anthrax samples to the highest bidder? Her vague talk of wanting him to come with her was no doubt a lie. The emotional outbursts, the pleas, the sex, the banter and saucy personality: everything about her had been a lie insofar as she had used it to keep him from seeing through her façade until he led her to Gorev.

Who was the garnish now?

A quiet knock sounded on the door. Holding her pistol out of sight, Sofia walked over and opened the door for two more KGB agents -- Odin and Svet -- who stepped quickly inside. Muscular and young, with shaved heads, they carried backpacks and were dressed in black fatigues. Around their waists were holstered Makarov pistols.

"The police are two houses away," Svet said in Russian.

"They are going from house to house," Odin added. "We saw them on our way in."

Sofia silently mouthed a curse.

"What do you want us to do?" asked Svet.

"You are certain they did not see you?" she asked in return.

"Of course not," Svet replied.

Sofia turned to her hostages. By now, Gorev had regained consciousness and was sitting up. His head was still oozing blood.

"I know most if not all of you speak Russian," Sofia said, pacing back and forth in front of them, "and that you just heard my colleague inform me that the police are knocking on doors. Colonel Talanov is right when he says we are not here to start a bloodbath. But if any of you attempts to raise an alarm when officers knock on our door, I will shoot the policemen and then I will shoot you, and the bloodbath we were hoping to avoid will become a reality. Does anyone *not* understand what I just said?"

Sofia made drilling eye contact with each person in the room, waiting for -- demanding -- nods of understanding. And one by one, the hostages began nodding. Gorev was first, then Anna. Sofia waited for Noya to respond but the girl kept staring at the floor with a vacant, faraway look and Sofia moved on to Franco, who nodded, then the two safe house residents, Alejandro and Carmen. She then looked at Pilgrim and Bixler.

"Do you really expect us to believe you're going to let us live?" asked Bixler in English.

Sofia slapped her palm several times with the long, silenced barrel of her Makarov. "You are perhaps thinking that you will wait until the police arrive at our door, and that you will cry out and become a big hero and save these people, like in a Rambo movie of Sylvester Stalin, is that it?"

"It's Stallone . . . Sylvester Stal-*lone,*" Franco blurted out.

Sofia glared sharply at Franco.

Franco averted his eyes. "Sorry, that just . . . popped out."

"Shut up!" barked Sofia just as the gate buzzer sounded several times in rapid succession, a sign of urgency and impatience.

"Remember what I say to you," Sofia said, looking hard at Bixler then around the room. "Any noise and you will die."

She motioned Alejandro and Carmen to their feet. Once they had joined her, Sofia grabbed Carmen by the arm. "You stay with me while you---" she pointed at Alejandro "---will answer the gate. Assure the police that everything is all right. Under no circumstances will you allow them inside this house. If you do, I will kill your wife. Do you understand?"

For emphasis, Sofia placed the barrel of her pistol up under Carmen's chin.

Frozen with fear, Alejandro could only stare at the gun while Carmen stood there, eyes closed, quivering with fear.

The gate buzzer sounded again.

"Do you *understand?"* repeated Sofia, pressing the gun harder against Carmen's throat.

"Threatening them won't help," said Talanov.

"Either this man goes out there *now* or I kill him and you're going out."

Glowering briefly at Sofia, Talanov walked over and clasped Alejandro on the shoulder. Alejandro blinked and looked vacantly at Talanov just as the buzzer sounded again.

"You need to answer that gate," said Talanov in a calm voice. "Your wife will be okay." Taking Alejandro by the elbow, Talanov ushered him to the door, where he made Alejandro turn and face him. "Look me in the eyes," he said. "Focus."

Alejandro did.

"Answer the gate," instructed Talanov. "Tell the police your wife is sick -- with the flu -- and that you're fighting it off yourself. Cough a few times. Make it convincing. You can do it."

Talanov nodded toward the door and stepped back, out of sight. Taking a deep breath, Alejandro opened the door and slipped outside.

Sofia glared at Talanov before shoving Carmen back toward the others and motioning for her to sit down. She glanced at Odin and Svet and nodded for them to draw their weapons. The two men withdrew their Makarovs and screwed silencers onto the barrels.

Outside, Alejandro walked along the darkened walk to the gate. "Who is it?" he asked when the buzzer sounded again.

"Policia Nacional," a voice barked back.

Alejandro unlatched the gate and saw three policemen standing before him. In the street beyond were two squad cars with flashing blue lights. Other officers were moving about in the darkness. Still others were arguing with protesters. One protester in particular was screaming that three of his friends had been killed by Russian spies, who ran down this street and disappeared.

"Do you live here?" an officer asked.

Alejandro wobbled slightly and stared off into space.

The officer snapped his fingers in front of Alejandro's face. "Do you live here?" the officer asked again.

"Huh?"

"What is wrong with you? I said, do you *live* here?"

"Yes."

"Are you alone in the house?"

"Alone?"

"Yes! Are you *alone?* Is someone with you?"

Alejandro swallowed hard and stared at the officer, unable to clear his mind of the terrified look he had seen in Carmen's eyes with a gun being held to her throat. What was she feeling? Was she crying? He knew she was afraid. So was he.

But what could they do? What could anyone do?

"Something is wrong with this guy," the officer said to his colleague. "Keep him here while I have a look."

Under no circumstances will you allow them inside this house. If you do, I will kill your wife.

Sofia's words were like an awakening slap when the officer took a step forward.

Alejandro sprang back and barricaded the sidewalk with his outstretched arms. "Wait, you can't go in. My wife is . . . very ill. And so am I." He turned away and coughed deeply, almost painfully, then cleared his throat and spat. "Some kind of flu she picked up at school, and of course gave to me. She's an English teacher, you know."

"I thought I recognized you," the third officer said brightly. "Your wife teaches my youngest daughter, Abrienda Díaz."

"Ah, yes, of course," said Alejandro. He turned away and sneezed. "My apologies for the coughing. Not to mention the mucous." He cleared his throat and spat again. "You cannot believe how much mucous one nose can produce. And if you multiply that by . . ."

"Never mind," said the first policeman, stepping back just as a police cruiser stopped beside Talanov's van just up the street. Alejandro saw four heavily armed officers get out and began shining flashlights in through the van's windows.

Alejandro coughed again.

"Have you seen anyone tonight?" asked the first officer. "Has anyone knocked on your door?"

"The buzzer sounded once but I didn't answer it," replied Alejandro. "Whoever it was must have moved on."

"Do not open your door or this gate for anyone the rest of the night. Do you understand? Not for anyone."

"What's this about? The protests?"

"Go ahead, I will take care of this," the third officer said to his colleagues, who bid Alejandro good night and moved on to the next house. The third officer continued, "This is much more serious," he confided. "Some ETA extremists claim a pair of Soviet spies -- a man and a woman, both tall, especially the woman -- beat them up and killed their companions."

"And you believe them?"

"We found the bodies. All of them had been shot. Witnesses where the murders occurred confirmed hearing shots and seeing two figures running away. The extremists -- who are out there arguing with us now -- claim the Soviets jumped from that black van---" he turned and pointed "---which is still there. So I repeat: do not open your gate for anyone until we have apprehended them."

"I remember the scare we had with those Turkish spies last year."

"You know about that?"

"I keep a careful eye on matters that may affect the security of our schools."

"Then you know what I am talking about."

"I do. But how do you know these are Soviet spies?"

"We have been tracking them since they arrived in Spain several days ago. The Americans are watching them, too, although you did not hear that from me. The two spies -- Aleksandr Talanov and Sofia Dubinina -- were confirmed as having checked in to the Gran Casino del Sol and, according to the Americans, are still there, although I do not see how this can be since they were seen here, within the hour, and the murders occurred here within that same time frame. Police units are on their way now to the casino."

"And you're conducting a search to see if the spies are holed up in someone's house?"

"Precisely. They fled the nearby crime scene on foot and have not yet returned for their van, so we are securing the area."

"Thank you, Officer Díaz. If I see or hear anything, I'll let you know."

"By the way, your next-door neighbor reported hearing what sounded like gunshots coming from your house."

Alejandro swallowed.

"Can you explain that?" asked Díaz.

"It, uh, must have been the corks from two bottles of Champagne that I dropped. French, no less."

"Your wife is ill and you're drinking Champagne?"

"No, no, of course not. They were on the counter and I was moving them when I accidentally knocked them onto the floor and they exploded. What a mess. And am I ever in trouble. They were French, no less, but I already told you that, didn't I?"

Officer Díaz stared curiously at Alejandro, who shuffled nervously in place.

"Look at this!" an officer shouted from the street.

Alejandro and Díaz looked to see a policeman emerge from the van.

"We've got changes of clothes -- a tuxedo and a party dress -- and boxes of nine-millimeter ammunition," the policeman called out just as a scratchy police radio in one of the patrol cars announced how officers had gained entry into the Talanov suite at the casino to find the only occupant to be a Russian call girl asleep on the couch. The call girl claimed she had been hired by a man whose name she didn't know. She said the man had paid her to call him Alex. Her description was of a muscular Soviet male -- stocky, in his early thirties -- with thinning hair. She said he was dressed entirely in black -- bomber's jacket, shirt, slacks -- which does not at all fit the description of a leaner, taller Talanov. A rope left dangling out the bedroom window suggests the man escaped by rappelling down the outside of the hotel."

Alejandro coughed. "I really must go."

"Of course," Díaz replied. "Give my regards to your wife. I hope things don't get any worse."

"So do I," Alejandro said, closing the gate. "So do I."

CHAPTER 18

"It is a good thing you convinced them to leave," Sofia said when Alejandro returned. "Tell me everything they said."

"They know the van outside is yours. They've popped open the lock and found ammunition, a tuxedo and a party dress inside. They know you're in the neighborhood and say you killed some people. They also know you're not in your suite at the Gran Casino del Sol, and that a man in black escaped from your room. They are now interrogating the Russian call girl who took your place."

Sofia ran a hand through her hair and began pacing the floor.

"What do we do?" asked Svet.

"We wait them out," said Talanov. "The police will rummage through the van and file their reports while others continue their search. Once they believe the neighborhood is safe, they'll haul away our van and leave a patrol car on the street while the others go home for breakfast. In the meantime we call the freighter and have them delay departure for twenty-four hours. This will give us time to make our move tomorrow night, once it's dark."

"If I want your opinion I will ask for it," Sofia declared.

Talanov held up his hands in a gesture of sarcastic surrender and returned to sit at the table.

Sofia paced back and forth in front of the hostages, her lips muttering angrily while glaring at Talanov. She stopped and pointed at Carmen. "You, fix coffee while I think."

A quivering Carmen, her eyes swollen from crying, sat huddled against Agent Pilgrim, her head on Pilgrim's shoulder, her arms folded tightly across her chest. Pilgrim had brought her over while Alejandro had gone out to speak with the police and Carmen had not moved.

"Move!" Sofia shouted.

Carmen sniffled a few times but did not budge.

Sofia stepped over to Carmen and slapped the Makarov in her hand. "I will ask you one more time."

"She's terrified. Unable to function," said Talanov, standing. "The kid. Get her to do it."

"My daughter is Noya, not Kid," Anna mumbled bitterly.

Bixler touched Anna on the arm. A signal to be quiet.

"I know they are going to kill us," said Anna. "So I want them to know our names."

"He doesn't care," said Bixler. "That's why he calls her Kid. To him, that's all she is. Like a rock or a chair."

Talanov strode into the living room and pointed at Noya. "Make us some coffee," he said.

"Stay where you are," commanded Sofia.

"Don't make this about us," replied Talanov.

"It is *always* about us," Sofia said with a sneer. She looked at Bixler and said, "You, make the coffee."

Talanov motioned for Bixler to remain seated and stepped over to look Sofia directly in the eyes. "I do not care that you are in charge. If that is what my orders say, then so be it. I *do* care when you make foolish decisions in an effort to prove something that does not require proof."

Sofia locked eyes with Talanov, her eyes boring into his in an attempt to stare him down.

Talanov remained where he was, calm and unwavering.

"Colonel Talanov is right," said Odin. "The woman is an American agent and the kitchen is full of potential weapons. Send the girl."

"She's a logical choice," added Talanov. "The least likely to pose a threat."

Sofia looked at Odin for a long moment, considering her

options before motioning Noya to stand. When Noya stood, Sofia grabbed her by the arm. "Your name. What is it?" she asked.

"Noyabŕ . . . Noya," she replied, averting her eyes.

Sofia took Noya by the chin and forced eye contact. "A girl with the name of November. How quaint. Like April or May."

Gorev was already shaking with rage but Bixler signaled him to remain calm.

Sofia looked Noya over. "You are a pretty girl," she said.

"Leave her alone," warned Talanov.

"I wondered what the Boy Scout would say," Sofia said. "You see, *Noya,* Colonel Talanov has placed me in a very difficult position. He has not shown me the respect I deserve. He keeps interfering with my authority, making decisions that are not his to make. What happens when you disobey, Noya? Your parents have to discipline you, don't they? They may not want to, but they know it is for your own good."

Talanov grew rigid with anger.

Sofia continued, "So I am left with a big decision. How do I teach Colonel Talanov a lesson? How do I let him know he has overstepped his authority by interfering in mine?"

"Let her go and we can talk," said Talanov. "The girl has no part in this."

"She has every part in this, Sasha," said Sofia. "She is a commodity of value, especially to you. The girl is powerless and I have the power. All of it. And I am willing to use it. And this flips a switch inside you. I saw it with the old woman. I see it now."

"I care only what is good for this mission," lied Talanov. Right now, he was willing to say anything to defuse this situation.

"But *I* am what is good for this mission," Sofia replied curtly. "Otherwise, Comrade Kravenko would not have placed me in command. He would have retained you. But he did not. He gave it to me. But you keep undermining my authority and making me look foolish. And that I cannot allow."

"Let her go," demanded Talanov, taking a step forward.

Sofia pulled Noya in front of her and jammed the gun to her head.

Talanov stopped.

Sofia saw him tighten his grip on his Makarov.

"If that gun moves from your side, Colonel, I will kill her," vowed Sofia. "And if you are thinking that you will shoot me after I shoot her, think again."

Hearing the sound of weapons being draw, Talanov glanced around to see Odin and Svet with their pistols trained on him. They were standing together, about three feet apart, about ten feet away from him. No chance at all of missing.

Talanov looked at Noya and saw her staring up at him with the same dispassionate eyes he had seen before. They were deep and brown but completely devoid of emotion. No fear, no worry, no . . . anything. He was trained to feel that way. She was a kid and kids were not supposed to feel that way. They were supposed to be alive with crazy dreams, emotions and hopes for the future. Obviously, this was no ordinary situation and Talanov realized that. Noya and her parents were running for their lives -- from the KGB -- *from him* -- and yet Noya did not seem to care that they had been caught. Why not? She had just witnessed the murder of her grandparents. Everything they had hoped for and dreamed about was over.

Nor did she seem to be afraid of Sofia's threats. And that *was* troubling, because she should be afraid. Were he in charge, Gorev and his family would be taken into custody and returned to the Soviet Union.

With Sofia, he was not so sure.

Which is why it bothered him that Noya was not afraid.

Kids were not supposed to feel that way.

"Is this how you want it to end?" Talanov asked, stepping between Sofia and her men and raising his Makarov. He knew Sofia had threatened to shoot Noya if he raised his weapon, but he could see in her eyes that it was a bluff. She was angry, unstable and a megalomaniac, but she was not stupid. One shot would alert the police and her grand scheme would be over.

Furthermore, by moving directly between Sofia and her men, Sofia was now in their firing line, meaning if they decided to shoot him preemptively, one or more of their bullets stood a good chance of going right through him and striking her. Which of course they would realize in a moment. That meant he needed to talk fast.

He said, "You shoot Noya. I shoot you. Your men shoot me and the police swoop in because of all the shooting. And none of us really want that. We all lose, and for what: the final word in who makes coffee?" He paused a moment, allowed his words to sink in, then said in a gentler tone. "Let the kid make coffee. *Please*. It is a logical choice -- one of your men even agreed -- so I am *asking* you to allow it."

He knew the kid -- Noya -- was watching him while he watched Sofia, whose eyes burned with a rage she was barely able to control. Her finger twitched on the trigger of her Makarov but she did not pull it. Her nostrils flared several times.

With an angry sneer, she lowered her weapon and pushed Noya toward the kitchen. To Odin: "Go with the girl."

Talanov responded with a nod of appreciation and stepped aside while Odin went with Noya to the kitchen.

In the kitchen, Odin leaned against the counter and placed his Makarov in full view. Noya stood in the middle of the floor, looking around, unsure.

"Make coffee," said Odin impatiently.

"I do not know what to do," Noya replied, looking at the variety of pots and pans hanging over a rectangular butcher's block table. Other pans and skillets were piled on a shelf beneath the table. Near the stove was a small wooden box with a tiny drawer in its side and a crank-style handle protruding out of its top -- a coffee mill -- and beside it was a canister marked, coffee. On the blackened burner on the stove was a tarnished kettle.

Odin rolled his eyes and motioned for Noya to fill the kettle with water while he ignited the burner. He checked the coffee mill's hopper and made sure it was filled with beans, then told her to crank the handle until the tiny drawer was full. Opening several cupboard doors, he found a coffee press and set it on the counter beside the mill. He then began taking a number of small white porcelain cups out of a cupboard.

In the living room, Sofia commanded Talanov to remain where he was while nodding for Svet to follow her into the dining room, where they began talking quietly. Talanov could not hear what they were saying although from their nods and gestures, he could tell it was something urgent. After several minutes, Svet pointed to his backpack over by the front door. Sofia nodded for him to get it. Svet brought it to the table. When Sofia looked inside, she broke into a big smile and patted Svet on the shoulder.

Talanov thought about what he had just witnessed. A commando's backpack always contained standard and optional items, depending on the nature of the assignment. Standard items -- first aid supplies, maps, weapons, ammunition, ropes, etc. -- would not generate that much of a smile. What was it, then, that had made Sofia so happy? What optional item or items did that backpack contain?

While Talanov pondered what that might be, Sofia dispatched Svet down a short hallway to find the back door. While Svet did that, Sofia strode back into the living room and faced the hostages.

"Where is a café?" she asked, "the nearest one that is open?" It was more of a demand than a request.

When no one answered, Sofia aimed her Makarov at Carmen.

"The Gato Gordo Café!" Alejandro blurted out. "End of the street, turn right, two blocks."

"Very good," Sofia said. She pointed at Anna, who was sitting huddled beside Gorev, eyes lowered, arms clasped around her knees, which were drawn to her chest. "Stand up," she said.

Anna scooted nearer to her husband.

"Stand up or I will kill you."

Gorev told his wife to stand. Anna whimpered that she was afraid but Gorev squeezed her hand and Anna timidly climbed to her feet, where she stood in place, feet together, hands clasped tightly together in front of her, head down, shaking with fear.

Svet came striding back down the hall in his heavy combat boots. When he entered the room, Sofia looked over at him and Svet nodded.

Sofia grabbed Anna by the arm and brought her forward. "Such a little mouse, so drab and plain," she said, snorting with contempt. "You, little mouse, are coming with me. Colonel Talanov, you and Agent Odin will guard the hostages."

"Where are you going?" asked Talanov.

"That is need-to-know," Sofia replied, motioning Svet to grab his backpack.

Talanov watched Svet hoist the backpack over his shoulder. When he and Svet locked eyes, Svet nervously looked away.

Svet's reaction was not a good sign. By going to a café, Sofia and Svet were risking capture in an area crawling with police. Taking a hostage with them was also not a good sign. Were he in charge, he would have done the same thing, which is why he understood why Sofia had done it: to maintain a means of control should Gorev somehow be tempted to escape. With Anna's life in the balance, Gorev would stay put and do as instructed.

As for the backpack and the enormous risk Sofia and Svet were taking, there was really only one logical reason: Sofia was planning some kind of a diversion and Talanov knew what it was.

A bomb.

The bomb scenario was an obvious deduction. By detonating an explosive device that killed dozens of people, the police would forget about a couple of Soviets, at least for the moment, which would be more than enough time to whisk

Gorev from the confines of the safe house. Soviet agents frequently carried plastic explosives on espionage missions, so it would come as no surprise for Svet to be carrying some. The Russian PVV-5A was a superior product, but using the powerful and wonderfully pliable C-4, especially here in Spain where America was widely unpopular, would assure the placement of blame squarely on the shoulders of the Americans once forensic analysts did their thing and Spanish authorities began pointing fingers.

It was both a logical and an unthinkable act.

But with Kravenko placing Sofia in charge, he was reluctant to interfere again and risk more lives, especially with two armed Soviet agents under her command. Plus, like it or not, detonating a bomb made sense. It would divert the police and allow them to escape from a situation he had created when he rescued that old woman. Plus, when he was eventually called before Kravenko -- and he most assuredly would be -- Sofia would be praised and promoted while he would be disciplined and demoted. Life as he knew it was over. Up until now, Kravenko and others had tolerated his cavalier behavior because he always delivered what he promised. Failure for someone in his position was simply not an option. And his actions from this moment forward would determine whether the remainder of his career -- if he had one -- would be spent in Moscow or Siberia.

Talanov refocused when Noya entered the room carrying cups of coffee on a porcelain platter. She was having a difficult time because the platter was heavy and the cups were beginning to slide.

Sofia told Noya to hurry up.

Noya's arms began to shake. Talanov stepped forward to help but Noya lost her grip. The cups slid off the platter and crashed to the floor, splashing coffee all over Sofia's feet.

Sofia cursed and jumped to the side.

"You clumsy stupid *girl!*" shouted Sofia. She kicked the cups away before backhanding Noya with the Makarov. Noya hit the floor hard, where she bounced once before rolling up onto her side, where she lie crying and bleeding.

Sofia yanked Noya to her feet and reared the gun back to hit her again.

Talanov grabbed Sofia by the wrist.

Dropping Noya, Sofia spun around to face Talanov while a tearful Gorev crawled over to his daughter. Nearby, Anna was sobbing, face in her hands.

"Mark my word," vowed Sofia. "You *will* answer for this."

"Mark *my* word," Talanov replied. "Hit that girl again and it'll be the last time you hit anybody . . . *ever.*"

"Do not make promises you cannot keep," said Svet.

Talanov glanced around and saw him circling to the right with his gun, removing Sofia from his line of sight. Glancing toward the kitchen, he saw Odin as well. Both men had him in their sights.

Sofia twisted free from Talanov's grasp and leaned to within inches of his face. "I know how quickly you rose, Colonel. Care to guess how quickly you will *fall?*"

"Don't get your hopes up too high."

Sofia dismissed Talanov with a sarcastic snort and kicked Gorev away from his daughter. To Odin: "Get that fucking kid into the kitchen and keep her there."

Odin holstered his pistol, grabbed Noya and muscled her into the kitchen.

"My daughter is *bleeding!*" cried Gorev.

"She will live," Sofia growled. She grabbed Anna by the throat and shoved her gun up into her face. "Remember this day, little mouse," she said. "It is the day I did not kill your daughter. But I will unless you do exactly what I say. Do you understand?"

Her reddened eyes swollen from crying, a quivering Anna sniffled and nodded.

Sofia handed Anna to Svet, who made her sit on the floor, where she gulped air and sobbed, mouth open, wanting to wail but knowing she could not, her swollen eyes looking desperately -- pleadingly -- at her husband, who looked back with equal helplessness.

"Your samples, where are they?" Sofia asked, glancing at Gorev before grabbing Pilgrim's medical bag and digging through vials of sedative, vaccines and antidotes. She located two single-use syringes in sterile packaging and tossed them one after the other to Svet, who caught and slipped them into his backpack. In the absence of a response, Sofia looked again at Gorev and said, "Do not make me ask you again."

"I do not know what you are talking about," Gorev replied.

Gorev had tried his best to sound convincing in his nonchalance, but in truth he was a terrible liar. Perspiration dots had already formed on his forehead and he was biting his lip nervously, eyes averted, hands fidgeting while he sat on the floor.

Nearby, Bixler rolled her eyes.

Sofia stared at Gorev for a long moment before exhaling wearily, shaking her head and looking toward the kitchen.

"Odin, shoot the kid."

"Wait!" Gorev cried out. He pointed to one of his suitcases and Sofia motioned for him to get it. Gorev struggled to his feet and walked unsteadily over to where their suitcases had been placed together on the floor. The one he chose was scuffed and worn, with leather corners and brown trim. He brought it over and placed it in front of Sofia.

Sofia told him to open it.

After glancing helplessly at Bixler, who looked away, Gorev laid the suitcase on its side, flipped open the latches and lifted the lid. He pried at the lining of the lid, near the hinges, ripping open a seam and folding back the lining to reveal a length of slender copper pipe. He unsnapped the pipe from where it had been mounted and pulled a wooden stopper from one end. When he angled the pipe into his hand, three glass ampoules wrapped with cotton and gauze slid out of their cushioned hiding place inside the pipe. Each tiny bottle was about two inches long, with a longer main section filled with blood, then a constricted "waist," then a "mouth" that had been plugged with a glass pellet and dense brown wax.

Gorev handed the ampoules to Sofia, who gave them to Svet, who placed them gently in his backpack.

"Now, the antidote," Sofia said.

With a deep sigh of regret, Gorev dug a final ampoule out of another secret pocket. It was shaped like the others but was full of pale yellow liquid. After pausing briefly, he handed it to Sofia, who inspected it with satisfaction before handing it to Svet, who placed it carefully inside his backpack.

"Wait here until we return," Sofia said, taking Anna by the elbow and leading her down the hallway and out the back door.

"What the *hell* is in those ampoules?" Bixler whispered harshly to Gorev, who was covering his face with his hands.

"That information is classified," said Talanov.

"If that's the case, why are you letting that psycho-bitch walk out of here with them? What's she planning to do?"

Talanov did not reply.

"Look, whatever's in those ampoules is obviously nasty stuff," Bixler continued. "So nasty it's top secret. So nasty it requires an antidote. So nasty the good doctor here had to transport it inside an insulated metal pipe in a secret compartment. Look at him, Talanov! The guy's freaking out!"

Bixler and Talanov both looked at Gorev, who was slumped forward, sobbing.

"Now, what the hell is your girlfriend planning to *do?*" demanded Bixler.

"My *colleague* is in charge of making sure those ampoules don't fall into enemy hands."

"Come on, Talanov! You can't seriously tell me you believe she took those ampoules for safe-keeping. You don't trust the woman any more than I do. She's unstable as all getout."

"How we choose to handle property stolen from the Soviet Union is not open to debate."

"Look, you and I both know your *colleague,* as you put it,

has turned against you. She's gone psycho and wants your head on a platter, which to me shows she's not really a colleague but an adversary. I can help. We don't have to be enemies. But you've got to tell me what's going on."

Just then, Odin came back into the room looking exasperated. "I can't get the bleeding to stop."

Talanov looked over at Pilgrim. "How well equipped is your bag?"

"Talk to me, Talanov!" said Bixler.

Talanov ignored her. "Your bag?" he asked Pilgrim again.

"It's a field kit," answered Pilgrim. "Emergency supplies, chemical ice packs, first aid . . ."

"Let me have it."

Pilgrim handed it to him while Talanov motioned for Gorev to follow him into the kitchen, where Noya was sitting cross-legged on the floor holding a blood-soaked dishtowel to her head. Several other blood-soaked dishtowels were wadded up nearby.

Placing Pilgrim's field kit on the floor, Talanov lifted Noya onto the counter. He then placed the medical bag next to her and dug through it to see if it contained any potential weapons.

As indicated, it was a well-equipped field kit, with enough instruments and supplies to collect and preserve blood samples, remove bullets, sedate nervous defectors, vaccinate against various infections and offer first aid. The packets containing scissors and forceps weren't much of a threat. But there were also two single-use suture kits. Inside each kit was a scalpel. Talanov tore open the suture kits, removed the scalpels, then put the suture kits back in the bag and handed the bag to Gorev.

Gorev dumped the contents on the counter and Talanov watched him go to work.

While Gorev attended to his daughter, Talanov thought about what Agent Bixler had said. She was right: he didn't trust Sofia any more than she did, not that he trusted Bixler, either, or her offer to be of help. The loaded question, of course, was what Sofia was planning to do with the ampoules. Was Bixler right? Was Sofia planning to release some of the anthrax in the Gato Gordo Café? The possibility was too horrific to entertain, even for someone like Sofia.

Talanov watched Gorev soak a cotton ball with hydrogen peroxide and begin cleaning the wound on Noya's head. The peroxide bubbled and foamed and Gorev dabbed away the excess using other cotton balls.

Glancing behind him, Talanov saw the coffee mill Noya had used. A dusting of coffee grounds had been spilled on the counter. Sitting on a wooden coaster next to the mill was a stainless steel carafe. Talanov peeked inside the carafe, saw there was coffee and filled a small porcelain cup.

"Anyone else?" he asked, gesturing with the cup.

No one replied.

"You'd think an American safe house would have a decent-sized mug," he remarked, downing the tepid liquid in a single gulp.

He paused to watch Gorev use an antiseptic towelette to clean the skin around the gash of dried blood.

"Americans are known for their mugs," Talanov continued, chatting casually while pouring himself a second cup, "which is one thing the Americans have done right. Europeans, on the other hand, love these ridiculously small cups."

Talanov saw Noya flinch when Gorev applied some lidocaine anesthetic cream to her wound.

"So, *Noyabŕ,*" said Talanov, "do you prefer *Noyabŕ* or Noya? Which one?"

Noya did not reply.

"Either way, it's a pretty name."

Noya did not reply.

To Gorev: *"Noyabŕ* . . . November. Why did you give her that name?"

Gorev did not reply.

"Come on, people, it's called chitchat -- distraction -- and it makes visits to the doctor's office that much easier, even when that office happens to be in a kitchen." Talanov took a sip of his coffee, waiting for an answer. "Well?" he asked again.

"Noya," she finally said.

"From the month of her birth," added Gorev.

"So, Noya," said Talanov, "tell me about yourself. What are your dreams? Your interests?"

Noya did not reply. She was sitting slump-shouldered on the counter with a sad, vacant look on her face. Her father was bent over her head, working gently to anesthetize her wound.

Talanov watched them for a moment.

"Dreams and interests?" he asked again.

Noya looked over at Talanov and saw him watching her.

"What does it matter?" she replied. "Such things are not possible."

"What do you mean? Everyone has dreams."

Noya said, "We are born and we die. That is it."

"Come *on*. You're pretty. You're smart. You'll go far."

"To where? In Soviet Union, there is nowhere to go. A slow death or a fast one, what's the difference?"

Talanov did not know what to say. He had never heard such depressing hopelessness spoken with such apathy and surrender. And while he knew kids were not supposed to act this way, he understood Noya's despair. Every one of their hopes and dreams had been dashed -- *by him* -- after which she witnessed the brutal execution of her grandparents.

"Look, I'm sorry about your grandparents," he said. "They didn't deserve what happened."

"You really should watch what you say," stated Odin from the doorway. "Such a remark could be . . . misinterpreted."

"As you no doubt will see that it will be," Talanov replied, glancing at Odin briefly before watching Gorev open an iodine swab and dab it on Noya's wound. To Gorev: "As my colleague over there will be happy to remind you, Doctor, I am no longer in charge, and while I am bound to uphold my orders within this new chain of command, I will make sure you and your family are treated fairly and safely."

"And I repeat: do not make promises you cannot keep," Odin said. And with a sarcastic chuckle, he disappeared.

After watching Odin leave, Talanov thought about what he had said: do not make promises you cannot keep.

Cannot or will not, he wondered.

He noticed Noya staring at him thoughtfully while Gorev avoided looking altogether. He could tell Gorev was purposely refraining from speaking his mind. His face said he wanted to. His eyes were angry and his lips were pinched. Talanov could guess what he was thinking: that all the promises in the world would not change his inability -- or unwillingness -- to challenge Sofia.

Talanov lowered his head.

"Dreams are for not for people like us," Noya remarked unexpectedly.

"What do you mean?" asked Talanov.

"In Soviet Union, we are told what we will become. It does not matter what we want. Then one day my father comes home and says he had found a way for me to have a dream . . . that we would go to America . . . that I would one day fly in a helicopter."

"Enough," said Gorev sharply. To Talanov: "I am sorry. All this nonsense about flying in helicopters . . ."

"Is that what you'd like to do?" Talanov asked Noya.

Gorev said, "She spoke out of turn, Colonel. Forgive her. She is young and does not know when to be silent."

Talanov ignored him. "Is it?" he asked her again.

Noya shrugged.

"The Soviet Union has the most advanced helicopters in use today. The Mi-24 -- also known as the Hind -- and the Mi-8. Plus the fours and the sixes. We lead the world."

"Not really," Noya replied.

"Oh?" asked Talanov, amused.

"Do you know who invented the helicopter?" asked Noya.

"Can't say that I do."

"The Chinese in 400 A.D., as a toy," she replied. "Leonardo da Vinci then designed an aerial screw, with Mikhail Lomonosov proving the concept in 1754 with a model that was powered by a spring. Many inventors had a part in its development -- Alphonse Pénaud, Gustave de Ponton d'Amécourt, Thomas Edison, Jacques and Louis Breguet, Paul Cornu and others -- but it was the Focke-Wulf Fw 61 -- first flown in 1936 -- that was the first functional helicopter. Henrich Focke was German. But it was the great Russian inventor, Igor Sikorsky -- he was born in Kiev, but the Ukraine was then part of the Russian Empire -- who created the first mass-produced helicopter, the Sikorsky R-4, once he emigrated to America. He also wrote a book -- The Message of the Lord's Prayer -- and another one -- The Invisible Encounter."

Talanov stared at Noya with utter astonishment. "How do you know all of that?"

Suddenly embarrassed, Noya looked away.

"Tell me," Talanov said.

Noya looked down and did not reply.

"Designing helicopters has always been her dream," Gorev explained. "The only time I see her smile is when she talks about propulsion mechanics, power density and anti-torque control. You would not believe all that she knows. She would make an excellent engineer."

"The Soviet Union needs good engineers."

Talanov waited for some kind of response but there was none. Noya sat in silence on the counter, shoulders slumped, wisps of hair covering her face while she looked down at the floor.

"Is that something you'd like to do?" he asked.

Noya kept staring at the floor.

Talanov said, "Designing helicopters is a noble ambition. A worthwhile dream. When all of this mess is over, perhaps I can make inquiries on your behalf."

Noya did not reply.

"What do you think?" he asked.

Noya shrugged.

"Is that a yes or a no?" asked Talanov.

"What does it matter?" she replied.

"I guess that depends on whether you want to just read about Sikorsky or go up into the sky after him."

Noya frowned and thought about that.

"It is one thing to have a dream," said Talanov. "It's another to do something about it. The difference between an R-4 and the dream of one was Sikorsky. He aimed for the sky and went after it."

After removing the atraumatic needle from the suture kit with its attached length of thread, Gorev began stitching Noya's wound.

"You speak of designing helicopters," he said. "My dream was to become a doctor, and I became a doctor to heal people and help them. But what was I made to do? Kill people. The KGB put me in a laboratory and I was told to engineer new viruses and bacteria. Anthrax was my specialty. I was then told to inject my new strains into prisoners, to see how quickly they died so that we could do this to our enemies. That is what the KGB did to my dream."

"Do you want her to hear all of this?" asked Talanov.

"What difference does it make? It is easy for you to tell my daughter to have a dream when you are the one who will crush it."

"You may want to watch yourself, Doctor."

"Or you will -- what -- exile me to Siberia? You are planning to do this, anyway. You have already killed my parents."

"What happened to your parents was unfortunate."

"Unfortunate," repeated Gorev. "You murder my parents and call it . . . unfortunate?"

Talanov did not reply. In truth, he didn't blame Gorev for being so bitter.

Gorev continued, "Operation Barbarossa. The codename for Germany's invasion of the Soviet Union during World War II. My father was there, Colonel, fighting against the panzer divisions of Hitler when he laid siege to Moscow. He lost three toes and two fingers to frostbite. But he survived. He survived the winter and he survived the Nazis. But he could not survive you. *You,* the people who should be protecting us."

"He didn't do it," muttered Noya.

Gorev leaned back and stared at his daughter. "What did you say?"

"He didn't do it."

"This man is *KGB,"* hissed Gorev, "and my parents -- your grandparents -- are *dead.* Other people are dead, too, and his colleague, that woman -- that *murderer* -- took my Anna -- *your mama* -- and he did *nothing.* He just stood there and let it happen. He will say it is because of his orders. *Rubbish!* I had orders, too -- to kill innocent people by infecting them -- but they were *wrong.* And I did something. Even though we were caught and it was for nothing, at least I did something. At least I *tried.* So do not think because he stands here and talks about helicopters and flying up into the sky that he is your friend."

Noya looked down, avoiding eye contact with her father.

Gorev said, "You mean *nothing* to him, Noya. Nothing! This man is a *killer."*

"I don't believe you," she said.

Talanov was the one to reply. "Believe him. It's how things are."

"Then why did you stop her from hitting me?"

Noya's words hung in the air, suspended, and Talanov did not know what to say. He *had* stopped Sofia from hitting her . . . threatened her, in fact, if she ever tried it again.

"You could have let her, but you didn't," said Noya. "And she was going to, but you stopped her. Why?"

"I just couldn't . . ." Talanov began. His voice trailed off.

"You are not what everyone thinks," Noya said.

For several seconds Talanov stared at Noya before rubbing his forehead and awkwardly looking away.

And for the briefest of moments, Noya smiled.

CHAPTER 19

"Colonel, we need to talk," said Bixler when Talanov brought Noya and Gorev back into the living room and told them to sit down. The gash on Noya's head had been neatly sutured and was now covered with flesh-colored tape.

"So, the Ice Man has some new friends," said Odin sarcastically.

"Can my daughter lie on the sofa?" asked Gorev, pointing to one of two matching sofas positioned against the wall beneath a framed print of some perky red flowers. "She needs rest and the floor is hard."

The sofa was a three-seater of tufted brown leather with polished, two-tone wooden armrests. It didn't look all that comfortable but would certainly be better than the floor.

"Go ahead," Talanov replied, handing Pilgrim her medical bag with a nod of appreciation.

On the floor in front of the other couch were Alejandro and Carmen. Alejandro had his arm around Carmen, who was staring at the floor, shivering. Pilgrim was sitting next to them, her arms folded across her lap, looking weary. To Gorev's right were Bixler and Franco.

Gorev patted a small decorative pillow into position and helped Noya lie down. He then sat on the floor.

"I need to go to the bathroom," said Franco, raising his hand. "I've held it as long as I can."

Talanov motioned Franco to his feet and told Odin to go with him.

"I think I can manage on my own," Franco said.

"I wouldn't want you getting lost," Odin replied.

Franco hurried down the hall walking almost cross-legged, with Odin close behind.

"No funny business, either," mumbled Franco, glancing over his shoulder at the beefy KGB agent, who growled something in Russian and gave him a token shove, a reminder about who was in charge.

"Okay, talk," said Talanov, turning to face Bixler, who got up from where she had been sitting in front of the fireplace.

"Now before you go chewing me out, I just had to stand up," said Bixler, rolling her shoulders and stretching. "My legs are asleep."

"Is that what you wanted to talk to me about?"

"Of course not," answered Bixler, shaking one leg then skirting the glass-topped coffee table to approach Talanov. On the coffee table was a brightly-colored ceramic platter. "Call me paranoid if you want," she said, "but after hearing what Doctor Gorev said in the kitchen -- that anthrax was his specialty -- I believe your mental-case girlfriend is going to set off a dirty bomb in a crowded café. Why else would she need a syringe?"

Everybody in the room looked at Talanov, wondering what he would say. Talanov could see it in their faces.

On the surface, an anthrax bomb made no sense. Sofia's goal was to create a diversion, which an ordinary explosion would do. The police would be drawn to the scene, thus clearing the street in front of the safe house. Mission accomplished. He also understood why Sofia took the ampoules. If anything happened here -- say, a surprise second visit by the police, or some other turn of events -- the samples would be safe. She was in command and the ampoules were her responsibility.

It was the syringe that worried him.

So he began thinking about everything Sofia had told him, including how much money there was to be made for people like them . . . people with specialized skills. At the time, her ramblings seemed just that -- ramblings -- someone inviting him to join her in some vague new career after the KGB, which seemed innocent enough in light of her belief that the Soviet Union was deteriorating from within.

Taking those syringes, however, changed everything and begged the question: *had Sofia hijacked Gorev's defection in order to sell his anthrax samples?* If so, it would explain why she needed him at the outset -- to track down Gorev -- which in turn would explain why she feared being pulled from the assignment by Kravenko. It would also explain why she had been so vague about the nature of her new venture and why she kept testing him to see how capable he was of detecting her lies. She was assessing his ability as well as his character. Could she tempt him to become a mercenary? Was he as good as people said?

Everything finally made sense. Sofia was planning on selling Gorev's samples, either to an existing client or the highest bidder, which is why she needed the syringes: to infect the C-4, which she would then detonate as a demonstration of the killing power she was offering.

"Are we taking a mental vacation?" asked Bixler. "Aren't you at least a little curious about what your girlfriend is doing?"

"Like I said, what we are doing is not your concern."

"The hell it's not. What she's doing is everyone's concern, and you know it. But she rattles your cage with threats about reporting you and you let her walk out of here. How can you be so stupid?"

"Ease off, Glenda," said Pilgrim.

"Ease *off?* We're talking hundreds if not thousands of lives, Donna!"

"And you're not helping with talk like that."

Bixler threw up her hands and turned away.

Pilgrim said, "Sorry, Colonel, Glenda can get a little aggressive. But she does have a point. Your colleague has C-4. She has ampoules of anthrax. She took *syringes.* Why would she need syringes if not to impregnate a bomb with blood from those ampoules? She took every syringe that I had. See?"

Pilgrim opened her medical bag and held it open.

Talanov instinctively leaned forward to look.

Bixler smashed his head with the platter.

Although Talanov sensed the attack an instant before it took place, it was not enough time to duck away from the blow.

Talanov hit the floor hard.

"You *hurt* him!" Noya cried.

"He'll be all right," Bixler replied, vaulting over Talanov to grab his Makarov just as Odin came running down the hall into the living room, his gun aimed squarely at Bixler, who was aiming Talanov's Makarov right back at him. "Asylum and one hundred thousand dollars cash if you help me deliver Dr. Gorev and his family to my Consulate," she said in Russian, her aim never wavering.

Odin's eyes darted back and forth between Talanov lying motionless on the floor and Bixler with her gun trained on him.

"I meant what I said," added Bixler. "Asylum -- which means a new identity in the United States or wherever you choose -- plus one hundred thousand dollars."

"Do you take me for a fool?"

"Only if you decide you want to shoot it out. If we do, Gorev and his family will still get away because you and I will be dead on the floor. That's being a fool. But not if you cooperate." To Pilgrim: "Donna, the propofol."

"What about him?" asked Odin, glancing at Talanov on the floor.

"We'll sedate him."

"Sedate is for pulling teeth. Let me kill him. Then we have deal."

"No!" screamed Noya, scrambling to sit up.

"You would kill your own man?" asked Bixler while Gorev held Noya back.

"It was our plan all along," Odin replied while Gorev and

Noya argued back and forth, with Gorev finally having to command Noya to stay put and be quiet.

Bixler's look of incredulity made Odin laugh.

"Talanov has outlived his usefulness," Odin said. "We use him now only as a guard until police are gone from street."

"But . . . why? He's one of the best that Moscow has."

"Because he *is* the best, that is why. He has become -- how do I say -- a threat to certain people in Moscow who do things a different way."

Bixler narrowed her eyes. "Are you saying Moscow wants him dead?"

"Not only Moscow," said Odin.

"Meaning you and Dubinina?" asked Bixler.

Odin grinned.

Bixler said, "Sounds stupid to me, killing the best man you've got, but -- hey -- what do I care? My offer still stands: asylum and one hundred thousand dollars. But you'll need to put down that gun."

"What is one hundred thousand compared to one million?" asked Odin.

"So *that's* why you want Talanov dead. You and Dubinina are planning on selling Gorev's formula. And Talanov was the fly in your ointment."

"Fly in ointment?" asked Odin with a frown.

"A problem you had to get rid of. Someone who stood in your way. The real problem, though, is whether you want to be alive with a hundred grand or dead with a million."

Odin thought about that.

"Well?" asked Bixler.

"What matters is killing Talanov."

"What matters is you giving me an answer," said Bixler. "Now, what's it going to be?"

Odin saw Bixler aiming the Makarov straight between his eyes. If he shot Talanov, the American agent would shoot him.

"You cannot allow Talanov to live," insisted Odin. "He is your enemy just as he is mine. We are together on this. If we do not kill him now, he will hunt us down. No one can escape the Ice Man."

"At the moment he's not your worry. I am. So why not play this smart and accept my offer? You'll get a new passport and a big chunk of money."

"And the Ice Man?"

"Not your worry. Now, for the last time, what's it going to be?"

"How do I know I can trust you?" asked Odin.

"Because you're still alive. Now, do we have a deal or not? If we do, then you need to lower that gun."

"Then what?"

"You go outside and get in our car. The black Mercedes."

"And if the police stop me to ask questions?"

"Do you speak any Spanish?"

"Only Russian, a little English and some German."

Bixler looked at Alejandro sitting with his wife. Carmen was still traumatized so Alejandro would not leave her side.

"My interpreter, Franco, will go with you, wherever the hell he is," said Bixler. "He speaks fluent Spanish and can handle any questions the police may ask. Which I doubt will be any at all since they've already been here once."

"And if I decide to run?"

"Go for it. I won't be chasing you down."

"If I ran, I wouldn't get paid."

Bixler shrugged.

Odin looked down at Talanov then back at Bixler. "All right, we have a deal."

"Good. Now, lower your gun."

"How do I know you won't shoot me?"

"If I'd have wanted to kill you, I'd have done it already and we wouldn't be having this conversation. Look, I'm trying to make this a win-win situation for everybody. Now, lower your gun and hand it over. That's the only way this can work."

Odin laughed. "I trust you, but I don't," he said. "I will lower my weapon, yes, as a sign of trust, but I will not surrender my ability to defend myself should something go wrong."

"How badly do you want what I'm offering?"

"How badly do you want my cooperation?"

Bixler chewed on his words for a moment. "All right, you win," she said, lowering her weapon while Odin slowly placed his back in its holster, both agents kept their eyes warily on each other until each was satisfied the confrontation was over.

"Glenda, I found a syringe!" said Pilgrim.

"Fill it with propofol," she replied. "Franco, get in here!" she yelled.

Franco peeked out of the hallway.

"Where the hell have you been?" demanded Bixler.

"Washing my hands," he said, showing Bixler his hands.

Bixler said, "Doctor Gorev, I want you to take Noya and go with Agent Franco."

"What about my wife?" asked Gorev. "We were told to wait here."

"By Talanov's partner, who has gone to set off a bomb. She's hardly the kind of person we're going to wait around for."

"She has my wife!"

"She killed your parents! Do you not get that? Unless we do something to stop her -- as in *right now* -- your wife does not stand a chance, never mind the thousands of people Dubinina may infect with *your* anthrax. Now, go and get in the car. Franco will take care of you until I get there." To Pilgrim: "Fill that syringe."

"What are you going to do?" asked Noya.

"Give him a sedative. We need him out of commission."

"He is already out of commission."

"He'll wake up."

"When?"

"I don't know . . . soon . . . in a while. I didn't hit him that hard. Don't worry, he isn't hurt."

"You broke a *platter* over his head."

"Look, I know you think this man is your friend. He isn't. Trust me on that."

"He stopped that woman from killing you. Perhaps he is more of a friend than you think."

"You're too young to understand."

"Maybe you're too old."

Bixler looked at Gorev and nodded toward the door. "Doctor, if you don't mind?"

Filling the syringe with propofol, Pilgrim suppressed a smile while Gorev scolded his daughter, who continued glaring at Bixler.

On the floor, Talanov moaned.

"Hurry," Bixler told Gorev just as Pilgrim withdrew the needle from the propofol, held it up and tapped the barrel with her finger.

"What about the bodies of my parents?"

"We'll make some kind of arrangement but right now I can't tell you what it will be," said Bixler, keeping a cautious eye on Talanov. "This is Spain and your parents were murdered by a Soviet agent. I do promise we'll treat them with the dignity and respect they deserve. Now, hurry. I'll let you know."

"Thank you," said Gorev. Grabbing his suitcase, he and Noya followed Franco and Odin out the front door.

Talanov began to move.

"Donna, the syringe!" said Bixler.

Pilgrim prepared to stab Talanov in the shoulder just as he struggled up onto one knee.

"Stay where you are," ordered Bixler, raising the Makarov.

While Alejandro and Carmen remained huddled by the fireplace, Talanov glanced first at Pilgrim then Bixler. "Good cop versus bad cop. I should have known," he said, rubbing the back of his head. There was actually a knot where Bixler had smashed him with the platter.

"One of the oldest tricks in the book," she said. "Like taking candy from a kid."

"Yeah, well, I've studied your American clichés, and the big problem you run into is how silly you look when they come back to bite you in the ass."

"Yeah, well, guess which one of us is down on his knees and which one of us has the gun," Bixler replied. "So if you don't want me pulling this trigger and messing up a perfectly clean floor, you'd best stay right where you are. Now, hold still and let Donna give you a little jab in the arm."

"And here I was, thinking we had a good thing going," said Talanov.

"Seeing you face down on the floor was pretty good for me. So that's where we need you to stay."

"Not when there's a bomb to defuse."

"So she *is* setting one off," exclaimed Bixler. "I *knew* it!"

Launching an attack from one knee can be a powerful tactic but is contingent upon two variables: strength and angle. The first is obvious: one must have the leg power to perform the maneuver. The greater the strength, the quicker the explosive thrust. The second can be tricky, for not only must the target be within range -- an extended arm's reach at most -- but the restricted angle of the strike field, which was an approximate one-hundred-and-twenty-degree field opposite the power leg, can easily be miscalculated, especially if the target is moving. Miss your target, especially if she is holding a loaded gun, and you can get shot.

Talanov knew he had the strength. He trained regularly and practiced these kind of moves. But his target, Bixler, had moved to a position outside his strike field. She was behind him now, at his "six-o'clock" position, which let him know she was a savvy agent.

It was obvious Bixler did not want to shoot him. For one thing, she wanted him sedated, not dead. For another, their banter -- as adversarial as it had appeared -- had been more like a sparring match. Had she been trigger happy, she would have already put a bullet in him. As it was, she had engaged him in a round of banter. She would definitely not allow herself to be pushed around -- which their banter had also told him -- but she was not the kind of person to shoot without strong justification.

Which is exactly what Talanov gave her when he attempted the impossible by launching himself backward in a twisting spin.

Bixler stepped back and pulled the trigger.

Click.

Talanov's hands clamped the Makarov as he turned into her, his back against her stomach. Continuing his twist and yanking upward, Talanov hinged at the waist and bent forward. Bixler felt herself being lifted off her feet and knew she was two, maybe three seconds away from being flipped over his shoulder. Her only hope was to go with the momentum, and kicking upward with her trailing leg, Bixler did a cartwheel over Talanov's shoulder.

Landing on her feet, Bixler reacted immediately with a front kick aimed directly at Talanov's abdomen. A solid blow to the solar plexus would disable even the strongest of men, and Talanov was already bent over from flipping her, his arms extended, his mid-section exposed. True, the Makarov had been ripped from her hands and Talanov was now in possession of it. But because it had misfired, Bixler knew it would be of no use.

Talanov saw the kick coming. There was no time to block it so he did the only thing he could do: he dove into it.

With his momentum already in a forward direction, Talanov rolled toward Bixler, like a barrel, hitting her thigh and truncating the force of her kick and toppling them both to the floor. Talanov landed on his back and Bixler landed on top of him, his hands on her breasts.

"Let *go* of me!" she yelled. She delivered a hammer blow at Talanov's face.

Talanov jerked left and raised his right shoulder, deflecting the blow while Pilgrim danced and hopped around the perimeter of the scuffle with the syringe, looking for an opportunity to jab Talanov.

Continuing the roll to his left and thrusting upward with

his hip, Talanov tossed Bixler off. She rolled up onto her feet a short distance away and tried a second front kick to the head just as Talanov was climbing to his feet. He blocked the kick with an arm. But Bixler's kick carried enough punch to knock the Makarov out of his hand.

"That cheap Russian hardware just saved your life," said Bixler, leaping forward with a third front kick that feinted first with the left leg before striking with the right. Talanov blocked the kick before grabbing Bixler and flinging her into Pilgrim, who almost stabbed her with the propofol before toppling onto the couch.

"Careful!" Bixler yelled at Pilgrim before jumping up to launch another series of front kicks at Talanov.

"I'm not the enemy here," Talanov replied, stepping backward while blocking her kicks.

"The hell you're not!" retorted Bixler, throwing a series of punches that Talanov batted away.

"Come on, Glenda, you saw what happened."

"You bet I did. You let your girlfriend walk out of here with a *hostage,* never mind the bomb she's planning to set off."

"I had no part in that."

"You sure as hell didn't stop her!" shouted Bixler. She aimed a side kick at Talanov's knee.

"If I'd have known what she was planning, I would have," answered Talanov, deflecting the kick downward with his hand. "As it was, I had no chance."

"My heart bleeds."

"Then let's join forces. Help me stop her."

"Not in a million years."

While Pilgrim, Alejandro and Carmen watched from their positions near the fireplace, Bixler flew at Talanov with a flurry of aggressive punches and kicks, which Talanov kept blocking left, right, up, down, outward, inward, backward.

"You fight like a *girl!"* yelled Bixler, unable to connect, frustrated that Talanov kept ducking and weaving, avoiding everything she could throw, not fighting back. "What are you, a man or a mouse?"

"Your clichés are as bad as your fighting."

Pilgrim laughed at the remark and Bixler glared at her for an instant before hurling herself forward in furious front kick combination -- another feint -- that masqueraded for a lightning roundhouse kick aimed straight for Talanov's head. Talanov caught Bixler by the ankle, ducked under her outstretched leg with a quick spin to come up behind her with his forearm around her neck.

"The syringe," Talanov said to Pilgrim. He gestured for her to bring it to him while Bixler tried to head butt and twist her way free. "She'll only get hurt if you don't."

Bixler yelled a string of profanities, but with Talanov's arm wrapped tightly up under her chin, it came out as gibberish.

Pilgrim instinctively shielded the syringe.

"I mean it, Donna," said Talanov. "A chokehold can be dangerous, even lethal."

Biting her lip with indecision, Pilgrim watched Bixler struggle helplessly.

"The longer you delay, the less chance I have of stopping Sofia," Talanov said. "Don't make me do this the hard way." He squeezed harder and Bixler's face began to turn red. Her eyes began to show panic as her air supply was cut off.

"Okay, don't hurt her!" said Pilgrim, hurrying over with the syringe.

"Donna, *no!*" mumbled Bixler, her words barely intelligible.

"In her arm, Donna," said Talanov, "and please don't miss. Trust me. We're on the same side."

"Are we?"

"Yes, we are."

"Then why not let Glenda go?"

"I think you know the answer to that. Look at the time I've wasted fighting with her. At the time I'm wasting now. If this goes on much longer, Sofia *will* set off that bomb. Now, are you going to help me or not, because if you're not . . ."

"All right!" said Pilgrim. "Just . . . don't hurt her, okay?"

"Then make it quick."

When Pilgrim approached with the syringe, Bixler started kicking and jerking in a final effort to break free.

Mouthing "Sorry," Pilgrim stuck the needle in Bixler's arm and depressed the plunger.

"How long until it takes effect?" asked Talanov.

"Thirty seconds, give or take," she said, "and she'll be out for roughly half an hour."

"Thank you," said Talanov, controlling Bixler with what looked to be a lifeguard hold across the chest while Bixler fought to get free. To Alejandro: "Got any wine?"

"Down in the basement. Why?"

"Your names again?"

"Alejandro and Carmen."

Talanov held Bixler's head down in a wrestling hold and looked at Pilgrim. "Donna, I want you to take Alejandro and Carmen to the basement and open a bottle of that wine. Once Glenda's asleep, I'll lay her on the sofa and prop a chair against the basement door, locking you in. Don't worry, once she wakes up, she'll let you out. Alejandro, I want you to give some of that wine to your wife. Make her drink it. Two or three glasses. The trauma of what Sofia's done will be with her a long time, but with your help she'll come out of it, especially if I can stop Sofia from setting off this bomb. Now, is there anything I need to know about the café?"

"It sits on a busy corner," said Alejandro. "Lots of traffic, and it can hold almost two hundred customers on a busy night, like tonight, not counting staff and those in the queue, who will be standing out front waiting for a table. The kitchen is to the rear and backs onto an alley, but there are many cooks and waiters near the back door, and lots of activity."

By now, Bixler had almost passed out. Talanov released her and she slumped into his arms, then revived slightly and tried clumsily punching him. Talanov got her in a bear hug, pinning her arms. Bixler tried head butting Talanov, who tucked his head, protecting himself.

"You don't give up, do you?" he said.

Her head bobbing deliriously, Bixler slurred a string of curses while Talanov carried her to the sofa.

"Nice fragrance, by the way. Chanel?"

"Fuck you," growled Bixler before passing out.

Talanov laid her on the sofa and turned to see Alejandro with the Makarov in his hand.

"I may be making the biggest mistake of my life, but here," said Alejandro, handing it over.

Talanov smiled his thanks and accepted the weapon.

"What changed?" asked Alejandro. "You're risking everything going after her like this. If you succeed in stopping her, you become a traitor and we both know what happens to those. If you don't succeed, you die in an explosion. Why do this?"

Talanov thought about Noya and what she had said. *You are not what everyone thinks.* She had seen something in him that he had not even seen himself, or had lost sight of. Here she was, a girl without hope who somehow caught a glimmer because of an impulsive action on his part to stop Sofia from hitting her. And here he was, a man neutralized . . . a man also without hope because he had surrendered to what he thought was the right thing to do. Problem was: he had accepted the wrong definition of right. He had accepted Sofia's definition.

It was time to accept his own.

"Why do this?" asked Talanov. "Maybe I'm not who everyone thinks. Don't ask me to define what that means because I'm not really sure."

"You'll need a car. Take mine. It's the piece of crap out front. There's a spare key under the mat. When you get to the café, park on the side street, where it's dark. No one will see you there. There's a walkway between a building and the backs of some shops bordering the café."

"Thanks," said Talanov, turning to Pilgrim. "Anthrax. How would she disperse it?"

"I don't know. I'm not a scientist."

"Neither is Sofia. Come on, Donna, *think*. What would she do?"

"Anthrax can be fatal if inhaled. The endospores would reproduce rapidly inside the host and kill it, with dark blood oozing from the mouth and nostrils. Exposure by ingestion -- eating tainted meat -- or through scratches or cuts -- is rarely fatal and can be treated."

"So Dubinina will try to get it into the air?"

"That's my guess. Which will be difficult since your samples are in vitro. Which means she would need to pack some kind of a dispersal agent in with the C-4."

"What kind of a dispersal agent?"

"A fine mist would be ideal -- like crop dusting or a fog -- that is somehow protected from incineration, which will be difficult if not impossible given she's detonating a bomb. Plus, there's not a lot of blood in those ampoules, so what she has won't go very far. If she had a viable medium and time to cultivate . . . I don't know, I just don't *know*."

"It's okay, don't worry," said Talanov, clasping Pilgrim on the shoulder. "If you don't know, then Sofia probably doesn't, either, and that may have bought us some time. I'm guessing she'll break into a store somewhere to see what she can find."

Pilgrim said, "A single gram of anthrax, if distributed appropriately, could kill one third of the United States."

"Then I'd better get moving. Okay, you three, in the basement."

"You're still going to lock us in the basement after everything we've done?" asked Alejandro.

"If I don't lock you in the basement, it won't just be Glenda who knows you helped me. Don't forget, the police are still looking for me -- never mind the CIA -- so let's just say helping me would not boost your chances for a promotion."

"Not that I think I want one. Good luck, Colonel."

"Take my medical bag," said Pilgrim. "We had no idea we were dealing with anthrax when I packed it, but there may be something in there you can use in case of an accident. If you come across any intact ampoules, get them into a sterile container and seal it shut. There are two in the bag."

"Why are you helping me?" he asked.

Pilgrim walked with Alejandro and Carmen to the basement stairwell. "For me, it was Noya," she said. "What you did . . . what she saw in you. Children often see what adults don't."

Talanov smiled and nodded. *You got that right.*

Pilgrim lowered her voice and said, "In the American Consulate in London is a man called La Tâche."

"Like the red wine from France?"

"Burgundy, Colonel, not red. You will like him. Give him a call."

"Why would I want to call him?"

Pilgrim smiled and shrugged.

Talanov eyed her for a moment. "Does he have a number?" he asked.

"Not one that I can write down."

"Tell me. I'll remember."

Pilgrim did. "If you call him, mention Irene."

"Who's Irene?"

Pilgrim smiled and clasped Talanov on the shoulder. "God be with you, Colonel."

And she disappeared down the stairs.

CHAPTER 20

Hearing the clamor of voices in the street, Talanov carefully shut the front door of the safe house and tiptoed along the darkened path to the gate. The high wall and dense shrubbery kept anyone from seeing him.

He peeked through a gap and in the glare of flashing lights from the patrol cars could see several officers trying to calm a small group of protesters. Some of the protesters were accusing Gorev and his family of being connected with the two Soviet agents who had not only killed their friends, but murdered other NATO protesters. The police were trying to calm things down but the group was getting angry. Standing in a group were Franco, Odin, Gorev and Noya. Gorev was holding Noya in front of him, arms around her, protecting her.

Talanov recognized two of the protesters. The first was Paco, the leader of the *Euskadi Ta Askatasuna* -- the ETA -- and Juan, his friend, whom he and Sofia had encountered on the road to the Gran Casino del Sol. Paco was recounting how his friends had been gunned down by the two spies -- both of whom he could identify -- adding that it was no coincidence these other Russians had been stopped on the same street where the van of the two spies had been parked. Paco was demanding that he be allowed to question these Russians his way. The officers said that was not going to happen.

"If these Russians are allowed to leave," said Paco, "the location of the spies goes with them. We must find out what they know. They are in this together."

"We don't know that," an officer replied.

"Then let me find out."

"I cannot do that. We have rules of interrogation."

"I don't," said Paco. He took the officer aside. "I promise the girl will not be harmed -- not permanently, anyway -- and it will motivate one of them to give us the answers we require. These spies have caused enough trouble. They must be stopped. As it is, we are getting nowhere. All I ask is that you and your men step over to your patrol car and call headquarters. Ask what they want you to do. In the meantime, my men and I will quietly do what needs to be done."

The officer looked over at Noya standing with her father, who was being questioned by another officer through Franco. When Noya saw the men looking at her, she lowered her eyes. The officer went over and spoke with his colleague, who shrugged and nodded. The officer grabbed Noya by the arm and brought her to Paco.

Gorev tried stopping them but the third officer held him back.

Paco grabbed Noya by the hair and pulled back, craning her neck and forcing her to look up at him.

"What have we here?" he asked.

"Leave her alone!" cried Gorev in Russian.

Paco had no idea what Gorev said but knew it was a cry of desperation. *He was getting close.* He ran his hand down to the top button of Noya's shirt and yanked it open.

Noya closed her eyes and began to cry.

"No!" Gorev cried out, rushing forward only to be blocked by Paco's men while the officers gathered together to watch. "I'll talk!" he shouted desperately, looking at Franco and telling him to translate. "Whatever they want to know. Just leave my daughter alone."

Franco translated what Gorev told him.

Paco grinned and unfastened a second button.

Franco sprang forward and grabbed Paco's hand. "Let her go. He said he would talk."

Paco shoved Franco away. "Not before I am through. Interfere again and I will---"

Hearing footsteps, Paco turned around.

"Looking for me?" asked Talanov, striding toward the group.

"That's him!" yelled Paco, pointing. "The spy who killed my friends!"

The officers went for their weapons but stopped when Talanov lifted his Makarov and they saw its long, thick silencer. Paco's men also backed away, their hands half raised.

Dropping Pilgrim's medical bag on a strip of grass, Talanov strode over to Paco and smashed the butt of his Makarov against his forehead. Paco's eyes rolled back in his head and he toppled to the pavement.

Talanov made a quick sweep of the others with his pistol.

"Are you okay?" he asked Noya.

Noya smiled and nodded.

Talanov handed her back to her father. "Doctor, get ready to go." To Odin: "I'll deal with you back in Moscow."

"What do you mean?"

"Amazing how chatty people become when they think you're unconscious. Your career as an agent is over."

The officers all turned toward Odin with stares of incredulity that said, *you, too, are KGB?*

With everyone staring at Odin, Gorev whispered something to Franco. When Franco protested, Gorev told him to hurry.

Franco said, "Dr. Gorev, the man beside me, is a defecting Soviet scientist and he fears for his life with these men. They are both KGB and he begs you to grant him asylum."

What Gorev had Franco say was understandable. By all appearances, Talanov was threatening to recapture him and his daughter. True, Talanov had rescued Noya and he was thankful for that, but Talanov was also preparing to take them into custody again. And that he could not allow, not when they were this close to freedom. Plus, he knew Talanov would be reluctant to gun him down in the presence of witnesses and police officers. This was his chance.

Unfortunately, Gorev had forgotten that Talanov was not the only person who was armed.

Odin pulled his gun, grabbed Noya and pulled her in front of him. The police went for their weapons but stopped when they saw Odin jam his pistol against Noya's head.

Everyone froze.

"Let her go," said Talanov. In the corner of his eye, he saw the hand of a policeman drifting toward his weapon. Talanov snapped his fingers and wagged his finger back and forth.

The policeman retracted his hand.

By now, Gorev was barely able to control his panic.

Odin crouched behind Noya. "Let her go? Do you think I am *stupid?*" He bobbed back and forth, not giving Talanov a clear shot. "The fact that you know what we were planning means there is no going back for me now."

With the police watching their every move, Talanov slowly circled Odin, following his movements as carefully as Odin followed his. Ordinarily, he would just shoot. No dialogue. No second chances. Just a bullet to the head. Yes, the risks were high but protocol was clear: *take out the threat, whatever the cost.* Which meant if Noya had to die, so be it.

But protocol had flown out the window the moment Noya entered his life . . . a young girl as devoid of feeling as he . . . a young girl who, like he, had surrendered to the initiatives of others. A young girl who had not wanted contact with him any more than he had wanted it with her . . . each of them alone in a crowded house until Sofia's cruelty changed everything.

The fact that he cared what happened to her was a problem. Right now he needed cold, quick, efficient movements. Right now he did not need to be concerned with secondary outcomes. Right now he needed to focus on Odin but all he could think of was Noya. In his peripheral vision he saw her calmly watching him. And he knew he dared not make eye contact with her, not even for an instant.

"I knew this moment would come," Odin said.

"What moment is that?" asked Talanov.

"If only you would have joined us. If only you would have said yes and become one of us. But you wouldn't, and so here we are, your gun on me and mine on the girl."

"Let her go and you'll live," Talanov replied. "You have my word."

Odin laughed. "Forgive me if I do not believe the Ice Man now that he knows people in Moscow wanted him dead, and that I was a part of this plan."

"Who organized the plan?" asked Talanov. "Who set it in motion?"

"What does it matter? I told Sofia you could not be bought, no matter how much Gorev was worth, which is not so much now that we have his samples. But she said you were like a dog on a leash, that she could make you do what she wished. But I knew differently."

And without warning, Odin shifted his angle of aim and fired. The maneuver required no sweeping arm movement. Just an unobtrusive flick of the wrist that was hardly visible. A distance of about four inches.

Odin's Makarov, which had no silencer, sounded like the amplified backfire of a tractor in the hushed moment of shock. The whitewashed walls lining both sides of the street bounced the sound all over the place, extending its echo. In the slashing blue lights of the patrol cars, Gorev, who had been standing ten feet to Noya's left, shuddered briefly and gasped before the agony of a bullet rippled through him and he fell.

And whereas Odin had been the center of attention up until that moment, Gorev now was. Odin knew everyone would instinctively shift their focus onto the flailing arms and the screams as Gorev hit the pavement and began writhing in pain. It had not been a fatal shot. Odin did not want Gorev dead. He wanted him screaming. He needed but a brief moment of distraction in order to swing his Makarov forward and drop Talanov where he stood.

Except that Talanov had not been distracted.

Ducking right and pulling Noya with him as a shield, Odin saw the tiny flash at the end of Talanov's Makarov. The flash was no larger than a dot and was the last thing Odin would ever see.

With Talanov's bullet hitting him between the eyes, Odin curled away from Noya and hit the asphalt, where he bounced once and rolled up onto his side, like a soggy sponge. Talanov had already grabbed Noya and was hugging her before Odin had settled into a motionless heap.

The three police officers went for their guns.

"Don't," commanded Talanov.

The three officers stopped and slowly raised their hands.

"The keys to your car. Where are they?" demanded Talanov.

No one spoke.

Talanov fired a shot between the legs of one of the officers and everyone jumped. The bullet ricocheted off the pavement and took a chunk out of the wall across the street.

"In the car," the officer replied.

"You and you, put Doctor Gorev in the back seat of the patrol car," Talanov told Paco and Juan, including them in the sweep of his aim.

All along the street, porch lights began clicking on.

Talanov told Noya to get the medical bag. She ran over, picked it up and ran with it to the patrol car, where her father was groaning and bleeding in the back seat. Talanov motioned Paco and Juan away from the car and they rejoined the others.

"Remember how your father treated your head wound?" Talanov asked Noya.

"Kind of," she replied.

"He needs you to do the same thing. Climb in and stay low until we're safely out of here. I'll talk you through it."

Noya climbed in and shut the door.

Keeping everyone covered, Talanov rounded the front of the car and paused by the open door. "All of you, lie down, on your stomachs," he said.

Everyone obeyed.

Talanov jumped behind the wheel, started the engine and peeled away just as the policemen scrambled to their feet, drew their weapons and began shooting. Several bullets shattered the patrol car's windshield and stung the air.

Once the sound of bullets striking glass and metal had stopped, Talanov sat up and thought about Alejandro's directions to the café. To the corner, turn right, two blocks down.

He just hoped he could make it in time.

CHAPTER 21

Talanov screeched around the corner. They were out of danger now although a total of five bullets had punched through one or both windshields and sent cracks radiating from the holes. Other bullets had hit the bumper and trunk. The police lights on top of the car were still flashing.

"Are you two okay?" asked Talanov, glancing over his shoulder.

"We are not hit," Noya replied, wiping strands of hair from her face.

Talanov could see Noya had cut Gorev's shirt away and was drenching the wound with iodine while Gorev winced and stammered instructions.

He looked back out of the cracked windshield. Never had an assignment gone so wrong. It should have been a simple case of tracking down a defector and bundling him back home. He had done it before. It wasn't hard. And finding Gorev had not been hard. Disliking Gorev had not been hard, either, at least not before he had met him. When he started this assignment, he regarded the man and his family as nothing more than traitors.

But then Noya happened, and everything changed.

Talanov clicked on the police radio and listened to a news report about protesters causing trouble down by the beach. Another report followed about hotspots of looting and robbing: televisions, stereos, bicycles, food, even blood from a surgical clinic. *Blood from a surgical clinic?* He thought about that. Thankfully, there was nothing yet about his stealing the patrol car but it would not be long. The officers would report the theft and call for back-up, and Franco, who had overheard Alejandro telling Sofia about the Gato Gordo Café, would then tell them where he was headed. Which meant if the police arrived to arrest him before he located and defused the bomb, Sofia would escape, the bomb would go off and Marbella would become a nightmare.

Talanov switched off the flashing blue lights, slowed at the intersection and steered the patrol car around a tight corner into the darkened side street Alejandro had told him about. He drove to an intersection with a dead-end street that branched off to the left, made a U-turn and returned to park near the entrance into the narrow walkway Alejandro had also told him about. He looked in the direction of his two o'clock position. The café was just over there, at the end of a row of shops. He could hear music and smell grilled meat. In the distance was the hum of traffic from the busy Mediterranean Highway that fronted the café.

"How's he doing?" asked Talanov, turning off the engine and swiveling in his seat. There were no streetlamps nearby so the interior of the car was dark. Houses lined the street but were protected by high walls and shrubs.

"I have cleaned the wound," answered Noya. "My father said the bullet has broken his shoulder. Most of the bleeding has stopped."

"Is there an exit wound?" asked Talanov. "A hole in his back?"

Noya shook her head no.

"We'll get him to the hospital as soon as I can," said Talanov. "Right now, I need to stop Sofia from setting off that bomb." To Gorev: "What am I dealing with?"

Gorev motioned for the medical bag and Noya handed it to him. He dug through the bag, found a plastic bottle of caffeine tablets and popped one under his tongue. He then forced himself to sit up, and after a couple of deep breaths, briefed Talanov on what had happened at Sverdlovsk in 1979 with the accidental release of anthrax spores into the atmosphere.

"Thousands of people died," explained Gorev. "It was covered up, of course, and blamed on tainted meat. What you may not know is that Anthrax 836 -- the strain that was released -- was only the beginning. My new strain is much more lethal."

"How sick does it make people?" asked Talanov.

"Not just sick, Colonel, they die. *Bacillus anthracis* -- which is all we know to call it right now because the engineered new strain has yet to be classified -- enters the blood stream and spreads rapidly -- within an hour -- and kills with ninety-eight-percent efficiency. It does, however, have a weakness. Unlike spores, which can lie dormant for years, this new strain can last only a few minutes outside of a nutrient host. Like cancer, it needs a steady supply of food to fuel its ability to voraciously reproduce."

"Meaning someone's body."

"Or, in this case, the blood inside those glass ampoules, which has been stabilized with a citrate-glucose solution during transport."

"Is your strain infectious?"

"Yes, if people begin coughing and sneezing, which other people then inhale. Otherwise, no."

"So, by exposing the population of a crowded café, who infect others with their sneezing, who in turn infect others and so on, this new strain could wipe out a whole section of the coast in -- what -- a few days?"

Gorev shifted position and winced. "Infecting a large group of people would be difficult if not impossible since the anthrax is *in vitro* and your colleague is planning to disperse it by way of a bomb. The heat generated by the blast would kill the bacterium."

"But the anthrax itself it has the potential to wipe out the region?"

Gorev nodded.

"What if Sofia injected your infected blood into a fresh

unit of blood?" asked Talanov. "How quickly would the unit become lethal?"

"Very quickly," said Gorev. "With the stabilizing influence of the citrate-glucose diluted, the bacterium would reproduce exponentially on the nutrients in the blood, especially as it warmed to room temperature."

"So, if Sofia raided a surgical clinic and stole several units of blood, she could make a biological weapon capable of infecting several hundred people, who in turn would infect thousands of others?"

"Yes, although as I mentioned to you before, she would still have the problem of dispersal. A bomb would most certainly kill the bacterium."

"Unless she found a way to insulate it against the blast. Assuming I can reach her in time, how do I destroy the stuff? Can I pour it down the drain?"

"We don't yet know its effect on marine life and whether averting one catastrophe would create another of greater consequence."

"What about heat or fire?"

"As I said, incineration would definitely kill it," answered Gorev. "In the absence of fire, the safest means of destroying it would be to simply pour it onto the street, away from others, without exposing yourself or any animals, of course. If a rat feeds on it, or if exposure occurs, the victim has less than a two-percent chance of survival."

"Thank you, Doctor. And just so you know, I really am sorry."

"For what?"

"Everything." To Noya: "Lock the doors and wait here. If I don't come back, the police will arrive soon and you'll be safe."

"And if you do come back?"

"I'm not sure that I will. No matter what happens, keep aiming for the sky. Sikorsky did. So can you."

Noya smiled.

"Send me a postcard from America," he said.

And with that, Talanov climbed out of the car and shut the door.

Dashing to his right, he paused in the shadow of a tree to unscrew the silencer from his Makarov. If he needed to clear the café, a few gunshots would do the trick faster than anything.

He did a quick scan of the layout. Behind him was a shady side street that led to the busy Mediterranean Highway. A barricade had been set up at the end of the street, cutting off access to the highway. A streetlamp at the far end of the street shone through the trees and cast mottled blotches of light on the ground.

Straight ahead was the narrow pedestrian lane running between the row of shop backs on his right and a store on the left that had been closed for several months, awaiting renovation. To his far right, beyond the shops, was a parking lot full of cars, most of which belonged to café patrons.

The lane ahead was dark, although at the end of the lane was a short alley, where a streetlamp bathed the area in light. On the other side of that alley was the back door to the café. Echoing down the lane was the passionate tempo of a Spanish guitar, sounds of laughter and clanging pans. Echoing down that lane was a reminder that lives were at stake.

He took a deep breath. *God help me.*

CHAPTER 22

Circling right, Talanov had to smile at the short prayer he had breathed. *Me, an atheist from the most atheistic nation on earth. Maybe I'm not what even I think I am.*

He had decided not to approach the café from the rear. If he were Sofia -- assuming she was in the restaurant right now acting the part of an ordinary diner in order to unobtrusively plant the bomb -- he would post a guard in the alley -- Svet -- calculating that if he, Talanov, made it past the police and came after her, the most likely point of access would be by way of the back door, through the kitchen. So he would enter by the front door like an ordinary customer.

Still dressed in his black fatigues, Talanov stuck the Makarov in the gun pouch near the small of his back. Rounding the corner, he walked along the edge of the parking lot. The row of shops was on his left, with the Mediterranean Highway straight ahead, beyond a sidewalk filled with people. He could see vehicles speeding by in both directions. In the parking lot to his right were more than a hundred parked cars.

The Gato Gordo Café was actually more of a restaurant than a café. It had started out as a tiny establishment with a small grill and some tables, but had been expanded twice to include live music, a bar, and a large elevated brick pit, where various cuts of aged Galician beef were grilled over a bed of fiery applewood coals.

With the sweet fragrance of caramelized meat filling the air, Talanov actually heard his stomach growl when he sidled between the bumper of a car and some shrubs. Being this hungry was a potential problem. He had not eaten in hours and if ever he needed energy to maintain focus, this was it. Glancing to his left, he could see smoke from the grill billowing out of a rooftop chimney.

The front of the café, which faced the Mediterranean Highway was a wall of bi-fold glass doors that could be opened or closed, depending on the weather. In front of this was a brick patio filled with small tables and chairs. The patio also contained a fire pit and a circular brick planter. In the middle of the planter was a thick, gnarly pepper tree that provided shade during the day. The patio was filled with chatting patrons. Candles in jars illuminated each table. A fire was dancing in the pit. The branches of the pepper tree was festooned with lights.

Talanov did a quick headcount. There were nearly forty people on the patio. Everybody seemed happy. Not a care in the world. He rounded the front of the café and saw a line of more than twenty people stretching out the front door, where an aproned waiter with curly black hair was taking orders for drinks.

Sixty people thus far, not counting those inside.

Bypassing the queue, Talanov squeezed past a cluster of people chatting in the doorway and approached a podium in the tiny foyer. The hostess greeted him but Talanov simply smiled and walked right past her.

Inside, he was greeted by a party atmosphere. The café was packed and nearly every one of the more than forty tables were full. The kitchen was to his right. All kinds of shouts and sizzles were coming from that direction. The pit, with its four cooks and massive stainless steel hood, was straight ahead. Swirls of smoke were being sucked up into the hood while the pit itself, made of bricks formed in the shape of a large horseshoe, were radiating a fragrant heat. The patio was outside to his left, while in a small area between the patio and the grill was a man on a stool, strumming a Spanish guitar, his eyes closed, his head keeping time to the music.

Seated alone at a small table was Sofia. At her feet was a large sequined handbag of colorful panels. She was slicing a bite off of her steak when Talanov pulled out a chair.

"Mind if I join you?" he asked.

Sofia stopped chewing and watched him sit.

Talanov unwrapped the other napkin, took the fork and speared a bite off her plate.

He popped it into his mouth. "Ummm, rib eye. *Very* good," he said, chewing. "I must remember this place."

Sofia used her napkin to dab the corners of her mouth.

"Let me guess," said Talanov, spearing another bite then pausing with the forkful near his mouth. "You came into the café, but because there was a line, strolled over to this table and paid the occupants a hundred dollars to vacate right then and there."

She held up two fingers.

"*Two* hundred?" he asked, surprised. "I forgot. The eighties. Inflation." He ate his bite of steak while Sofia watched him, amused. "So I'd like to start off by thanking you," he said.

"Are you hoping to keep me occupied until the police arrive?" she asked.

Talanov pointed to Sofia's plate inquiringly and she shrugged agreeably.

"Technically, it's Odin I should thank," he said, scooting her plate toward him and cutting off another bite, "and not for what you might think. By the way, I *am* flattered that you offered me so many opportunities to join your scheme. Agent Bixler offered Odin a hundred grand to go with her. You should have heard what he said: 'What's a hundred grand compared to a million?' But Agent Bixler -- bless her -- asked him whether he'd rather take the hundred grand *she* was offering and live or the million *you* were offering and die. Care to take a guess what he said?"

Sofia was glaring now.

"Don't worry," Talanov continued, talking while he

chewed, "Odin got a little out of hand and I had to kill him. Still, selling Gorev's nasty little creation to the highest bidder -- especially after a demonstration here in the café of what you're offering -- would definitely buy you an island somewhere. But that's not what I want to thank you for. What I really want to thank you for -- sorry, thank *Odin* for -- is letting me know how I was betrayed in Moscow."

"Not that it will do you any good."

Talanov smiled. "I'm here, aren't I? Don't count me out just yet."

"Odin told me you couldn't be bought."

"I'm afraid the lad got rather chatty with Agent Bixler, thinking me unconscious on the floor. He explained why you needed me -- to locate Gorev -- and why you were so argumentative about our flying openly into Spain."

"I couldn't have Kravenko pulling us off the assignment because of your reckless disobedience of his orders, now could I? However, to your credit, I was wrong about the effectiveness of your methods. I underestimated you, Colonel."

"And here I was, thinking you were just an inexperienced little Barbie Doll, when all along it was part of your plan."

"Men frequently underestimate women."

"This really *is* good steak."

Sofia smiled indulgently. "As you no doubt know, Colonel, success in our line of work is very much a game of strategy, endurance and skill, like the game of soccer, which you seem to adore so very much."

"Not to be pedantic, but soccer was Zak's game, not mine."

Sofia's smile turned cold. "Then let's hope the metaphor will not be lost on you."

"Your point?"

"The penalty kick in soccer is a free shot defended by only the goalkeeper twelve yards away. Twelve yards between life and death, where reaction speed makes all the difference. If the goalie anticipates in the right direction, he prevents the other team from scoring. If not . . ."

Sofia glanced past the doorway into the kitchen to a short hallway leading to the bathrooms. Standing in the hallway was Svet, holding Noya by the arm. In his hand was a syringe full of blood.

Talanov saw the terror in Noya's eyes as she looked desperately back at him.

Sofia said, "Yes, Colonel, I figured you would somehow escape and attempt to interfere."

"Leave Noya out of this," he said.

Sofia leaned forward with controlled rage. "I'm afraid it is too late for that, just as it is too late for the girl's miserable mouse of a mother. You should have heard her beg before I put a bullet in her head and Svet threw her body into the dumpster. As for the police arriving . . . well, they are chasing a spurious report I called in about two Soviet spies attempting to flee the country out of Algeciras."

Talanov stood and reached for his gun. "Then I'm afraid you leave me no choice."

"Oh, but you do have a choice," answered Sofia with a poisonous smile. "And the life of your little friend over there depends on which choice you make."

CHAPTER 23

Talanov turned in time to see Svet stab the syringe in Noya's arm.

"The choice is yours, Sasha," Sofia said as Svet muscled Noya into the kitchen. "Me or her?"

With a roar, Talanov forgot about his gun, reached across the table and yanked Sofia out of her chair with both hands. "The antidote! Where is it?" he shouted.

"Who knows?" Sofia replied.

By now, the café had grown quiet and everyone was looking.

"So, you can stay here and fight with me," she continued, "or you can go after your pretty little friend and *hopefully* get her to the hospital. Every second is critical, I'm told, for the two-percent of people who manage to survive."

Impulsive, emotional decisions are much more explosive than cerebral decisions. It's raw power versus filtered power. It's why emotional people -- those who become angry or frightened -- can perform superhuman acts of strength, such as lifting a car off a trapped child.

Talanov was not the emotional type. He was cerebral: calculating and cold.

Except now when he exploded toward the kitchen. He didn't think about whether or not to do it. He just did it. Diners were sent sprawling out of their chairs. Tables were overturned. Glass and silverware went flying.

And he had made the exact choice Sofia knew he would

make.

Talanov was aware Sofia had planned it this way and that he was playing right into her hand. That she'd pegged him accurately. He was predictable but right now he didn't care. He would find Svet and kill him and get Noya to the hospital.

At the kitchen doorway he glanced back. Sofia was already making her way toward the door.

Of the diners he had pushed over, two were British officers -- both captains -- with food on the fronts of their uniforms. They were pushing back from their table to come after him. Others were shouting and cursing. Still others were shaking their fists.

Talanov was set to race into the kitchen when he saw something that changed everything.

Sofia's handbag under her table.

"It's Talanov, that Soviet spy!" Sofia shouted from the doorway. "Somebody call the police!"

It was a natural reaction for people to look first at the person doing the shouting -- Sofia -- then where she was pointing -- at Talanov, who had already offended and angered half of the patrons in the café. Murmurs of "tackle him . . . take him down," began to ripple through the crowd. Neighboring tables of young men began nodding in agreement. *We can do this. We'll be seen on TV!*

Talanov glanced a final time toward the kitchen. If anyone deserved life, it was Noya.

He heard the scrape of chairs scooting back. Saw more than a dozen young men jump up from their tables. The two British captains were closing in. Others were cheering them on.

Pulling out his Makarov, Talanov fired five shots in a left-to-right pattern in the ceiling. The café went instantly quiet before turning into a stampede. The two captains were hit by the onslaught and forced back toward the front door.

Above the crowd, Talanov yelled, "There's a bomb. *Everyone out!"*

At the mention of "bomb," panicked diners jammed the

doorway trying to get out. Others poured over the patio wall like Wildebeest fleeing a lion.

With their angry eyes still on Talanov, the two captains muscled their way through fleeing diners.

Talanov saw the two British officers coming toward him. "Captain!" he shouted above the clamor. "Get these people out of here *now!*"

The two officers kept pushing his way.

Talanov knew he did not have time for a discussion right now. A bomb was about to go off and that left him with two choices: either shoot these two captains on the spot or enlist their help.

Shoving several tables aside, Talanov met the two soldiers and shoved his gun in their faces.

Both men took a step back.

Talanov said, "Yeah, I'm that guy. And I get it that you want to tackle and hold me for the cops after a few get-even punches. But if you've been watching the news, you'd know my colleague was a KGB agent named Sofia Dubinina. Six feet tall, Chinese, a ruthless killer. Well, that's who just ran out the door. And *that* is what she left me to contend with."

He pointed at the sequined handbag.

Said the taller of the two captains, "She ran off and left it. So what?"

"There's a bomb in that bag, that's what. And it's set to go off any minute. It's also been laced with anthrax, which means if we don't clear this café *right now,* hundreds if not thousands will die."

The captain looked again at the bag then at Talanov. "Okay, you've got my attention. But if this is some bullshit line . . ."

"Have a look for yourself," said Talanov, pushing chairs aside and approaching the table. "She planted the bomb here because she wants to demonstrate the killing power of a deadly new strain of anthrax. To show how easy it is to use, and how quickly it spreads."

"Why'd you run toward the kitchen?"

"Because her partner -- she had two but I killed one -- stabbed a syringe full of infected blood into the arm of a young girl named Noya Gorev."

"But you stopped. You didn't go after them."

"And I will forever hate myself for that decision," said Talanov, looking the captain in the eye. "But I couldn't because of this." He knelt onto one knee and gingerly unzipped the bag. Inside was a digital timer with just over three minutes remaining. Wires ran from the timer into four cakes of C-4 plastic explosive, which had been surrounded by chemical ice packs and six glass jars filled with blood. The entire assembly had been taped together with flesh-colored medical tape and nestled inside a thick bed of broken glass. It looked like a cooler full of ice but in fact was a bag full of shrapnel.

"What do we do?" asked the captain.

"Get it out of here, away from these people," the other officer replied while people around them continued to scramble and push their way out of the café. Others, however, were curious as to what was happening and began filtering back in, lured by the prospect of seeing a bomb or the KGB agent they had been hearing about on the news.

"And take it where?" answered Talanov, noticing the gathering crowd.

"Is that really a bomb?" people began asking. "Did you really kill all those people?"

Talanov fired two more shots in the ceiling and the onlookers scattered.

"Gentlemen, right now we're on the same side," Talanov told the two captains. "So I'm asking you -- begging you -- to get these people out of here."

"You got it, Colonel," they said.

While the two captains began yelling and ordering people out the door, Talanov ran into the kitchen and saw three cooks filling their pockets with steaks they had wrapped in plastic. They were dressed in work clothes of white linen and were covered with greasy stains.

Talanov flashed his gun. One of the cooks raised his

hands as if it were a hold-up. Another fell to his knees and began to pray.

"Get up!" barked Talanov in Spanish, pointing at them with his gun. "Degreasers. What do you use?"

"You are not here to kill us?"

"Answer me!"

"Methylated spirits. We use it to clean the floor and our equipment."

"Bring me all that you've got."

The three men ran into a storage room and brought Talanov several large cans. Motioning them to follow, Talanov lifted an empty stockpot from the stove and led them out of the kitchen. "Over there," he said, clearing a path to where Sofia's handbag was still on the floor. "Fill that bag and this stockpot with spirits," he said, placing the stainless steel pot on the floor next to the bag.

The men obeyed.

"Now, get the hell out of here," said Talanov.

"What about our steaks?"

Talanov shot a hole in the floor.

While the three cooks fled, Talanov ejected his empty magazine and put in a fresh one. He then ran into the kitchen, grabbed a dishtowel, tied a knot in the end and soaked it in oil from the deep fryer. He then set it alight from a burner and ran back into the dining area. After glancing around to make sure everyone was gone, he tossed the flaming towel into the stockpot. The vapor cloud of the spirits ignited with a bright flash just as Talanov ran through the kitchen and out the back door.

And what he saw stopped him in his tracks.

Gorev was lying on the dirty asphalt of the alley, near a dumpster, writhing and groaning. His stomach was a mass of blood and Noya was bent over him, sobbing. She looked up when she heard Talanov running toward her.

"He shot my father," cried Noya. "He just laughed and shot him for no reason."

"Come on," yelled Talanov, hoisting Gorev into his arms

and starting to run just as the café behind them exploded. A thunderhead of flame annihilated the roof and sent fiery debris into the sky.

The blast knocked Talanov and Noya to the pavement. Talanov landed on top of Gorev and rolled completely across him. His gun skidded away. Behind them, the café became a raging inferno when another explosion occurred. Talanov could feel the heat on his back.

Noya was lying a short distance away.

"Are you all right?" Talanov asked, crawling over to her.

"My arm, it's burning," she said.

"From the explosion?"

"No. From the needle."

Talanov knelt beside her and carefully pulled up her sleeve. In the light from the blazing café, he saw the large swollen red area where she had been stabbed. He touched it lightly and she flinched.

"Let's get you and your dad to the hospital," he said. "You'll be okay."

"I'm afraid she won't," said Svet.

Talanov spun around and saw Svet holding his gun. In Svet's other hand was a tiny vial. Svet grinned and held up the vial. "Not without this, she won't, and now that you have ruined our demonstration -- our *five-million-dollar* demonstration -- I especially wanted you and your little friend to see what happens next."

And with a bitter sneer, Svet dropped the vial of antidote on the asphalt and stomped on it. When he did, Gorev's wail of despair could be heard over the cracking of the burning café.

Said Svet, "Our good doctor there knows what is in store for his daughter. He is, after all, the one who created the monster inside her. But with his daughter now carrying the infection, we do not need him or his antidote anymore."

Svet racked a cartridge into the chamber of Talanov's Makarov. "By the way, Colonel, I know about the first cartridge being a dud. I use the same trick myself."

And after racking in a second cartridge, he shot Gorev in the chest.

"And now you," growled Svet. "We can't have our new incubator reaching a hospital, now can we?"

When Svet aimed the pistol at Talanov, Noya ran screaming into him, her fingers like claws, punching and scratching just as Svet pulled the trigger.

The Makarov kicked in Svet's hand and a casing went singing through the air.

The 9mm bullet struck Talanov in the shoulder and sent him crashing into the brick wall of a building, where he slid to the pavement just as Svet backhanded Noya with the pistol. Svet watched her stumble and fall with a gash on her forehead. He then laughed at Noya got up and came at him again.

"I will come back for you in a moment," he said, punching her to the pavement.

And setting his sights on Talanov, he walked over to finish the job.

CHAPTER 24

"A pity you will not get to see her die," Svet said. "I hear anthrax is a horrible death." He grinned at Talanov lying against the side of the building holding his shoulder. Blood was oozing through Talanov's fingers while the café behind them burned. Both men could hear Noya crying and coughing.

"Your time is coming," said Talanov, glancing toward Gorev's moans then looking up at Svet. "Maybe not by me, but I promise you'll pay."

"Do not make promises you cannot keep," Svet replied with a grin. "Do you not remember how I tell you this before?"

"It will happen, don't worry. Keep looking over your shoulder."

"Too bad you did not take your own advice, because there you are on the ground and here I am with your gun, and there she is, your little friend, who is now our laboratory animal. Such a pretty animal, too, so full of spirit and fight, defending you the way she did, like a kitten, bearing her claws. Too bad she will never reach motherhood. Oh, but wait -- she *is* a mother, isn't she -- of a new disease!" Svet laughed. "So, before I kill you, I want you to remember me in the café with your little friend. Remember me stabbing the syringe into her arm. Think of her screaming now as fever begins to eat away at her and---"

Out of the darkness, a massive hand clamped Svet's wrist

and wrenched it upward to the inside, diverting the gun barrel away from Talanov while twisting the weapon out of his hand. Another hand clamped Svet by the neck and lifted him completely off the ground. Svet tried punching the dark hulk of a figure looming in front of him but it was like hitting the trunk of a tree. Svet kneed the man and kicked him, but to no avail. Svet was like a ragdoll hanging in midair, flailing and wriggling, eyes bulging, unable to breathe.

Zak scowled at the Makarov he had taken and tossed it on the pavement. He then turned his fury on Svet. "You should have looked over your shoulder."

Suddenly, came the sound of running footsteps. Zak looked and saw a group of college students round the corner of the burning café. They stopped when they saw Zak holding Svet by the neck. They stared for a long moment, then saw Talanov holding his shoulder. Then they saw Gorev bleeding all over the pavement.

The students all turned and ran except for one in a Houston Oilers baseball cap -- an American -- who dashed over and knelt beside Gorev. He pulled off his t-shirt, wadded it into a ball and pressed it to Gorev's chest. He then placed Gorev's hand over the shirt.

"Hold this. It will slow the bleeding while I get help," he said in English.

Gorev grabbed the student by the back of the neck and pulled him close, attempting to speak.

Exhaling a deep ominous growl, Zak looked back at Svet. "I heard," he said. "And I saw what you did."

And Zak began to squeeze.

Svet tried clawing Zak's face in a final desperate attempt but Zak grabbed his fingers and broke them. Svet tried screaming, but it came out as a muffled gargle with Zak's hand around his throat. Svet locked eyes with Zak . . . saw his rage in the flickering light from the burning café. Seconds later, Svet's eyes rolled back in his head, and after a few twitches and jerks, he went limp.

After a final crushing squeeze, Zak tossed Svet's body into

the same dumpster where Svet had dumped Anna Gorev. He then ran over to where Talanov was kneeling beside Gorev and the student in the baseball cap. Gorev was unconscious and Noya was looking on with a blank stare. Her face was streaked with dirt and her clothes were torn and stained.

"What's your name?" asked Talanov.

"Joe Abernathy," answered the student.

"Tell me again what Gorev told you."

"Melissa in time," answered Joe.

"Melissa in time?"

"The words came out in gasps. Then he was out."

"But he didn't say who Melissa was or where we could find her?"

Joe shook his head.

Noya coughed slightly and Talanov leaned over and felt her forehead with the back of his hand. "She's got a fever. Can you help us to the car?"

"After what you did inside? Anything you need, Colonel. I'm here."

"Have you got a handkerchief?" asked Talanov. "Noya is starting to cough and we need to cover her mouth."

"Sorry."

Talanov saw Gorev was wearing a long sleeve shirt and asked Zak to rip out a sleeve. Zak grabbed the shoulder and pulled out the sleeve like it was a perforated sheet of paper in a notebook. He handed the sleeve to Talanov, who tied it gently around Noya's mouth.

"Okay, let's go," said Talanov.

Joe helped Noya stand while Talanov struggled to his feet. Zak picked up Gorev and hoisted him easily over his shoulder.

They hurried toward the car.

"Does your father call you Melissa?" Talanov asked Noya while they ran.

Noya shook her head.

"Do you know anyone by that name?"

Noya coughed and again shook her head.

Half a dozen more university students -- four boys and two girls -- came running down the lane after them.

"*La policía!*" a freshman named Luis called out, asking his friends if anyone spoke Russian.

"I speak Spanish. What's going on?" answered Talanov.

"Some local *pitufos* were telling everybody they had seen you," answered Luis.

"So we steered the police across the street," added his girlfriend, Justine, "but they will figure the truth out soon enough. So you must hurry."

"Reporters are here, too," said Luis, "and they are talking to everyone. Lieutenant Barraza, the police spokesman -- another *pitufo* -- said you were dangerous, that what happened in the café was the latest in a long string of crimes. I told them it was not true, that you had saved our lives."

"The reporters did not want to believe us," added Justine, "but we were all saying the same thing -- all of us -- and it made Barraza look like the *pitufo* that he is. I told them what happened, Colonel, how the Chinese woman planted the bomb. How you fired your gun to chase everyone out. How I came back and saw the timer and all that broken glass. How you chased us out again and then -- *ka-whoom* -- a massive explosion ripped off the roof. Incredible!"

"But I think the reporter believed us," said Luis. "We were all saying the same thing and people who were listening to us started to agree. There were even two British soldiers and they began telling the same story to the reporter. They made Barraza look like a fool."

"*Pitufo,*" others agreed.

"What do you need us to do, Colonel?" asked Justine. "How can we help?"

"Why are you doing this? asked Talanov.

"You saved our *lives,*" answered Luis.

"We do not like the police, anyway," said Justine. "Álvarez, the Comandante, is always sending the police to push students around -- nightclubs and rallies and protests -- so this is a way we can push back."

"And do something good, like you did for us," agreed another.

"What happened to the girl?" asked Justine.

"One of Sofia's men stabbed her with a syringe."

"Sofia? The Chinese woman?"

Talanov nodded.

"Why would he do that?"

"To make her really sick. They were hoping I'd rush Noya to the hospital and let their bomb go off."

"And you chose to stay?"

Talanov did not reply.

"How can we help?" asked Luis. "What do you need us to do?"

They reached the end of the lane, where it met the side street where Talanov had parked. To the right, beyond the building fronting the street, they saw a police car easing through the crowd of onlookers filling the street. Its lights were flashing but the street was packed and the going was slow. The driver hit the siren and people began jumping out of the way.

"Hurry, they are coming," said Luis just as Noya began to cough.

"Can one of you get her some water?" asked Talanov.

Luis sent one of his friends.

The last of the crowd parted and the squad car sped toward them.

"Block that car! We have to get Gorev and Noya to the hospital."

The students ran into the street waving their hands back and forth. The squad car skidded to a stop and an officer yelled for everyone to get out of the way. The group responded by sitting down in the middle of the street. An officer jumped out and began dragging the young people out of the way, two at a time. But as soon as he returned for others, the first pair would run back into the street and sit down again.

"Put Gorev in the front seat," Talanov told Zak while he

placed Noya in back.

"Are you okay to drive with that shoulder?" asked Zak.

"There's a medical kit on the floorboard. I'll take a couple of caffeine tablets and clean the wound later."

A young man came running up. "It's the best I could find for something wet," he said, handing Talanov a can of beer. Talanov nodded his thanks and handed the can to Zak. "Do your best to keep Noya awake." Zak nodded and climbed into the back seat.

Before sliding behind the wheel, Talanov paused and sniffed the air. *Lemon balm.* He motioned for Joe.

"What is it, Colonel?" asked Joe.

"Grab me a handful of that ground cover," he said, pointing to the lemon balm growing beneath a tree.

While Talanov got in and started the engine, Joe ran over, twisted off a handful of leaves and brought them back.

Talanov gave some to Noya. "Eat this, it will stop your coughing," he said, tossing the remainder on the dashboard. To Joe: "The hospital. Which way?"

Joe yelled at one of the students.

"That way," the student said, pointing down the dead-end street. "There's a barricade at the end but you can go around it. You'll end up on the Mediterranean Highway and will have to go right. Flip around as soon as you can and head back east. The hospital is about a mile down on your right. Five stories. You can't miss it."

"Thanks," said Talanov. "I owe you for all you've done."

"Not as much as we owe you," said Joe. "Good luck, Colonel."

Talanov shifted into gear and roared down the darkened street. At the end was a knee-high barricade mounted on thick wooden posts. Talanov veered left and drove over an oleander bush, crushing it as he bounced over the sidewalk and curb and into the busy highway. Cars screeched and swerved to avoid hitting him as he fishtailed into the flow of traffic to the blasts of horns.

The police radio was on and an excited dispatcher

squawked that Talanov was seen driving away from the café with hostages in a police car. The dispatcher interrupted herself to say Talanov and the hostages were now heading west on the Mediterranean Highway.

"Hostages?" yelled Talanov angrily. "Do they not *care* what those students were saying?"

Gunning the engine, Talanov roared into the left-hand lane and made a squealing U-turn at the first break in the median. Heading back east, he saw that a barricade of police cars had been set up ahead, where they were inspecting every car.

The police dispatcher squawked another report that said Talanov had made a U-turn and was now heading back east.

"Hang on," said Talanov, steering the police car up onto the sidewalk. Pedestrians leaped out of the way as the car flattened small trees and sent trashcans flying. The officers manning the barricade saw him coming and ran up onto the sidewalk, their guns drawn. Talanov roared toward them full throttle, the engine whining as another trashcan was sent cartwheeling across the tops of several stopped cars. Across the street to his left was the burning café.

Hesitant to shoot, the police shouted for Talanov to stop. But Talanov flew straight at them, horn blaring, lights flashing. At the last minute, the officers jumped out of the way as Talanov roared past, flattening another sapling before veering back into the street and racing away toward the east. The officers sprinted to their cars and peeled away after him, sirens screaming. The police radio was still broadcasting reports about what direction Talanov was headed.

Talanov looked in the seat beside him at Gorev, who did not appear to be breathing. He then looked at Zak in his rearview mirror. "How is she?" he asked.

"Getting worse," Zak replied.

"Can I have some water?" asked Noya. Her voice was weak and her coughing had subsided after eating the lemon balm.

Zak opened the beer and gave her a swallow.

"The hospital is up ahead," said Talanov.

"Who's Melissa?" asked Zak, "and how do we reach her in time?"

"If I had access to Gorev's files, I could check to see if there was someone named Melissa who worked with him. Judging by the name, which sounds American, I doubt we'll find her working in a Soviet lab."

"Maybe she's his contact in America?" suggested Zak. "Someone who knows his research?"

Noya laid her head against Zak's shoulder and closed her eyes. Zak shook her lightly to keep her awake.

"If she is," said Talanov, "the Americans are not going to tell us. Hold on, we're almost there."

Because Talanov was dividing his attention between the road ahead and Zak in the rearview mirror, he did not see the police car shoot out of a side street to his left. Its headlights were off, so there was no warning as the car shot across both lanes of traffic and rammed them in the rear fender.

The crash sent them spinning clockwise into a parked car, with the other car plowing into a van immediately behind.

Three shots exploded chunks of glass in on Zak and Noya.

Talanov ducked and looked around to see Sofia push open her car door and climb out.

"It's Sofia!" Talanov yelled. He jammed the gearstick in reverse and hit the gas. The car squealed back and smashed into Sofia's car just as she fired three more times -- *thunk, thunk, thunk* -- and jumped out of the way.

"Where the hell did *she* come from?" yelled Zak, protecting Noya with his arms.

"She knew we'd have to come to the nearest hospital," Talanov said, shifting into Drive and hitting the accelerator again just as Sofia jumped back in her car, reversed away from the van she had smashed and sped after them.

"Obviously, she's been following our progress on *her* police radio," said Zak. "They're broadcasting our every move."

"We've got no gun, no way to defend ourselves," said Talanov, looking worriedly in his rearview mirror at the headlights closing in. Farther behind were the flashing blue lights of the police.

"Noya needs help *now,*" said Zak, feeling her forehead.

"I know," Talanov replied. "But we've first got to lose Sofia and I'm not sure how to do that. She can handle a car better than anyone I know."

"Can I have some water?" asked Noya.

Zak offered her another swallow of beer but Noya didn't want it.

"We'll get you some as soon as we can," said Talanov.

"Aleksandr Talanov, can you hear me?" a woman's voice crackled over the police radio.

Talanov grabbed the microphone out of its bracket. "Agent Bixler! Is it you?"

"Yes, it's me! And what the *hell* do you think you're *doing?*"

"And a pleasant good evening to you, too," Talanov replied just as Sofia fired again. The bullet punched through both windshields and narrowly missed hitting Talanov in the neck.

"Listen to me!" shouted Bixler. "The police have orders to shoot you on sight, and the only reason they didn't turn you into Swiss cheese a moment ago is because you've got hostages in the car."

"They're not hostages," yelled Talanov, swerving around two cars. "We're trying to get them to the hospital to save their lives." He switched on the lights and siren.

"Two officers saw you force Gorev and his daughter into your car."

"We didn't force them. Noya's sick and Gorev's been shot. Talk to the people who helped us. They'll verify what I'm telling you."

"A lot of people are saying a lot of things," said Bixler, "and most of them are about you shooting up the place before setting it ablaze."

"I set that fire to incinerate the anthrax. There was a timer counting. Noya had been stabbed. I had to act fast."

"Why not switch off the timer? Or pull out the wires? Why risk infecting the *entire continent* by blowing a café to smithereens? The explosion was heard on *Gibraltar,* for crying out loud! Flames are *still* billowing over fifty feet in the air."

"I didn't try any of that because I couldn't tell what the actual configuration of the bomb was, or if you can even pull out wires without setting the whole thing off. It's pretty easy to give advice when you weren't there."

"Look, just pull over and wait. We're right behind you."

"Were you dropped on your head as a child? *Sofia's* right behind me and she's shooting at us. The moment I stop, we're dead."

"Why didn't you hand Noya over to the paramedics? They were at the café. Why run?"

"Because she's got *anthrax* -- one of Sofia's men deliberately infected her -- and I was not about to leave her in the street or risk getting both of us shot by some trigger-happy cop."

"They have antidotes they could have given her."

"Not for this stuff. She needs a hospital. So does Gorev."

"You can't keep running forever. Someone's bound to get killed."

"Listen, before Gorev lapsed into a coma, he said something about reaching Melissa in time. You need to find out who Melissa is and whether or not we can reach her. Was she a contact, a colleague . . . someone who knows of his work?"

"We're not doing anything until you pull over."

"I *can't* pull over!"

"You will if you want my help."

"Come on, Glenda! I'm not the enemy!"

"The *hell* you're not."

"Glenda, stop, he's not the enemy," said Pilgrim, interrupting.

"He *drugged* me," Bixler shouted, her voice crackling over the radio. *"With your help!"*

"Because he needed to stop Sofia from setting off that

bomb. Which he *did,* in case you'd forgotten. The anthrax was incinerated. Hazmat is there as we speak and so far they've found nothing."

"He blew up a café!"

"And if he hadn't? Come on, Glenda, you were not about to let him go."

"Whose side are you on, anyway?" snapped Bixler.

"Noya's. And she doesn't have much time. So will you *please* let me handle this? Colonel, this is Agent Pilgrim and we're in one of the police cars behind you. Tell me exactly what Gorev said about Melissa."

But Talanov was focused on his fuel gauge. A minute ago the gauge showed their tank being nearly full. Now it was just over half. He glanced in the side mirror and saw a tiny plume of liquid spraying out behind them.

"What's wrong?" asked Zak.

"Sofia shot holes in our tank."

"Colonel?" asked Pilgrim.

"All I know is what an American student named Joe Abernathy told me. I'd been shot in the shoulder and he ran to help Gorev. Gorev could barely speak and told Joe we needed to reach Melissa in time."

"Was Gorev speaking Russian or English?"

"Like I said, Joe was an American, so Gorev probably used words he knew Joe would understand."

"But you don't know that for sure?"

"No, I don't. According to Joe, Gorev said two words: Melissa and time."

"Aside from the name, is there a Russian word that sounds like Melissa?"

"None that I know of."

"What about 'time?'"

"*Vremya* is the Russian word for 'time,' so if Gorev said the word, 'time,' he was speaking English, not Russian," answered Talanov, weaving around three cars, with Sofia staying close behind.

But when Sofia passed the same three cars Talanov had

just passed, she shot the front tires of the two lead cars.

In his rearview mirror, Talanov saw the lead car's tire explode. He even heard the explosion and saw the car nosedive into the pavement and flip in a twisting cartwheel motion, round and round, end-over-end. It then took a bizarre high bounce and landed on top of the spinning second car an instant before both cars were hit by the third car for a screeching metal-on-concrete collision. Other cars hit their brakes but not in time to avoid skidding and crashing into one another for a massive multi-car pile-up that completely stopped traffic on the Mediterranean Highway.

"So we're talking about . . . watch out!" shouted Pilgrim over the sound of screeching tires.

"There goes any police protection we may have been hoping for," said Talanov just as Sofia sped forward and rammed them from behind, causing their car to swerve back and forth.

"Talanov, what just happened?" shouted Pilgrim.

"Sofia happened, that's what. Find Melissa! It's Noya's only hope."

"We'll be stuck in traffic for hours."

"I'm not interested in excuses, Agent Pilgrim. I don't care what you have to do. Call your Consulate, call Langley, call your fucking President. Just *find out who Melissa is and find out now.*"

CHAPTER 25

Traveling at speeds approaching a hundred miles per hour, Sofia rammed Talanov again and sent his car veering into the center divider. Talanov regained control, cut right across the highway and up an embankment of flowers to an exit ramp. With an angry curse, Sofia cranked her steering wheel right and skidded in front of two cars, where she gunned the engine and bounced her way up the embankment, following Talanov.

The ramp merged with a shady street that crested a small rise. There it split. The right fork angled toward a quiet housing development fronting the beach. To the left was a bridge spanning the highway. Talanov crossed the bridge, turned left again and raced down a ramp onto the highway again. In the distance, her could see the massive collision Sofia had caused. Lines of headlights stretched into the far distance. Blue lights were flashing everywhere. The flashing lights of ambulances had joined them. One of the crashed cars had burst into flames. Even farther away, he could see fire leaping from the café.

By now, Talanov's car was making a loud tapping noise and he was running low on fuel. Black smoke was spewing from the tailpipe. With Sofia closing in on him, his only chance was to slow down as they approached the hospital, which was now on the other side of the highway, and allow her to pull up beside him. He would then hit the brakes and cut right onto the shoulder and stop, hoping her reaction time would cause her to speed by and give him enough time to jump out with Noya and sprint across the highway, using the blocked lanes of traffic on the other side as cover.

But if he tried the maneuver from the right-hand lane, she would unquestionably know what he was planning. His best shot was to stay in the left-hand lane, near the center divider, and allow her to draw even with him on the right. He would then hit the brakes, crank the car hard to the right and hopefully lose her long enough to stop on the shoulder and make a run for it. Right now, getting Noya to the hospital was all that mattered. If the police shot him afterward, so be it.

Talanov could see Sofia gaining. He couldn't be too obvious about slowing down, but since they were already nearing the hospital, he needed her alongside of him *now*.

They passed the crash site on his left. The hospital was just ahead. He saw a clear spot where there were no cars in either lane. In the left lane where he wanted to be, he let up on the accelerator.

Sofia was right behind him.

His police car was blowing smoke and starting to sputter.

But Sofia would not pull up beside him. He kept glancing in the rearview mirror -- willing, praying, *begging* her to come alongside -- but she just stayed there, right on his tail.

They sped past the hospital and Talanov's heart sank.

His strategy had failed.

They raced through a stop light, where the Mediterranean Highway again became the main thoroughfare through a tourist district. There were landscaped apartments and more stop lights at side streets. There were shops and nightclubs and restaurants. They flew past a car lot. Then a real estate office. Then the café, which was still billowing black smoke into the sky. Fire trucks were all over the place. There were chemical, biological, radiological and nuclear -- or, CBRN -- units dressed in protective gear. Police were holding back onlookers while they worked. The café had been cordoned off.

Talanov pounded on the steering wheel with frustration.

The hospital was out of sight. Sofia was still on his tail. His car was making noise and he was low on fuel. What was he going to do? Sofia knew what he knew, that she simply had to stay behind him because sooner or later his car would quit.

He glanced in the rearview mirror and saw Zak holding Noya by the chin, talking to her quietly.

"How's she doing?" he asked.

"We need to do something and fast," Zak replied. "How's Gorev?"

Talanov looked over at Gorev lying motionless beside him. His chest was hardly moving. "Alive, but barely," he said.

"Can I have some water now?" Noya asked again, her voice but a whisper.

Traffic was slowing. In the distance a stoplight had turned red. If he stopped for that light, they were dead.

It was now or never.

They were still in the fast lane. A median divider was on their left. Two cars were on their right, with a distance of about thirty feet between them. When they passed the first car, Talanov cut sharply between them. The first cars hit the brakes just as Talanov bounded up over the right-hand curb and through a knee-high brick wall backed by a cedar hedge. They crashed through the hedge, bouncing and fishtailing between several palm trees and across an open lot.

Sofia reacted but not quickly enough. The first car honked and swerved but kept going, which cut off Sofia from following Talanov.

Talanov bounced across the open lot toward the hedge on the other side. He crashed through it and onto a residential street, where he cranked the steering wheel right and sped down the street.

"We've lost her for now," said Talanov, breathing a sigh of relief. He switched off the patrol car's blue flashing lights.

"We've got to find water," said Zak. "She's burning up and I'm having trouble keeping her awake."

"How about her coughing? Has it stopped?"

"The lemon balm seems to have worked."

And yet in spite of that small victory, Noya was still fighting a losing battle. Talanov knew it and Zak knew it. She needed water and needed it now, as much to quench her thirst as cool down her body.

The street he was on curved gently into a local business district. There were shops and offices, most of them closed. A concentration of storefronts and tiny walled courtyards. Vintage streetlamps among the palm trees lining the streets gave the small precinct a friendly feel.

They came to an intersection. On the opposite corner was a restaurant. A neon sign in the window advertised fine Sicilian dining. In front of the restaurant was an outside dining area with several small tables and some chairs. Overhead was an awning of red, white and green.

Except the restaurant was closed, which meant if he wanted water he would have to break in.

Talanov had no qualms about that. Right now, he would do anything to get Noya some water.

But as he paused at the stop sign, his eyes were drawn to a burning car two blocks down. Hungry tongues of fire were raging out of its broken windows and a thick plume of smoke was pumping into the night sky. Nearby, shouting protesters had smashed the front window out of a storefront and were jumping out of the opening with televisions, which they were throwing into the burning car. One of the televisions exploded and the protesters jumped back and cheered.

With his focus on the blazing car and associated activity, Talanov did not see the group of eleven protesters walking single file along the sidewalk to his immediate left. They had been veiled in the shadow of a building. One carried a transistor radio that was playing eighties pop.

"Hold it, there's a cop," one of the protesters said.

The group stopped just as Talanov stopped at the sign. Talanov's eyes were on the Italian restaurant again. Through the glass pane of the front door he could see neon signs advertising German beer and French sparkling water. EU cooperation at its best.

One of those patio chairs through the door should do the trick, he thought, unaware of the protesters watching him.

"That cop car's a piece of shit," a protester said. "Look at how shot up it is."

"Is that guy even a cop?" another one asked. "He sure as hell isn't Spanish."

"Maybe he stole the car."

"Maybe he's that *Russian* who stole a police car," said the guy with the radio. "They said he got away, and that he's still in the area."

"It's got to be him," said another. "Look, I see people inside. They said on the radio that he took hostages."

"It is. It's *got* to be him!"

"Come on. Let's see if it is."

Hearing voices, Talanov saw the group coming toward him. Flooring the accelerator, he squealed right around the corner and sped away. In his rearview mirror, he could see the group run after him briefly before breaking off.

"Dammit, why *now?"* he yelled.

Talanov did a quick assessment of where they were. Sooner or later, Sofia would find him. She knew he needed a hospital, and with minimal traffic in this part of town, it would not be difficult to spot him in this car.

Ahead was a stop light. There was no cross traffic so he ran the light. In the far distance he could see traffic was flowing again on the Mediterranean Highway.

At the next intersection he looked left and right for another café. The engine sputtered and he glanced at the fuel gauge. The tank was nearly empty. If he couldn't find another café, at least he was heading in the right direction, toward the hospital.

Suddenly, a police car shot out from a side street and smashed into them, sending both cars into out-of-control spins across the intersection. There were screeches of spinning tires and the groans of metal crushing metal. Talanov's car bounced over a planter of flowers and crashed into a clothing store. His engine continued to clack loudly as chunks of glass from the store window fell to the sidewalk and smashed.

"Are you okay?" yelled Talanov, jamming the gear stick into reverse and hit the gas. The tires made a deafening whine as the police car strained to break free from its sandwiched position between the building and the other police car.

"We're fine," Zak yelled just as Sofia yanked open the passenger door. She grabbed onto the door frame an instant before the car pulled loose and hopped backward, its engine hissing and tapping, its tires spinning. Hoping to throw her from the car, Talanov cranked the steering wheel and spun the car in a counterclockwise direction. He then hit the brakes and Sofia flew backward against the open door. He then shifted into Drive, stomped on the gas and spun the steering wheel in the other direction. The car leaped forward and slammed Sofia face-first into the door post. And yet she still continued to hold on.

Pushing herself away from the door post, Sofia grabbed Gorev by the shirt and rolled him out of the car.

In his rearview mirror, Talanov watched Gorev's body hit the pavement and slide to a stop.

Sofia glared at Zak. "Well, well, Major Babikov, what a surprise." With one hand on the door post, she reached for the gun in her belt.

Talanov hit the gas and yanked the steering wheel back and forth. The car swerved from side to side in a wild zigzag pattern along the darkened street. With its engine snicking and clattering, the crippled patrol car did not have much more to give. But it had enough to nearly throw Sofia from the car and prevent her from pulling her gun while she hung on with one hand, half in and half out of the car.

"Save Gorev!" shouted Talanov to Zak. "TAG, on three, two , one . . ." He hit the brakes and the car skidded forward, its tires smoking before Talanov punched the accelerator and the car shot forward again.

TAG, which is an acronym for Touch-And-Go, was a standard aircraft maneuver of touching down on the runway and taking off again without coming to a full stop. In his training courses of agents like Talanov, Zak had adapted the technique to enable his men to jump from moving ground transport vehicles. When the driver hit the brakes, the agents would dive from the door and hit the ground, where they would do several shoulder rolls before coming up onto their feet, just as Zak did now.

When Talanov accelerated forward after the TAG, Sofia was again slammed face-first against the door post. This time, however, she grabbed onto the post and worked her way into the car.

In the backseat, Noya struggled to breathe.

"Your *dǎoshī* did not train you well," Sofia yelled.

When Talanov snapped his head toward her with a dumbfounded stare, Sofia laughed.

"You think I did not know about your time in the mountains?" she asked, her expression hardening as the car raced clacking and whining down the street, the wind whipping her hair. *"I was there,* Colonel -- at *Lóngshù* -- years later but trained by the same *dǎoshī.* And *still* they talked about you -- *by name* -- breaking their own rules, just as you have broken them now for her, but not for me. I gave you *every opportunity,* but you refused. You would not let me in. And yet you let *her* in. What is she to you, this pathetic, dying girl?"

"You wouldn't begin to understand."

"Perhaps not, Sasha. But maybe you will understand *this.* "

And Sofia aimed her Makarov and fired.

CHAPTER 26

Noya did not make a sound when the bullet struck her. She jerked slightly and her eyes fluttered momentarily before slowly easing closed.

With the sound of the Makarov still ringing in his ears, Talanov jerked his head around in time to watch Noya's slender body deflate with a gentle sigh. The sight of the grotesque hole above her heart made every cell within him scream. In fact, Talanov did not hear the wail of his own voice in the aftermath of that moment. It was the horror and agony of his grief that cried the loudest.

He had seen death before. Not lots of times, but enough. Enough to know it didn't shock him, and sometimes death was necessary. He had shot people himself, and in every case there had been a reason. Someone was trying to kill you. Someone was trying to kill someone else.

This time it hadn't been necessary. In fact, it made no sense at all. Noya was an innocent bystander to everything that was happening. There was no reason for Sofia to kill an innocent person. Noya was also the incubator for the anthrax Sofia so desperately wanted. So there was no reason to kill her for that reason, either.

Why, then, had Sofia done it?

Talanov knew the answer.

It has always been about us, Sofia had once told him.

He had rejected her, and not just professionally but personally -- in spite of her best efforts to seduce him . . . in spite of her assurances to Odin and Svet that she could turn him, which in turn made her look foolish and desperate. So the shooting of Noya was her way of finally getting even. Of destroying the one person he cared about. Of having the last laugh.

What was worse, Talanov had sensed what she was going to do an instant before she did it. His response had been to yank the steering wheel right in an effort to use the centrifugal force of the moving car to divert her aim.

He reacted a fraction too late.

He knew what came next: Sofia would shoot him in the head before pushing herself out of the moving car. Like he, she had been trained to tuck and roll and protect herself from injury. She may end up with some broken bones, but she would live.

But just as Sofia miscalculated Talanov's response to her temptations, she also miscalculated his reaction to her vengeance.

Instead of hitting the brakes, which she assumed he would to -- a TAG, as it were, where she could shoot him and jump -- Talanov floored the accelerator.

Having braced herself for the opposite, Sofia lost her balance.

Talanov grabbed the Makarov and wrenched it upward.

A bullet exploded through the roof.

They continued wrestling for the weapon while the patrol car hurtled forward at full throttle.

On the opposite corner of the intersection ahead was a large brick building. It looked like a bank, with an oversized foundation and reinforced embellishments. It looked solid as a cliff. Which was just what Talanov wanted. He would end it all here and now.

His grief over Noya's death was simply too much. Yes, Sofia had been the one who pulled the trigger. But he was responsible, too. If he had not taken this assignment, she would still be alive. She would be alive to grow up and follow her dreams.

But he *had* accepted the assignment, and he could not change that now. He could, however, make sure Sofia's killing spree ended tonight. She would never again kill anyone.

He was not sure he could hang on. The pain in his wounded arm was excruciating. But he knew he couldn't give up, not until he had driven his car into the side of that building.

Then Noya coughed. It was barely a sound, it was so weak, but it was a cough.

Noya was alive!

Talanov hit the brakes at the last minute and cranked the steering wheel right. He would have preferred to go left but his arm already felt like someone was ripping it from its socket. Going right was his only option.

With pain from his wound almost blinding him, Talanov stiffened his arm to keep the steering wheel in a fixed position.

The car sputtered and coughed.

Come on, come on, he thought. *Don't give up on me now.*

The car skidded in a clockwise direction and Sofia was flung toward him as the car broadsided the building, allowing him to twist the gun away and hit the gas. The rear tires began spinning and whining and the car lurched forward again, throwing Sofia against the seat. Gritting her teeth, Sofia hung on as the car whined and wobbled its way up to sixty miles per hour.

Regaining her balance, Sofia slugged Talanov in the face, grabbed the pistol and tried ripping it from his hand. When that failed, she rammed his hand against the roof of the car once, twice, three times.

Talanov still hung on while doing his best to keep the patrol car in the middle of the street.

Sofia pulled her black knife from its sheath near her ankle.

Talanov saw the glint of steel.

He stomped on the brakes and threw Sofia against the windshield.

But while the maneuver threw her off balance, it also nestled her in a secure pocket with her back against the dashboard. With the car's forward momentum keeping her in place, Sofia drew the knife back and prepared to stab Talanov in his chest.

Talanov hit the gas again but Sofia was in a braced position with her knees against the seat.

She swung the knife toward him in a wide arc.

Talanov blocked downward with the Makarov.

The black knife sunk into the seat near his thigh.

Sofia yanked back to swing again.

Talanov lifted his gun and fired twice, the force of the bullets punching Sofia out the door with a shocked look on her face. In his rearview mirror, he watched her body bounce and flip several times before rolling beneath a parked truck.

In the backseat, Noya coughed again. Throwing down the Makarov, Talanov gritted away the pain and gripped the steering wheel with renewed resolve to save Noya's life.

"Vody," he heard her whisper before coughing deeply, painfully.

Noya desperately needed water and Talanov felt a tear run down his cheek. Never had he felt so helpless. Never had he felt so incapable of doing what needed to be done. Never had he seen such courage and strength as he was seeing in this precious young girl.

Up ahead was an intersection. The hospital was somewhere in a general direction off to the left. He wasn't sure where. He just knew he needed to go left.

He braced his arm for the turn.

Then something caught his eye. Beyond the intersection, on the left-hand side of the street, was a fire hydrant.

Water!

Gritting his teeth, Talanov aimed the patrol car for the hydrant. Hitting the brakes at the last minute, the car skidded into the hydrant and bounced back as the hydrant snapped and shot a powerful geyser of water up into the sky.

Talanov jammed the car into park and jumped out. Ripping out one of his sleeves, he soaked it in water, and after grabbing a mouthful for himself, ran back to squeeze some of the cool liquid into Noya's mouth. Up and down the street, porch lights came on as the hydrant thundered water into the air.

"*¿Qué está pasando?*" someone yelled.

"We've got to hurry," Talanov told Noya, dabbing her forehead with the wet sleeve before laying it across her neck. He gave her the rest of the lemon balm. This was it. It was all he had.

Her eyes met his.

Don't die, he thought, touching her forehead with the back of his hand. It was raging with fever. "What I wouldn't give for a helicopter right now," he said.

Noya smiled. "Sikorsky R-4B."

Another tear rolled down Talanov's cheek.

She squeezed his hand. "Do not be afraid. I am not."

I am, Talanov thought.

"I will always remember you," she said.

"As the one who got you into this mess."

"As the one who got me out." She smiled again. "You are my hero. You taught me to aim for the sky."

Talanov fought back more tears. *How can a girl so close to death be so full of life?*

CHAPTER 27

Zak paused to catch his breath and laid Gorev on the landing of a three-story office building. The landing was set back in the face of the building and would hide them in the shadows.

He had chosen to get off the main street where Gorev had been thrown, not only because of Sofia but also because the police had been given orders to shoot them on sight. The directive had been issued specifically against Alex, but because the police had seen him with Talanov loading Gorev and Noya in the patrol car, he did not want to take the risk of getting shot. That meant he would try and stick to those darkened side streets that ran parallel with the Mediterranean Highway. In another three blocks, he would then turn right and head toward the hospital.

By some miracle, Gorev was barely alive. Not only had he lost a lot of blood but he had also been thrown out of a car. Looking right, Zak saw two police cars speed past with their lights flashing. He needed to keep moving.

He had heard gunshots earlier and hoped Alex was not on the receiving end of those shots. He had never met an adversary like Sofia. Not only did her training match anything he or Talanov had been given, but she possessed a quality neither of them possessed: *hatred*.

And hers was personal.

For Talanov.

From what he had seen, it had not always been that way.

Following them around the Gran Casino del Sol, he saw the way Sofia looked at Talanov. Saw the way they worked together seamlessly, as one, as if on stage, with the eyes of the world watching, which in a very real way they were. He had seen many teams operate in the field, paired as couples like these two had been, but never with such flawless precision. It was the little things that created a convincing façade: the flirtations, the manners, the bickering and bantering, the affection and the sex -- all of which was an act, of course -- although perhaps therein lay the explanation. Perhaps it had become more than an act for Sofia, so that when the charade ended and Talanov withdrew, she felt betrayed and vulnerable.

And from what he had observed thus far, Sofia was not a person to betray.

After pausing in the shadows of a doorway to let a car pass, Zak looked both ways before dashing across the street with Gorev in his arms. Thankfully, Gorev was not that heavy.

One more block, he thought, trotting in the corridor of shadows near the line of storefronts. Between him the street was the added protection of a row of evenly-spaced palm trees. Between each tree was a tiled concrete bench that no doubt allowed the old men of Marbella to watch the young women of Marbella. It was a time-honored tradition.

Headlights approached them from the rear and Zak ducked into the recessed doorway of a gift shop and sat down, out of sight. He did not think he had been seen, thanks to the row of trees, but moving targets were visible targets, even in the darkness, especially at eye level, so remaining low and motionless was important.

Sitting with his back against the angled window with Gorev in his lap, Zak could hear the car making a grinding noise as it came toward them, as if a bent wheel rim was rubbing against a fender well. Russia had many dilapidated old cars that sounded this way, but he had seen relatively few in Spain. In fact, the only car he had seen recently that sounded like that was---

A sputtering police car sped by him.

Talanov.

Zak let out a shout but it was a weak one because he was tired and Gorev was in his lap weighing against his diaphragm. Zak struggled to his feet and ran with Gorev into the middle of the street, where he began shouting in Russian for Talanov to stop. But the street was dark and Talanov was already turning the corner, and the car was throwing black smoke and making all kinds of noise.

With Gorev still in his arms, Zak ran as fast as he could to the corner, hoping to stand under the streetlight and start waving his arms. With luck, Talanov would look in his rearview mirror and see him.

Zak was breathing hard when he rounded the corner and began shouting at the top of his lungs. His arms and legs were burning. He could therefore be forgiven for not hearing the approaching group of protesters discussing the repeated shouting for "Talanov" they had just heard. But forgiveness was not in the hearts of anyone in this group as Zak suddenly found himself in the midst of fourteen angry young men.

"You are Russian, a friend of the spies," one of them said as the group began forming a circle around Zak. "We heard you calling for Talanov."

"I'm trying to save this man's life," Zak replied.

"Then it is not his lucky day."

The attack came from Zak's rear as he knew that it would. Mob behavior was usually cowardly at heart, which meant they would first try to jump him from behind before attacking him from all sides like a pack of hyenas. He could literally hear the split second of hushed silence that preceded most attacks.

Bending forward and to his left, Zak rolled Gorev toward the men who were standing there. He needed both a distraction and some kind of strategic momentum if he hoped to come out of this alive.

The men jumped back just as Zak hopped to the right and

did a tumbling shoulder roll toward the four men who were standing there.

He came surging up toward them, his hands loose and ready.

Zak grabbed the first man, who weighed about the same as Gorev, and spun him in a complete circle as if he were throwing a discus or hammer. Zak released the screaming man, who flew horizontally into the two men who were attacking him from the rear. All three of them fell to the pavement in a tangled heap of arms and legs.

Zak was on the perimeter of the group now, which is where he wanted to be. He was no longer surrounded and the mob was stunned and disoriented.

His first object was to take out the men nearest him and several quick strikes did the trick, first to the man on his left, with punches to the solar plexus and an elbow to the chin, then to the man on his right with a side kick to the knee and a backfist to the forehead. That left a dozen men in the broken circle, three of whom were still trying to untangle themselves on the pavement. His next move was to systematically blitz his way around at least half of the circle before the others had time to react. Time was his enemy, not only because he was tired from carrying Gorev, but because the longer it took him to disable his opponents, the longer the others had to mount a counterattack.

The first three went according to plan. As Zak had hoped, the others stood watching his mesmerizing martial-arts ballet as he took down the three men with elegant efficiency.

But not all of the group responded as he had hoped.

Scrambling to his feet after having been knocked down, one of the men rammed Zak from his blind side and tackled him to the ground. Zak flipped the man off and rolled on top of him, but before he could crack one of his giant fists across the man's jaw, another man grabbed Zak by the neck and yanked him off. The group then set upon Zak with their feet. Zak was able to deflect their blows for a while, but they were soon hammering him from all directions. Vicious kicks to his head, back, kidneys, groin and face. Zak tried seizing a foot to drag one of the men down on top of him for protection, but his hands were stomped and kicked away. Before long, all Zak could do was curl up in a ball.

Zak was starting to lose consciousness when he heard the brief yelp of a siren. Through his closed eyelids, he saw flashing blue lights.

The kicking stopped. A car door slammed. Boot steps hurried toward him.

"What's going on?" a policeman demanded.

I'm going to survive, thought Zak as the boots stopped nearby.

"This man is a friend of the Russian spy, Talanov," a voice answered.

"How do you know this?"

"He was yelling for Talanov to stop -- in Russian -- when Talanov drove by."

The policeman used his boot to roll Zak onto his back. "Talanov had a friend with him at the café," he said, "and this man fits his description. Who's the other man there on the ground?"

"We don't know. He was with the Russian."

"Who shot him?"

"We don't know. The Russian was carrying him."

"And you heard this Russian yelling for Talanov?"

"Yes. But Talanov did not hear him and sped off down the street."

"Call this in," the policeman yelled to his partner in the car. "Tell them Talanov's colleague is down."

"Is there a reward for this man?" one of the protesters asked. "You should give us a reward."

There was no reward and the policeman said so. The protesters objected and an argument ensued, but the policeman held firm. There would be *no* reward.

"Now, stand back!" the policeman barked. "I have orders to shoot Talanov and his colleague on sight, and if you continue to provoke me, one of you may get shot, instead. Do you understand me?"

In the hushed moment of silence that followed, Zak could hear the policeman's gun slide out of its holster.

And he realized, *I'm going to die.*

CHAPTER 28

The sound of the gunshot echoed in the stillness of the night. The mob was silent, gathered around Zak and looking on, and there was no traffic noise to drown out the sound. So the echo seemed to hover for a moment before dissipating into the night.

Zak lay there curled up on the pavement, panting, his heart racing, waiting for the aftershock of pain.

But the pain never came. What came was a deafening screech of tires.

When the radio crackled that Talanov's colleague was down, Bixler did a squealing U-turn in the middle of the street. Thankfully, she was not that far away, having been part of the dragnet of patrol cars out looking for Talanov.

Speeding down the street, she saw the circle of people two blocks ahead, in the glare of a streetlight. She veered toward them and hit the brakes. The patrol car skidded to a stop just as Bixler jumped out and fired.

She had purposely aimed high, above their heads. She didn't really want to shoot anybody but would love to see a few of them piss their pants.

The group ducked before scattering in all directions, like flapping chickens. All except for the policeman, who *was* down on all fours. When he finally stood, Bixler was striding toward him with her pistol aimed straight for his chest.

The policeman raised his hands.

Bixler saw the officer was unarmed and looked around for

his gun. It was nowhere to be seen. Seeing movement in the corner of her eye, she turned spun toward the policeman's squad car and ordered the other officer out.

"Is Babikov okay?" she asked Pilgrim.

While Bixler kept her gun trained on the officer getting out of the car, Pilgrim ran over to Zak. "Are you all right?" she asked, rolling him onto his side.

Bleeding from his nose and mouth, Zak nodded.

"Can you get up?" asked Pilgrim. "We lost track of Talanov. We're here to help."

Zak nodded again and Pilgrim helped him unsteadily to his knees.

Three shots suddenly rang out.

Bixler was struck twice in her upper back and there was a suspended moment when time stood still. An awareness of having been shot was her first thought. Then came the echo of gunfire overlapping the sensation that she had been hit. Then came explosions of pain tearing through her in all directions.

She did not want to die. Not wanting to die was her very next thought: a begging, desperate plea that she would somehow live. And in that moment, she felt that she would.

A conviction that evaporated an instant later.

Bixler tried to breathe but could not. Nothing seemed to work. Her body would not respond. Instead, she stiffened and wobbled for an instant before her circuitry failed and she collapsed with a gargled gasp.

Pilgrim screamed at the sight of her partner hitting the pavement.

Two more shots rang out that missed Pilgrim by inches.

Zak saw Pilgrim dive to the side of her friend. Saw the muzzle flash from the pistol being fired from the darkness off to his left. Heard the sound of those shots echo away into the night.

Every inch of Zak's body ached from having been repeatedly kicked and beaten. But adrenaline is a powerful hormone which, in combination with a palette of other hormones, can have deadly consequences to anyone standing in the way of someone like Zak.

Zak's pain melted away as the explosive chemicals triggered an instantaneous reaction that saw him do a lightning dive for the pistol that Bixler had dropped. Tucking his shoulder, Zak grabbed the weapon before doing a shoulder roll and coming up smoothly onto both feet while twisting to fire four times at the shooter in the darkness.

The man stumbled forward and fell.

Leaping over the two women like a hurdler, Zak met the two protesters closing in on Pilgrim from her blind side. He batted away their punches and flattened them both. He then charged the others like an enraged water buffalo.

The remaining protesters turned and ran.

Zak chased them briefly to make sure they knew he meant business, then returned to Bixler's side.

"Check Gorev's condition," he told Pilgrim.

The two Spanish policemen started to get up but Zak told them to stay where they were. Sticking Bixler's gun near the small of his back, he lifted Bixler into his arms and ran with her to the car. He opened the door and laid her carefully on her side in the back seat. Her back was a mass of blood. Zak scooted in beside her and ripped the sleeves from his shirt.

He glanced up when he heard the trunk lid open and slam. Seconds later, Pilgrim slid behind the wheel.

"Gorev's dead," she reported. "I'm sorry."

Zak looked away for a moment then nodded.

"I put his body in the trunk," added Pilgrim.

Zak nodded.

Pilgrim started the engine, shifted into gear and raced away down the street. Glancing around, she asked, "How is she?"

"Both shots are to the upper back, near her shoulder. One is a clean wound -- in and out -- just inside the medial border of the scapula, so the bullet must have passed between the ribs. The other is still in there, probably slowed if not splintered by the density of the scapula."

"Sounds like you know anatomy."

"We were trained to know many things."

Passing streetlights filled the car with bursts of light.

A voice on the police radio issued a demand for the two female American agents to surrender the Soviet spy they had stolen.

"That was fast," said Zak as Pilgrim reached over and switched off the radio.

"Good news travels fast. Bad news, faster," whispered Bixler, then coughing.

"You must stop talking," said Zak. "A bullet may have damaged a lung."

Bixler nodded.

"Thank you for saving me," said Zak.

"Police radio. We heard what was happening," said Pilgrim.

"I must admit, until now I have never liked Americans."

"How many Americans do you know?" asked Pilgrim. She locked eyes with Zak in the rearview mirror.

Zak smiled sheepishly and shrugged.

"I thought so," she said. "But since we're confessing, I must admit I've never thought much of you Russians, either. Until now, that is. The hospital is just ahead."

"Why do you do this?" asked Zak.

"Glenda. Once you've earned her respect, she'll put her life on the line for you and not bat an eye."

"Thank you again for what you did," said Zak.

Bixler suddenly started gasping and Zak lifted her up into a sitting position. This caused the fluid in her lungs to drain downward, enabling her to breathe. When she finally caught her breath, she nodded.

"Did you ever locate Melissa?" asked Zak.

Pilgrim paused to look at Zak in the rearview mirror.

Zak responded with a curious stare.

Pilgrim said, "Are you sure those samples were anthrax? I ask because Washington heard from Spain's Hazmat people, who found no evidence of anthrax in and around the burned-out café. You can imagine how foolish this makes us appear since Glenda and I were the ones who called in the Hazmat people. We're now being blamed for creating -- and I quote -- an outbreak of wild and unsubstantiated rumors. Not only that, Washington had been pressuring Moscow to come clean about what they were doing over there, but after the release of this report, has had to backpedal and apologize. Furthermore, Moscow has denied knowing anything about a defecting doctor."

Zak said nothing.

Pilgrim continued, "So the official word now is that there never was any anthrax, a position that is sure to be strengthened now that Gorev is no longer alive to contradict that position."

Zak said nothing.

"So I need to ask you something off the record, Major," she said, "because if Gorev was indeed defecting with samples of anthrax, then we've still got a big problem. Again, this is off the record."

"What is your question?" asked Zak.

"Should I quit looking for Melissa? If you tell me to quit looking, I will, and I hope to God you do, because then I'll know for sure that Noya's in no further danger. But if you say nothing, you are -- quite literally -- admitting nothing yet telling me everything I need to know to try and save that young girl's life. So I'll ask you again right here and now: should I quit looking for Melissa?"

And Zak very pointedly did not reply.

CHAPTER 29

The roadblock of police cars ahead filled the darkened street with flashing blue lights. A total of seven cars had been driven into angled positions to form a barricade. Officers with rifles and pistols had taken up posts behind the barricade.

With his car clacking and hammering as it inched along, Talanov pounded the steering wheel one last time. He could see the hospital from here. It was right across the busy Mediterranean Highway, which was no more than twenty feet on the other side of the roadblock. Noya had a fighting chance if he could get her to that hospital. He would willingly go to jail in exchange for Noya getting help. But with the police having orders to shoot him on sight, and with more than a dozen weapons trained on him at this very moment, he simply could not take the risk of Noya getting shot by some trigger-happy moron wanting to make a name for himself.

The police radio was full of shouting about where he was. A police helicopter had been following him overhead, reporting his every move. He could hear the thumping of its rotor as it hovered in the sky. A second chopper had also joined in. In his rearview mirror he could see police cars emerging from the side streets and falling in with the other police cars closing in on him. He slowed down as he passed the last side street. He looked left and right. Speeding toward him from both directions were more patrol cars, their blue lights flashing. He was boxed in.

Suddenly, the focus of the police chatter on the radio

changed. The second helicopter -- a news helicopter -- was being ordered to leave.

They're getting ready for the kill, thought Talanov, *and they obviously don't want any pictures.*

Talanov thought about what Bixler had asked him about simply turning Noya over to the paramedics. Perhaps her suggestion would work here. He could stop the car, get out and lay Noya down on the street and move away with his hands raised. The only reason the police weren't shooting right now was because they knew she was with him in the car. So this option at least afforded her a chance. However, once he stepped away, even with his hands raised, there was an excellent chance they would gun him down. If that happened, at least he would be clear of Noya.

But would they rush her to the hospital? Or would they be afraid to help her because of the anthrax scare? Would they let her die in the street? The thought of everyone just standing around in a wide circle was infuriating. He had tried everything and failed. His only choice now: to keep trying.

In the end no one would know how hard he had tried, not that it mattered and not that he could ever atone for what he had done. No, he had not pulled the triggers that shot Gorev, his wife and his parents. Nor had he been the one who shot Noya or stabbed her with the syringe.

He was, however, the one who tracked them down.

He was, however, the one who failed to detect Sofia's intentions, and there had been plenty of signs.

And even though Sofia was now dead, the consequences of her actions -- and his -- had destroyed a family wanting nothing more than a new chance at life.

From the cacophony of chatter over the police radio came a booming voice in Russian. *"Aleks! Ty zdes'? Vy menya slyshite?"*

Hitting the brakes, Talanov yanked the microphone from its bracket. "I'm here, I can hear you!" he replied.

"Are you listening to this?" asked Zak.

"Listening to what?"

"The news. Turn on your radio!"

Talanov switched on the car radio just as the news helicopter descended out of the sky into view just above the police barricade. It was hovering thirty feet above the squad cars and Talanov could see the agitated officers waving it away. An officer with a bullhorn shouted for the chopper to vacate the area.

Turning up the volume, Talanov heard recorded interviews with Luis and Justine and some of their friends, including Joe Abernathy, the young man in the Houston Oilers baseball cap. They were talking over one another and praising Talanov for saving their lives. Others were pleading for people to help Talanov, saying he was trying to save the life of Noya Gorev. Two British captains were then interviewed and said much the same thing. The reporter then came back on and promised regular updates on Talanov's race to save young Noya Gorev.

"What is happening?" asked Noya, hearing her name. She tried to sit up but was too weak. Her eyes were barely open. Tangles of hair had fallen over her face.

Talanov did not answer. He was listening to the voice of the Spanish news reporter, who was describing the location and number of police cars that had been set up to block Talanov's access to the hospital.

"I can see Talanov from here!" the reporter said. "He has stopped in the middle of the street!"

There was silence on the radio for a moment, and in that moment Talanov heard the distant clatter and whine of car engines.

The police, he thought. *They're closing in.*

But when he looked in his rearview mirror, he could see the police cars behind him had stopped.

Talanov switched off both radios and listened. The whining and clattering grew louder.

He waited in the hush of expectation.

Suddenly, a stream of old cars and vans squealed and bounced out of a narrow alley halfway down the block. The cars turned toward him and roared past. In the lead van was Luis and Justine, then Joe Abernathy, then their friends, and their friends. Many of the cars screeched to a stop in front of the side streets, blocking the police cars coming that way. The rest made screeching U-turns to form a protective wall of steel behind Talanov while the news helicopter continued to hover overhead. Others formed a human funnel into the alley and began waving and shouting for Talanov to hurry.

"Hang on, Sweetheart," said Talanov.

Pressing the accelerator to the floorboard, Talanov squealed into the alley to cries of *"Te amamos, Noya!"* When he had disappeared, students ran into the mouth of the alley and sat down, blocking any attempt by the police to follow.

The concrete pavement in the alley was cracked and broken as the crippled police car bounced and hopped its way along. The whitewashed walls of backyards were little more than a blur. Twice he hit trash cans and sent them clanging and bouncing off the walls.

Emerging at the other end of the block, Talanov made a hard right, where the car backfired once and died.

"No!" shouted Talanov, trying repeatedly to restart the expired engine as the vehicle rolled to a stop.

Jumping out, he lifted Noya out of the backseat and began running with her in his arms. He could see the hospital on the other side of the highway.

Noya felt eerily light as he ran, as if she were wasting away in front of him. Talanov looked at her unconscious body. Her head was flopping back and forth, so Talanov hoisted her closer to his chest. His wounded shoulder was screaming in pain.

In the sky above, he could see the police helicopter. It was close enough that he could see the pilot's lips moving as he communicated with units on the ground. He could hear the sirens of police cars behind him. Could hear the throaty roar of their engines. Up ahead, a stream of officers began running toward him. They knew exactly where he was and that he was on foot.

As the squad cars behind him screeched to a stop to cut off his retreat, a line of twenty armed police officers took up positions ahead. At the command of a ranking officer, they aimed their weapons.

From a loudspeaker attached to the helicopter came a demand for Talanov to stop.

Talanov kept running straight at them.

"Halt, or you will be shot!" the loudspeaker barked.

With Noya still cradled in his arms, Talanov staggered to a stop in the middle of the street. He was panting and stooped. He was favoring his wounded shoulder, which was a dried mass of red.

For a long moment, no one moved. It was Talanov against twenty armed policemen. The only sound filling the night was the thumping of rotor blades. Even traffic on the busy Mediterranean Highway had stopped: four lanes and hundreds of cars stretching in both directions. Headlights and taillights as far as one could see. People had been following the news reports of what was now being called The Race to Save Noya, and were standing on top of their cars, watching and waiting to see what would happen in the dramatic standoff unfolding before their eyes. More people began filling the sidewalks bordering the street. Word was spreading quickly, and the students who had raced to help Talanov earlier were now lining the street.

Talanov began walking toward the troop of officers. Exhausted to the point of collapse, his shoulder aching, he pushed himself forward, step by step, one foot after the other.

He stumbled over a crack.

Two pairs of arms caught him from behind and kept him from falling. It was Luis and Justine, panting and winded from their run.

"Get back," he said. "Noya's sick. There's a chance she may be contagious."

"How come you're not sick?" asked Luis.

"I don't know, I honestly don't," said Talanov. "I gave her some lemon balm and all I can think of is that it stopped her coughing. Coughing is how it is spread."

"If it's good enough for you, then it's good enough for us," said Justine.

Talanov said, "I mean it. Get back."

Without answering, Luis and Justine positioned themselves on each side of Talanov, one hand under each elbow, an arm each around his back. They called for others to join them but no one did.

"This is Comandante Álvarez of the Civil Guard," a man with a bullhorn shouted from the troop of police officers. "I need that young man and that young woman to step away from the target. I repeat: *step away* from the target."

Luis gave Álvarez the finger to cheers and applause from the crowd.

"Colonel Aleksandr Talanov, you are ordered to lay down that hostage and surrender yourself!" barked Álvarez over the bullhorn.

Talanov, Luis and Justine marched steadily onward. Several of their students friends came running up from behind and joined in. Soon, others from the crowd began falling in behind.

"This is your final warning!" announced Álvarez.

Talanov and the others kept walking.

"Keep the target in your sights!" Álvarez yelled to his men, raising his hand. *"Steady.* On my command . . ."

"Comandante, are we really going to fire?" asked Lieutenant Barraza in a low voice, glancing worriedly back and forth between Álvarez and the dozens of people marching with Talanov. "The crowd is watching."

"Do you know how much damage this man has caused?" hissed Álvarez. "He *killed* people. He blew up a *café.* We have been chasing him all over town!"

"The people regard him as a hero. If you shoot him here in full view while he is trying to save this girl, you will not survive the backlash much less the wrath of the crowd. Especially if the girl dies, which by the look of it she may have already."

"What do you suggest?" asked Álvarez just as Talanov stopped two feet from the tips of their guns.

While Barraza whispered in Álvarez's ear, Talanov looked both ways along the line of troops. The news helicopter continued to hover overhead. The downdraft from the rotor blades whipped hair and flapped collars and shirts.

"How many of you have children?" Talanov shouted in fluent Spanish.

Most of the officers licked their lips and shifted nervously in place. Others glanced quickly around before adjusting their grips on their weapons.

"From your reactions, I'd say two-thirds," answered Talanov over the thumping of the rotor blades. "What would you be doing right now if this were *your* daughter? Huh? You'd be doing the same thing. At least your daughters have you to protect them. This girl has me: the guy you've been trying to kill. So if you're going to shoot, then either do it or get out of my way, because I need to get to that hospital."

The officer standing directly in front of Talanov nodded a discreet salute and holstered his weapon.

"Sir, you'd better act now," whispered Barraza as other policemen joined in by holstering their pistols and raising their rifles.

Álvarez brought the bullhorn to his mouth. "Let Colonel Talanov through!" he yelled as a huge cheer went up from the crowd. "Form an escort! Clear the way!" he then shouted as policemen began clearing a corridor through the huge crowd that had gathered behind them. Other officers ran into the gridlocked Mediterranean Highway and got drivers to inch their cars forward. Still others cleared a path through the spectators all the way to the front door of the hospital while the news helicopter followed Talanov's progress from overhead. People everywhere were clapping and cheering.

With Noya's motionless body cradled in his arms, Talanov, Luis and Justine followed the pathway cleared for them. Through the crowd. Through the traffic. All the way to the sidewalk in front of the hospital, where a medical team in blue scrubs was waiting.

Talanov gently placed Noya on the gurney.

"We'll take it from here," said a doctor. "We'll get her into surgery for that bullet and run some tests to see what she's got."

Talanov grabbed the doctor by the wrist. "Run your tests later. I know what she's got."

"If this were the real thing, Colonel -- and I know you know what I'm talking about -- this girl would be dead right now. But it's not. And she's not. Hazmat confirmed a false alarm."

"It wasn't a false alarm, Doctor. I know who made the wretched stuff, and I killed the bastard who gave the wretched stuff to Noya. So if you don't give her an antidote as in *right now* . . . don't make me finish that sentence. Humor me. Just give it to her, okay?"

The doctor swallowed. "As soon as we're inside. I promise."

Talanov nodded his appreciation and stepped back while an attending physician inserted an IV of hydrating fluid into Noya's slender arm. A nurse placed an oxygen mask over her face while a second nurse laid a cool pack over her forehead. When everything was secured, they rushed her away.

With people still clapping and cheering, Talanov walked with Luis and Justine toward the hospital. By now, the news helicopter had landed on the roof and a camera crew had made its way down the elevator to the ground floor and was rushing toward him.

Álvarez materialized with two officers.

"We'll assist Colonel Talanov from here," Álvarez told Luis and Justine. He straightened his uniform as the camera crew approached. The accompanying officers took hold of the students' arms and started to escort them away.

"We aren't going anywhere," Justine replied, twisting away.

Added Luis, "Colonel Talanov needs a doctor and we're going to see that he gets one."

"I will make certain Colonel Talanov receives the best of care," responded Álvarez, flashing a smile of yellow teeth.

"As if we're going to believe you," said Justine. "You're the *guripa* who wanted him killed."

"Comandante," said Talanov appeasingly, "I'm grateful for your generous offer, but the truth is, I would not have made it this far without these two. Allow me the honor of completing the journey in their care."

With an appreciative smile, Talanov clasped Álvarez politely on the shoulder before continuing with Luis and Justine.

Ahead of them, a cameraman began filming.

Álvarez motioned for Barraza. "See to his admission and make sure that he remains overnight for observation. Approve whatever costs are involved and give no one -- especially Talanov -- any cause for alarm. Later tonight, when the commotion has died down and the media have gone, I want him shackled and taken to jail. In a week, the people will have forgotten he ever existed. Then we can show NATO how Spain deals with spies."

CHAPTER 30

Inside the hospital, with dozens of spectators gathered around, Talanov sat quietly in a wheelchair while being interviewed by a reporter. Standing next to him was Nurse Marmol, a rotund woman of fifty with unnaturally black hair. She was gently cutting away the blood-soaked shirt from his shoulder. Up at the admissions counter, Barraza filled out a sheaf of forms approving payment for Talanov's treatment.

While Nurse Marmol worked, Talanov introduced Luis and Justine to the reporter and recounted how they had helped him. When the reporter began speaking with them, Talanov asked the nurse how Noya was doing.

Marmol shrugged while looking at the wound. "This shoulder doesn't look good."

"Bullets tend to do that," remarked Talanov.

"Then maybe you shouldn't play with guns."

"Tell that to the other guy."

A man in blue scrubs approached. "I'm here to prep Colonel Talanov for surgery," he said.

Nurse Marmol looked up and saw an orderly standing in front of her.

Talanov looked up and saw Franco.

"Doctor *Babikov* is waiting," Franco said.

"Babikov?" asked Marmol with a frown. "Never heard of him."

"He's a consulting Russian physician. He insisted I bring Colonel Talanov to him at once."

"I do not know who this Doctor Babikov is," said Marmol, her glare still in place. "Wait here until I find out."

"What's going on?" asked Barraza.

"This orderly was just taking me to surgery," Talanov replied.

"I know nothing about this," said Marmol. "Which is why you're going to stay where you are until I find out what is going on. What is your name?"

"Franco."

Marmol pointed a scolding finger at Franco then turned toward the admissions counter, where a gray rotary phone was visible.

Barraza looked suspiciously at Franco.

"The reason she knows nothing," explained Talanov, motioning Barraza closer and speaking quietly, "is because of the, uh, *infection.* As you can imagine, no one can know about this. That's why this orderly needs to rush me to quarantine."

"Then I must go with you," said Barraza. "I am not to let you out of my sight."

"Okay, let's go," said Talanov. "If being locked in the infectious diseases ward won't bother you, it sure won't bother me. To tell you the truth, I'd appreciate the company."

"Infectious diseases ward? For how long?" asked Barraza.

"Shouldn't be more than -- what -- forty-eight hours?" asked Talanov, looking at Franco.

"Seventy-two, to be safe," Franco replied.

"Can you wait here a few minutes?" asked Barraza. "I need to call and ask."

"Sorry, Lieutenant," said Franco, "but the contagion latency period and subclinical lymphatics are way past the intrinsic incubation threshold for a potential carrier's margin of safety."

Barraza gave Franco a blank look.

"He may be *contagious,*" whispered Franco. "Which means we leave *right now.*"

"Yes, yes, of course," said Barraza.

"Meet you in the ward, then," said Talanov as Franco began pushing him toward a set of double doors that led into a wide corridor, where the elevator was located.

"One floor up, through the vacuum chamber at the far end of the building," said Franco.

Barraza nodded and watched Franco push Talanov through the double doors into the corridor.

Hurrying over to the admissions counter, Barraza saw Nurse Marmol drumming her fingers impatiently on the counter, having obviously been put on hold. Barraza watched Franco wheel Talanov into the elevator. Running a hand across his forehead anxiously, he glanced at his watch three times while pacing back and forth. Finally, he tapped Nurse Marmol on the shoulder and asked, "Will you be long?"

Marmol glared at Barraza, then furrowed her brow when she did not see Talanov and Franco. An instant later, the hospital chief of surgery came onto the line. Marmol refocused and asked him about a visiting Soviet doctor named Babikov.

"Never heard of him," said the chief of surgery. "What's this about?"

"He was brought in to help with Talanov."

"Talanov, I know about," said the chief of surgery. "Comandante Álvarez says we are to admit him for treatment but hold him overnight for the officers who will take him into custody. But Doctor Babikov? We have no such person."

Nurse Marmol slammed down the phone. "Where is he, where's Franco?" she yelled. She pushed by Barraza and stormed into the center of the foyer, where she stopped and turned in a full circle. "Where are they? Where did they go?"

"To quarantine," answered Barraza. "One floor up, end of the building, through the vacuum chamber."

"You *idiot!* We have no vacuum chamber up there! One floor up is *gastroenterology!*"

Marmol raced to the elevator while Barraza rushed outside and flagged down several officers.

"Call the Comandante!" he shouted. "You two, come with me. The rest of you, seal the building. Talanov is trying to escape."

The officers sprang into action.

Barraza stuck his hand in the elevator doors, which were in the process of closing, and they opened again to allow him to step in with his men. Already in the elevator, Marmol glared at him for a long moment before dismissing him with a disdainful huff.

One of the officer's walkie-talkies squawked and the officer brought it to his mouth. Álvarez had been patched through and was demanding to know what happened.

The officer handed the walkie talkie to Barraza, who filled him in. Álvarez responded with a scathing rebuke that brought a satisfied smile to Marmol's lips just as the doors opened on the floor above. She went immediately to the nurse's station while Barraza sent his men running from ward to ward.

"Scour the building and *find him!*" yelled Álvarez, the walkie-talkie broadcasting his voice along the sanitized linoleum corridor like a megaphone. "I want updates every ten minutes until he's apprehended. Take everyone who helped him into custody!"

"Yes, sir," squeaked Barraza, switching off the walkie talkie just as his men came running back to say Talanov and Franco were nowhere to be found.

"Did they see anyone in a wheelchair?" asked Barraza.

"There are people in wheelchairs everywhere," one of the men said. "But no one matching Talanov's description. However, several patients and two nurses asked if Talanov could stop by for a visit."

After mumbling a curse, Barraza called to make sure Talanov and Franco had not escaped the building. Officers manning the exits assured him they had not. He then called for additional personnel to help with the search before directing his men to the stairwells with orders to meet him on the floor above. He then glanced toward the nurse's station and saw Marmol and three nurses smirking. When he turned toward the elevator, he heard them giggle.

Moments later Barraza stepped out of the elevator on the floor above, where he went immediately to the nurse's station. He showed his badge and asked if anyone had seen Talanov.

"Talanov is *here?*" asked the nurse. "In our hospital -- here -- *tonight?*"

"Yes," answered Barraza. "We are looking for him now."

"Can you get me his autograph?" asked the nurse.

"Absolutely not. Talanov is a wanted man."

The nurse called out down the hall. "Everybody, come quick! Talanov is here, *in the building.*"

"You mean, *here,* on our *floor?*" came a chorus of excited replies.

"No!" snapped Barraza, "he is not. I mean, he may be, I don't know. That's what we're trying to find out."

"If he's not here on our floor, where is he? We want to see him before he goes."

"I *don't know* where he is. That's why I'm standing here asking if *you've* seen him."

"No need to be grouchy," said the nurse.

The walkie-talkie squawked again in Barraza's hand. It was Álvarez demanding an update.

Barraza groaned and told him they had not located Talanov yet. He then listened while the loud voice of Álvarez again chewed him up one side and down the other for his incompetence. Before signing off, Álvarez filled him in on some additional information they had learned about Talanov and the Americans.

The echo of footsteps drew Barraza's attention and he saw a team of four men hurrying toward him. He looked at them expectantly but they shook their heads.

After disconnecting with Álvarez, Barraza called downstairs and chewed everyone out for a variety of unclear reasons. He then told his men to search the remaining two floors above.

At the end of nearly fifteen minutes of intense searching, the answer was still the same: *Talanov was nowhere to be found.*

Barraza's walkie-talkie sounded again. Could Barraza get an urgent message to the Comandante, whose walkie-talkie was busy? Barraza asked what the message was, and what he heard brought a smile to his lips.

So when Álvarez called several minutes later, Barraza was ready.

"Comandante," he said after Álvarez blasted him again, "it does not matter how Talanov escaped the hospital. What matters is how he plans on leaving the country."

The suggestion made Álvarez pause.

Barraza said, "Let us start with what we know. We know, for instance, that Talanov is wounded and will require medical help."

"That much is obvious," growled Álvarez.

"Of course, sir. But he is known everywhere by now and will find it difficult if not impossible to obtain treatment without being recognized. May I suggest we alert all the hospitals and clinics?"

Álvarez grumbled his approval.

"We also know that Talanov had help from an orderly," Barraza continued. "No one fitting the orderly's description was known to be an employee of the hospital, so we are left to conclude the man was an imposter. Nurse Marmol described him as being Spanish."

"Which tells us nothing."

"Of course, sir. But with Talanov featuring so prominently in the news, including his escape from the hospital and his earlier pursuit by the Americans, an employee of the Gran Casino del Sol phoned to report how Talanov had been under surveillance there by the Americans. The employee's descriptions of the American team included two female agents named Bixler and Pilgrim, plus a male agent named Franco, whose description fits the one we have of the orderly. We also have a report filed by two of our officers about Agents Bixler and Pilgrim rescuing Talanov's injured KGB colleague from a mob of extremists, whereupon Agent Bixler was shot.

When I checked admissions here at the hospital, I discovered Agent Bixler had been admitted with two gunshot wounds. She is in critical condition and Agent Pilgrim is with her now. Agent Franco, however, is nowhere to be found, nor is Talanov's injured colleague. I have sent men to question Agent Pilgrim but I do not expect her to cooperate. Sir, I realize this is all very preliminary, but since time is of the essence, I suggest we focus our attention on the Americans. If they helped Talanov's KGB colleague, they may well be helping Talanov as well, and Agent Franco is nowhere to be found. A Nurse Marmol described him as a very dangerous looking man."

"Why would the Americans do such a thing? They hate the Soviets as much as my second wife hates my first."

"That we do not know, sir. We know only that a connection exists. Thanks to additional information received from the casino, we know the type of vehicle the Americans were driving and what its number plate was. The remaining question is *where* to look."

"Go on."

"I therefore concur with what you are no doubt thinking," said Barraza smoothly.

"Which is?"

"That we alert passport control at all border crossings, train stations and airports, as well as along the waterfront, especially those ports with Russian freighters getting ready to depart."

Barraza could hear Álvarez cover the mouthpiece of his phone in order to say something to someone. A discussion then took place that lasted nearly a full minute before Álvarez uncovered the mouthpiece again.

"The Soviet freighter, Providenija, is leaving Málaga in two hours," he said. "Get up there and see what you find."

"Comandante, there is no way I can search an entire freighter in two---"

"You can and you *will* Lieutenant Barraza or you will be *Corporal* Barraza by morning."

Barraza swallowed hard and squeaked a reply.

"You escorted him into the hospital," yelled Álvarez, "and *you* allowed him to vanish. So *do not* come back empty-handed. If you do, heads will roll, and I guarantee you one will be yours."

CHAPTER 31

The Spanish port of Málaga was normally a forty-five minute drive up the coast. But with traffic being so light this early in the morning and with speeds averaging eighty-five miles per hour, Barraza and his men arrived in just over twenty.

The pedigree of the port was certainly impressive: the Phoenicians were there as early as 1000BC. But after its rise over the centuries to become a major European port, Málaga found itself overshadowed by the northern industrial power-houses of Rotterdam and Hamburg, which in turn surrendered dominance to the Asian super-ports of Shanghai, Singapore and Hong Kong.

Looking from the city toward the sea, the port had two modest, triangular-shaped bays. In the left triangle were quays 1 and 2, and in the right triangle were quays 4, 5 and 6. The Providenija was berthed at Quay 6, on the inside of a small concrete peninsula projecting out into the water.

Accompanied by two officers of the SVA -- the *Servicio de Vigilancia Aduanera* -- the Spanish "Customs Surveillance Service" -- Barraza's motorcade of seven cars passed through the security gate and roared out onto the peninsula. Several tower cranes stood silently in the darkness of the quay, while the Providenija itself, which was moored with thick ropes, was festooned with lights.

A black van was parked at the foot of an aluminum gangway that angled up to the stern of the freighter. Barraza stopped near the rear door of the van and focused his flashlight on the license tag.

"The Americans," he said. "They are here."

Piling out of their vehicles, Barraza and his men followed two officers of the SVA up the noisy gangway onto the elevated quarterdeck of the ship, where four stories of superstructure rose above them. They stepped through a hatch and climbed up the flights of steel mesh steps to the top floor, where the ship's bridge was located. Positioned like a penthouse across the entire top of the superstructure, the bridge was the command center of the freighter. Windows looked out over the massive deck of the ship. On the flat roof of the bridge was a forest of antennae, radar and weather instruments. Inside, counters of radar screens, navigation equipment and controls were lit up with glowing lights. Charts and maps were laid out on a large square table.

Barraza barged in holding his badge up for everyone to see and demanded to speak with the captain.

"I'm the captain," growled a burly, bald-headed man. Dressed in bib coveralls and a stained white singlet, he had been studying a map of the Mediterranean with the pilot and helmsman.

Barraza told the captain they had a Customs warrant to search the ship. "Or," he added, "you can take us immediately to Colonel Talanov and Major Babikov and save us all a lot of time."

"I know of no such men," said the captain.

"Then you leave me no choice but to search the ship," answered Barraza.

"No one searches my ship," said the captain, who outweighed Barraza by a good sixty pounds and stood a full head taller. His neck was as thick as Barraza's thigh.

With the attitude of a Jack Russell taking on an ox, Barraza held up the warrant. "This allows me to do whatever I wish."

"Your paper means nothing," said the captain. "You are standing in the Soviet Union."

"And you're sitting in Spanish waters. Which means you're going nowhere until I say so."

The two men glared at one another for a long moment. It was a standoff, with Barraza's men and the two merchant marine officers wondering who would blink first.

"Talanov and Babikov. Where are they?" demanded Barraza.

"I told you. I do not know who they are."

"Whose vehicle is that on the wharf?"

"How would I know?"

"It's parked in front of your ship!"

"If it had been parked on a Soviet wharf, I would know. But it is parked on a *Spanish* wharf. You figure it out. If I had known it was there, I would have stripped it of parts."

Barraza ultimately won the contest of insults and wills, and each room in the ship's accommodation was thoroughly searched, including the captain's quarters. Every door and hatch were unlocked and opened. Visual inspections were made of the kitchen, TV room, clinic, lower decks, engine room and hold. Every corridor, crawlspace, storeroom, ladder, stairwell, cabinet, air duct, storage compartment and locker was further scrutinized. No potential hiding place was overlooked.

Talanov and Babikov were nowhere to be found.

As Barraza stood on the deck of the freighter gazing south toward the inky waters of the Mediterranean, he heard the banging of a halyard on an aluminum mast. Looking left toward the noise, he saw the silhouettes of numerous sailboats and powerboats moored on the far side of the bay. Farther to the south was a tiny harbor filled with more sailboats. Could Talanov and Babikov be hiding in one of those boats, waiting for the freighter to exit the port's narrow strait? In the darkness before dawn, it would be an easy task for a small craft to come alongside the slow-moving freighter and climb up a ladder that would be lowered for them.

Looking again at the van parked below on the wharf, Barraza realized he had fallen for Talanov's diversion. By convincing Franco to park his vehicle in plain sight near the freighter, he knew exactly what would happen: anyone following would assume they were hiding on board the freighter. Since they weren't, no amount of searching would produce any results and the ship would be cleared to sail, leaving the door open for a boarding at sea.

Barraza knew he had been tricked. Big time. Talanov had laid down the bait and he had pounced.

But as clever as Talanov had been, his little scheme had a glaring weakness: if they wanted to board this ship, sooner or later they would have to emerge.

And when they did, *he and his men would be waiting.*

CHAPTER 32

Several hours before dawn, three incidents occurred simultaneously.

First, the Providenija sailed pretty much on schedule. To be precise, it was an hour and seventeen minutes late, but it nevertheless departed Málaga with relative ease before setting a course east, toward the Aegean Sea, where it would pass through the Bosporus, the Sea of Marmara and the Dardanelles before entering the Black Sea, where it would angle northeast toward the deep-water port of Novorossiysk.

Having taken up positions at numerous observation points, Barraza and his officers watched the giant freighter glide past. Harbor authorities in powerboats accompanied the Providenija as far as fuel would allow while other of Barraza's men searched the marina. They went from boat to boat, knocking on hatches and windows, rousing occupants and otherwise doing their best to find Talanov and Babikov cowering in some hidden corner.

The ship captain saw Barraza's men scampering about like ants and gave them a long grinning blast on the horn. The bellow echoed across the water and washed abrasively over Barraza like salt spray.

The second incident occurred thirty miles to the southwest, in Marbella, where a group of nine weary ETA extremists shuffled along a darkened residential street near a local business district. They were laughing and passing around large bottles of locally-made sangria. In the lead was Paco, who finished the contents of one of the bottles and tossed it over his head, where it tumbled end-over-end through the air before smashing in the middle of the street.

The group heard a moan and stopped.

"What was that?" Paco asked.

The group reversed direction and fanned out to investigate. Paco and several of the others pulled out their *navajas* and flipped open the blades. The knives made metallic clicking sounds as the blades locked into place.

The group began searching for the source of the moan.

"*Ayúdame* . . . help . . . me," a woman's voice called out from beneath a truck.

"There's someone here," said one of the girls, kneeling and looking beneath the vehicle.

The men gathered around and saw the twisted shape of a woman trapped beneath the truck's muffler and fuel tank. One of her legs was bent beneath her at an impossible angle. Her head had been wrenched backward and her face was pressed against the inside of a tire. Dried blood from two bullet wounds had streaked her face and matted her short black hair.

Pocketing their knives, Paco and his men grabbed the bumper and lifted while the two girls, Inez and Tia, carefully dislodged the woman, who barely made a sound while being pulled out.

"My God, she's been *shot!*" exclaimed Inez as everyone gathered around. Inez slid her hands under the woman's head and elevated it slightly. She then tipped one of the sangria bottles to her lips. The liquid sloshed over her partially-closed mouth and ran down her face.

The woman jerked and coughed.

"*¿Quién eres tú?*" demanded Paco, asking who she was.

The woman groaned.

After a long moment, Paco repeated his question.

With labored breaths, the woman slowly opened her eyes and looked up at each of the silhouetted faces staring down at her.

"Why isn't she talking?" someone asked.

"She's been *shot,* you moron," said Inez.

"Leave her as she is," remarked one of the men. "She'll only slow us down."

"She needs help," Inez replied.

"Shove her back under the truck," said another.

"We can't just leave her here!"

"We sure as hell aren't taking her with us."

"What's she doing stuffed under a truck, anyway?" asked another. "If the cops show up, we'll get blamed."

"You're right, come on, let's go," said Paco.

"My name . . . is Xin Li," Sofia whispered. "And I have money."

"Check her pockets," said Paco.

Two of the men rifled through the pockets of Sofia's torn and bloodied fatigues.

"Nothing," they said. "She's got nothing."

"What do you mean, you have money?" said Paco, kneeling beside Sofia and grabbing her by the face. "Where is it?"

"Help . . . me," Sofia repeated.

"Tell me or you die!" commanded Paco. He pulled out his *navaja,* clicked open the blade and rotated it in front of Sofia's face.

"Briefcase," Sofia whispered.

"Where is it? How much?" demanded Paco.

"Help . . . me," she said again.

"You'll get help when we get that money," Paco replied, lowering his face to within inches of Sofia and looking her over. A wrinkle formed on his brow. "You look familiar," he said.

"My name . . . Xin Li."

"I know you," said Paco. "You're that bitch in the Ferrari!" He pointed to the scab left on his forehead by the butt of Talanov's Makarov. "Remember this?"

"Talanov . . . shot me," said Xin Li.

Paco grabbed Xin Li by the throat. "And I will finish what he started unless you give me your money. Then you will tell me where your boyfriend is. I have a score to settle. Now, *where is it?"*

He again flashed his knife in front of Xin Li's face.

If killers have a weakness, it is in the blind spot created by their weapons. One can easily become careless with the unquestioned advantage a weapon provides.

It was an old adage taught to Xin Li -- Sofia -- ten years earlier by the same *dǎoshī* who had taught it to young Aleksandr Talanov six years before that. Hence, it was understandable that Paco felt in complete command. The woman lying on the pavement next to him had been shot twice. Her breathing was raspy and shallow. Her left leg and arm were broken. Her face was swollen and raw. She could barely talk and had barely moved. She posed no threat.

Thus, it came as a complete and very brief shock when Xin Li grabbed Paco's hand -- the hand grasping his *navaja* -- and yanked it across the side of his throat. The action was so clean and quick that Paco hardly felt it. In fact, Paco's first thought was that Xin Li had tried unsuccessfully to grab his knife away from him.

He started to backhand her when he felt something warm and sticky running down his chest. Seconds later, the remainder of the group was standing around Paco, who lay writhing on the pavement, with his life draining onto the street in a spreading pool of blood.

"Help . . . me. I pay," Xin Li whispered.

Inez said to the others, "Paco was a prick and you know it. Come on, she needs our help."

Slowly, the group gathered around and gently picked up Xin Li.

"We'll take her to my house," Inez said. "It's only three blocks from here."

The third incident occurred in the open waters of the Mediterranean thirty miles to the southeast of Málaga. Talanov and Zak were standing beside Captain John Krell on a small landing outside the bridge of the cargo ship Robert Dole. The crisp, pre-dawn wind blew their hair in erratic gusts as the freighter rose and fell on the swells.

"Thank you for welcoming us, Captain," said Talanov.

"Glad to help," said Krell. "When Donna called and said you needed a ride, I didn't think twice. She and Glenda are two of the best, and I mean *best*. Glenda can be a little fiery at times, but that's why she's so good at what she does. Skeptical as hell. Loyal to a fault. But once you prove yourself, she'll give her life protecting you."

"She nearly did," said Zak. "I owe her my life."

Krell smiled sadly and nodded.

"Any word on how she is?"

"Argumentative," answered Krell. "And pissed off. Donna's with her now, trying to keep her in bed."

"Did she tell you who we were?" asked Talanov.

"She filled me in."

"Then as an American you know there could be trouble if you get caught helping a couple of Russians."

Krell waved that away. "The crew and I had actually been following events on the radio, and for a while I thought they had you. Man, that took some guts doing what you did, standing up to the cops that way. So when I got Donna's call that you were on your way, I was happy as a pig in mud."

Talanov looked over at Zak. "Happy as a pig in mud. Bixler would definitely like that one."

"Clichés are clichés for a reason," laughed Krell. "I can hear her saying it now."

They all laughed.

Talanov asked, "How did she manage to get that news chopper to give us a ride?"

"You've got Franco to thank for that. Donna said he sweet-talked the reporter. Made some promises she's not sure he can keep."

"Good on him for trying," said Zak. "She was cute. Daniela something-or-other."

"What I want to know is how you gave those cops the slip," said Krell.

"When we got Bixler to the hospital, Pilgrim told me to

get up to the rooftop. When I asked what for, she said I needed to trust her. So I did."

Krell looked at Talanov. "And you?"

"After trying so long to kill me, the Spanish police became *very* chummy to the point of offering to pay for any and all medical treatment I may require, which of course meant I would be kept overnight for observation and rest. No need to guess what they were planning for me once the crowds had dispersed and the media had gone home. I would be taken into custody and no one would ever see me again."

"How did you get away?"

"Franco, who showed up dressed as an orderly with this wild story about needing to get me to quarantine. You Americans are an interesting lot."

Krell laughed. "Backatcha, my friend. So Franco took you up to the rooftop and put you on the chopper?"

Talanov nodded. "And here we are."

"What amazes me is how you figured out what the Spanish cops were planning," said Krell. "How did you figure that out?"

"The crickets," Talanov replied.

Krell responded with a look of confusion.

Talanov recounted his time in a monastery as a boy and how his *dǎoshī* had taught him to see and hear what others do not, especially when words were being used to distract or deceive. He recounted how he was taken by his *dǎoshī* to the edge of a cliff at the base of Khan Tengri, barefooted, deep in the night, in the absence of any moon. One wrong step and he would fall over two hundred feet to his death.

"My *dǎoshī* said, 'Listen to the chorus.' When I asked what that meant, he said, 'You cannot see but you can hear, and even when you hear, you must also smell, and taste and feel.' He then taught me to question even what he said. 'If I say, "Go left," you must stop and listen and decide if this is a wise course of action. Listen to the voice of the crickets. Go where they guide you. Crickets do not lie because they are many, not one. Listen to the chorus. They will not lead you astray.'"

"So," said Talanov in conclusion, "I learned to walk where I could quite literally hear the crickets. No sound meant no crickets, which meant an absence of solid ground . . . a precipice. Even the smell of a precipice is different. Rocks and soil smell one way. Open space another. It also feels different on your skin. Mountain updrafts versus the directional difference of wind blowing over a terrain. The chorus."

Krell nodded but Talanov could tell he did not understand.

"One moment the police were trying to kill me," explained Talanov. "The next moment they were smiling and helpful. Why the sudden change? Because people were watching. So I listened not to what the police were saying, but to what they weren't."

The door to the bridge opened and the pilot leaned out and said, "You and your friends will want to hear this."

"What is it?" asked Krell.

The pilot glanced nervously at Talanov.

"Spit it out, Beau. What's going on?"

"The girl -- Noya Gorev -- has died."

CHAPTER 33

Standing on the bridge with Krell surrounded by consoles full of electronic equipment, Talanov and Zak listened to the news reports streaming over the various radio and shortwave channels. He even watched a faint black-and-white television interview from a station in Palma, where Pilgrim and a bandaged Bixler were shown leaving the hospital surrounded by a crowd of reporters. Without removing her sunglasses in the glare of camera lights, Bixler paused to make a brief statement about the bravery of young Noya Gorev and how she had lost her valiant fight against a virulent form of influenza.

Talanov noticed the way Bixler spat out the word, influenza. How she clenched her jaw and angled her head, looking down and to the side with measured breathing, a sign of controlled but deeply-seated anger. When asked by reporters about the whereabouts of Talanov, she excused herself and left.

Bixler's body language told the obvious, that the story had been a lie. Noya had *not* died of the flu although Bixler had been ordered to say so. The reason was equally obvious: to quell any lingering fears about anthrax. Bixler was one of the few people this side of the Iron Curtain who knew the truth, and Bixler was being gagged. Talanov could tell she was angry, but orders were orders, regardless of the truth.

Welcome to my world, he thought.

Leaving the lighted bridge for the cleansing abrasion of some sea spray, Talanov descended the flight of metal steps and thought about someone he rarely allowed himself to think about, the memory was so painful. He saw himself as a boy of twelve lying doubled-up on the grass near an ancient peach tree, sobbing and bleeding and holding his stomach from being repeatedly kicked by the three Chinese boys standing around him. They were laughing and calling him *Lèishuĭ* -- teardrops. The boys then turned to the twelve year-old Chinese girl standing nearby. Long wisps of shiny black hair framed the sides of her face. The rest was tied in a sloppy ponytail near the top of her shoulders.

One of the boys walked over and grabbed her by the chin. "If *Lèishuĭ* interferes again, I will break his arm," he told her before nodding to his friends, who began kicking Alex again.

A shout from a monastery balcony sent the boys scurrying off through the trees, and soon Alex's *dǎoshī*, a bald-headed old man with powder blue eyes and a gangly white beard, was bent over Alex with a damp cloth infused with aromatic herbs. The girl remained standing nearby.

The *dǎoshī* knew the girl's name -- Zhao Ting -- but he was the only one who did. The use of names was forbidden at *Lóngshù*.

"You must never let them see you cry, young *Xuěbào*," the *dǎoshī* told Alex in Russian. "In doing so you tell them, 'This is how you can wound me.'"

Xuěbào meant "snow leopard" in Chinese.

Alex kept sobbing and did not reply.

"He tried to protect me," said Zhao Ting in Chinese.

The *dǎoshī* looked thoughtfully at Alex.

"Why did he do that?" asked Zhao Ting. "Since the first day he arrived, you have made us fight each other. I have beaten him every time."

"And yet he is the one who protects you?"

"Yes, *Dǎoshī*. I am the lowest in the group, the only girl, and when the boys pushed me down, he defended me."

"Has he spoken to you?" asked the *dǎoshī*.

"No."

The *dǎoshī* scrutinized Zhao Ting with a frown.

"I speak the truth," she replied. "He has said nothing."

"Have you spoken with him?"

"No, *Dǎoshī.*"

"And yet he persists in defending you."

"I do not know why. This is the fourth time he has tried, and every time the boys circle him, kicking and punching until he goes down. Then they attack without mercy. The boys push me on purpose, knowing what he will do."

The *dǎoshī* continued staring thoughtfully at Alex, who was lying motionless on the grass with the damp cloth still covering his face. His sobbing had stopped and his chest moved up and down slowly.

Suddenly, the *dǎoshī* stood. "Every tree must be pruned," he said. "Without pruning, a tree bears no fruit."

The *dǎoshī* brought a hand to his mouth and uttered a single word -- sharply, like a gunshot -- barked more than shouted. His voice carried on the gentle wind rustling the leaves in the peach grove. Seconds later, Zhao Ting heard voices and looked to see the three older boys running toward them through the trees. They were barefooted, each in his karate uniform, his *gi.*

"What are you doing?" she asked.

"By speaking, young *Xuěbào* has broken the rules."

"He did *not* speak!" insisted Zhao Ting. "You forbade us to speak, and we have not -- *he* has not -- not even when we fought."

"Ahhh, but he *has,*" the *dǎoshī* replied. "He spoke through his actions, which is why I had the boys push you, to find out what his actions would say."

"You *made* them do this to me?"

"To see what he would do. He responded as I thought, which is why young Snow Leopard must now be pruned. You will never see him again."

"But *why?*" Zhao Ting cried out.

"Take her and go," the *dǎoshī* told the boys.

Two of them grabbed her by the arms. When Zhao Ting screamed, Alex ripped the cloth from his face. When

---

Zhao Ting saw him stand, she broke away from one of the boys with a lightning roundhouse kick to the face and a back-kicking the other in the stomach. When the boys topped backward, she sprinted to Alex's side.

Without making eye contact, Alex and Zhao Ting looked toward the same clump of grass in front of them and smiled, knowing they had bonded without touching, without speaking.

The *dǎoshī* rubbed his chin thoughtfully.

The leader of the boys chastised the other two and commanded them to their feet. He then cast his angry glare on Zhao Ting. "Did I not tell you what would happen if *Lèishuǐ* tried interfering again? Too bad he did not learn his lesson."

The conversation had been in Chinese and Alex did not speak Chinese. But he understood expression and body language and these told him what he needed to know.

Alex assumed his fighting stance and Zhao Ting did the same, ready to fight beside him, knees bent, body balanced, feet spread and positioned one forward and one back, fists near the face, ready to strike.

Without breaking eye contact with his opponents, Alex held up a hand. It was a sign for Zhao Ting to hold her position. When she lowered her hands, Alex approached the three boys. Using his hands -- pointing first at the boys and himself and slapping his fist in his palm -- he said, "This contest is between you and me." He then pointed at Zhao Ting and shook his head.

"No!" Zhao Ting said, jumping to his side and glaring at the three boys looking angrily at her, especially the two she had kicked. "If you fight him, you fight me."

Alex looked at his *dǎoshī* and said, "I want these three to know the sting of defeat. By *my* hand, not hers, will they taste the salt of their own blood."

The *dǎoshī* translated what Alex had said and the leader of the boys grinned.

Alex said, "Give me your word she will not be harmed -- will not be touched -- ever again."

The *dǎoshī* nodded and translated.

The three boys nodded.

Taking Zhao Ting by the hand, Alex led her to a cool grassy patch beneath the branches of one of the ancient peach trees. Pausing to look down at the grass at their feet, her hand still in his, he waited until she looked down at the same patch before smiling and squeezing her hand. Releasing her, he returned to his position opposite the three boys, where he bowed and again resumed his fighting stance, one twelve year-old boy against three fourteen year-old boys, who began circling for the kill, just as they had in each of their previous fights.

But this time Alex began circling them in a wide elliptical pattern of his own, throwing them off balance. In every other contest, he had fought them from a stationary position at the center of the group. This time he was a moving target. The boys' impulse was to contain him as before, thereby forcing them to run in an even wider circle.

But scrambling to contain their moving target not only split the boys' focus, it isolated the boys from one another, allowing Alex to spring on one of them with a flying sidekick that caught him in the face. The boy stumbled forward and fell, where he lay moaning and dazed with a bleeding nose.

Although Alex was nearer to the second boy -- the one Zhao Ting had back-kicked in the stomach -- he turned and sprinted toward the leader. The sudden move caused the second boy to sprint after him.

The second boy was closing in quickly when Alex abruptly changed direction with a quick hop to the side and a spinning front kick to the second boy's jaw. The boy's teeth clacked together and his head snapped back before his knees buckled and toppled facedown onto the grass with a bloody mouth.

The remaining boy -- the leader -- stared with disbelief at his two friends lying on the grass. He then looked at Alex striding toward him.

"We did only what we were ordered to do," the fourteen

year-old said, his hands held up in surrender. "The *dǎoshī* told us to do it."

The older boy was speaking Chinese and Alex did not know what he was saying.

Except for one word.

Dǎoshī.

Alex stopped a few feet away and narrowed his eyes. *"Dǎoshī?"* he asked.

The fourteen year-old nodded and pointed toward Zhao Ting standing beneath the peach tree. When Alex instinctively looked, the fourteen year-old leaped toward him and kicked.

But Alex had already read the involuntary warning signs broadcasted by the older boy -- his shifting posture, the clenching of fists, the quick sucking in of a breath -- and spun away to come up under the boy's extended foot, where Alex grabbed him by the ankle, yanked to the side and pulled the fourteen year-old's feet from under him. When he hit the ground, Alex dropped beside him and hammered an elbow into his thigh, splitting the muscle.

The boy screamed and grabbed his leg.

Alex then punched him in the nose to give him a taste of his own blood before rolling up onto his feet.

But when he turned, Zhao Ting and his *dǎoshī* were gone.

Refocusing as the early morning spray off the Mediterranean stung him in the face, Talanov remembered racing to the monastery, where his *dǎoshī* was waiting in the Spartan main hall, flanked by two other mentors, both Chinese and both of indeterminate age. The hardwood floor echoed the slap of Alex's bare feet as he ran in and stopped.

"Where is she?" he demanded.

"You broke the rules, young *Xuěbào.*"

"I did not. You said, no names . . . not to speak. And we didn't."

"The voice of actions speaks louder than words."

"You *told* them to push her down. You *wanted* me to defend her."

"How does he know this, Master?" one of the two flanking mentors asked. "He does not speak Chinese."

Talanov pointed accusingly at the mentor. "See, *he* knows. And he's worried that I know. No, I don't speak your stupid language. But his actions speak louder than *his* words. I *know* what you did. *Where is she?"*

"You are angry, *Xuěbào?"*

"Yes, I'm angry! I did what you wanted me to do -- what you *trained* me to do -- and now you're punishing me. What kind of a *dǎoshī* are you?"

The mentors flanking the *dǎoshī* stepped forward with clenched fists but the *dǎoshī* held them back.

The *dǎoshī* said, "I have spoken. She is gone."

"You're lying."

"You are challenging me on this?"

"I can see it in your eyes. You think I'm some dumb kid, but I know truth when I see it, and I don't see it in you. Besides, isn't that what you taught me to do out there on that cliff -- question what you say . . . listen to the crickets? The crickets may not lie but *you sure do."*

The *dǎoshī* did not reply.

Alex turned away in disgust. "Some friend you turned out to be."

The eighty-four year-old *dǎoshī* sprang on Alex and flipped him with a quick maneuver that slammed him down onto the hardwood floor. The sound of Alex hitting the floor echoed in the emptiness of the room.

"You think because I teach you that I am your friend?" the *dǎoshī* asked, pinning Alex with a forearm across his throat, two rigid fingers pronged over his eyes. "I am your *mentor,* not your friend."

"I don't care what you say, anymore," said Alex, barely able to speak because of the arm across his throat, "so go ahead and beat the crap out of me if you want. When I get up, I'm going to find her."

The *dǎoshī* stared hard at Alex for a moment before rolling effortlessly up onto his feet.

And that's when Alex heard the faint sound of sobbing.

"I'm coming for you!" he shouted. He scrambled to his feet but the *dǎoshī* backfisted him in the face, knocking him to the floor with a split in the skin above his eye.

"Don't let them take you, I'm coming!" yelled Alex, wiping the blood from his face and climbing to his knees only to have the *dǎoshī* kick him in the stomach.

Alex collapsed, gasping for air.

He then heard the rattle of a bicycle.

He tried getting up again.

The *dǎoshī* darted behind him, flipped him onto the floor and punched him in the back of the head.

Everything went black.

More sea spray hit Talanov in the face and broke his reverie. He was standing at the very tip of the bow, staring out at the open water ahead. The sun was shining and the morning sky was clear. Beneath him, the sea was churning and foaming as the freighter pushed onward through the water.

A thought then hit him: maybe Bixler had lied to the reporters. Maybe Noya was alive and she was covering it up. Maybe the CIA had helped Noya disappear to America -- to protect her from anyone wanting to kidnap her back to the Soviet Union -- *people like him* -- in the same way the news helicopter had helped him and Zak disappear. Maybe, just maybe . . .

He gripped the railing angrily. There was no 'maybe,' and he knew it. There was no hope. In spite of her sunglasses, he had seen the look on Bixler's face. He had seen her constrained anger and resentment. If Noya were really alive, Bixler would not have shown the emotions she had. She would have been analytical and detached in her statement about Noya's death, like a politician shoveling bullshit to a gullible public. As it was, she was seething and bitter.

Talanov's thoughts turned a final time to the girl whose name he never knew. He remembered telling her that he was coming for her, and he had tried, but in the end he had been powerless to do so. He remembered running to the gate and looking down the winding dirt road into the valley below. But there was no sign of her or a bicycle. He even ran down that road for more than a mile but stopped when he realized she was truly gone, and he did not speak Chinese, nor did he have any idea where they had taken her. He did not know what her name was, or where she lived or how to begin looking. So he stood there knowing his only choice was let her go, and to this day, he had no idea what ultimately happened to her, his first and only friend, his first and only love. He could still see her deep, dark eyes framed by that long, shaggy hair that was always bunched up in some kind of a rat's nest of a knot. When they were sparring and she was kicking and punching and knocking the wind out of him, her eyes seemed to smile with affection.

The voice of actions speaks louder than words.

That is what his *dǎoshī* had seen and that is what his *dǎoshī* had wanted: for him to care about the girl whose name he did not know, so that when she was taken from him, a permanent scar would remain.

Talanov remembered wanting to cry that day. But he did not. Instead, he shoved her memory away just as he shoved his *dǎoshī* away. The one person he cared about most had been ripped away from him by the only *other* person he cared about -- his *dǎoshī* -- who had turned on him like the weather of Khan Tengri, which lures you onto its slopes with its majestic, friendly red afternoon glow, only to trap and kill you.

For a while, he tried hating her. It was no use. How can you hate someone who makes you so happy? He just hated the ache that he felt now that she was gone. He hated the ache he felt when he remembered her shy smile and laughing eyes, or that tangle of silky black hair falling in straggly wisps around her face. He hated wanting so desperately to find her but knowing he couldn't. And before leaving the monastery, he vowed never to let anyone make him feel so unhappy and lost again.

And in that moment, *ledyanoĭ chelovek* -- the "ice man" -- was born.

Yes, it took every bit of strength that he had not to let them see him cry. And he didn't, nor had he cried since -- ever -- not once.

Until now.

Standing alone on the bow of the freighter, Talanov grabbed the railing with both hands and let the tears run down his face. Years ago he had been powerless to go after the girl whose name he never knew, just as he had been powerless this time to save Noya. He had tried desperately to find Melissa. He had pushed himself to limits he didn't know he had. He had tried everything and still he had failed.

And a young girl who was just beginning to catch a glimpse of what life could be was dead.

CHAPTER 34

With the early morning lights of Marseille reflecting off the water in fluid ripples, Talanov and Zak stood beside Krell as the harbor pilot guided the Robert Dole expertly toward a floodlit wharf. On their right was the northern tip of a thirty-foot-high breakwater that was nearly four miles long. It stood protectively between the open sea and the numerous commercial docks and marinas of Marseille. On their left were several giant tower cranes, a number of long low warehouses and several yards full of steel containers. Adorned with lights, two of the tower cranes motored slowly along the wharf on steel tracks.

Krell knew how to sneak Talanov and Zak past the customs officials, and within minutes they were standing among the shadows and sounds of the waterfront: the fuss of seagulls, the drum and groan of containers being moved, the whine of gears and the screech of steel as a freight train made its way off into the darkness.

"If ever you need another ride, you be sure and look me up," said Krell.

"Thank you, Captain," said Talanov, extending his hand.

Krell shook hands with Talanov and Zak before pointing toward a pair of warehouses with forklifts moving in and out of large gaping doorways. A trail of workers were entering one of the warehouses. The morning shift was arriving. He said, "Go between those buildings and across the parking lot. There's a gap in the fence to the left of those tower lights.

Directly beyond are the tracks. Cross them and angle up toward those cars moving along *Chemin du Littoral,* where there's a lot of bars and bistros. From there, you can flag down a cab or hoof it into the city."

After final handshakes, Talanov and Zak made their way past the warehouses, through the parking lot and across the tracks. They stuck to the dark patches between the tower lights so as not to attract attention. A damp sea breeze surrounded them with the smells of fish and salt.

Within fifteen minutes, they had reached *Chemin du Littoral,* a two-lane street that curved along the base of a hill. The street was already busy with early morning traffic and Talanov and Zak waited for a break before crossing to the other side, where a string of bistros and bars stretched in both directions. Built above these small establishments were apartments that had been stair-stepped into the face of the hill. The flat roof of one residence was the patio of the apartment above it, and so on up the hill. Lights were on in a few of their windows but most were still dark.

Some of the bars and bistros were just opening their doors. Aproned kitchen staff scrubbed sidewalks with soapy water and stiff brooms. Others were still open for the early-morning shift workers heading home. The music spilling out of their doorways was a mix of accordion, Edith Piaf, Jacques Brel and eighties pop. Drifting out of those same doorways were the smells of fried food, cigarettes and beer.

The two men walked along in silence. Talanov had his hands in his pockets and his posture was slumped.

"Thinking about Noya?" asked Zak.

Talanov was actually thinking of La Tâche, the man Donna Pilgrim had said he should call at the American Embassy in London. La Tâche was obviously CIA, adopting as he had the codename of a famous French wine, which meant he should think of adopting a cover name as well if he was seriously considering giving La Tâche a call. The problem as to whether or not he should make the call was this: was there too much distance between him, a KGB colonel, and the CIA for a working relationship to ever be possible? Or were they too much alike? Was the CIA any better than the KGB? The CIA had their own kill squads and dirty secrets, just as the KGB did, and yet if anyone could help him stand up for the Noyas of this world, it was America. And only the CIA possessed the muscle and resources to make things happen the way he knew they needed to happen. And yet if he got caught phoning the CIA -- if it somehow reached Moscow that he had done so -- his life would be over. Not that they hadn't already tried. Still, he was just not sure phoning La Tâche was worth the risk.

So Zak's question about Noya came as a welcome relief. In fact, he took it as a sign that he had been thinking in the wrong direction. Forget La Tâche. There are other ways.

Talanov looked over at his friend and smiled. "Noya was an extraordinary girl," he said. "I never once heard her complain. In spite of everything she suffered, she never once complained."

They walked past several men staggering out of a bar.

"And smart, too," Talanov continued. "You wouldn't believe how smart she was. She *loved* Sikorsky."

"The aircraft designer?"

Talanov nodded. "Knew all about him. How he made a small rubber-band-powered helicopter when he was twelve. How he emigrated from Russia to America after World War I. How he designed and developed a number of helicopters and fixed wing aircraft, as well as a propeller-powered sleigh."

A long moment of silence passed while Talanov smiled at her memory.

He said, "Did you know Sikorsky also wrote a book called *The Message of The Lord's Prayer?*"

"He wrote a book on prayer?"

"And another one called, *The Invisible Encounter.* Sikorsky was an engineer, a man with a scientist's brain who was also a devout Christian."

"Is that so hard to believe?"

Talanov thought about the simple prayer for help he had breathed back in Marbella. He thought about the police car he had stolen and all the punishment it had taken in his desperate race to save Noya. How it kept going and going and going, much as he had in the face of everything thrown against him.

"I guess not," he confessed with a sigh.

"Besides, who are we to argue with Igor Sikorsky?" said Zak with a grin.

Talanov chuckled and looked back out to sea. "Gorev told me the only time he saw Noya smile is when she talked about Sikorsky and helicopters. That's why he wanted to defect: so Noya could follow her dream. Like Sikorsky, to aim for the sky."

Zak did not reply.

"I killed her dream, Zak."

"You weren't the one who jabbed her with that syringe."

"It never would have happened if I hadn't tracked them down. She didn't deserve that. She deserved to fly helicopters and get married and have kids and grow old with dozens of grandkids running around."

"Quit torturing yourself. This is precisely the reason we are trained not to care. To prevent us from going through what you're going through now."

"Do we not violate this training ourselves?" asked Talanov. "Look at us, you and me, and all we do for each other. We're like brothers."

"Sometimes, you think too much."

"And you know I'm right."

"And *you* are forgetting Gorev's culpability in what happened. He subjected his family to the risks of his defection. He knew we would come after him."

"And they knew I'd find him. Were counting on it, in fact. And those same people ordered me killed. I have no idea who *'they'* are, but they somehow convinced Kravenko to put Sofia in charge without telling me. And she nearly pulled it off. She had me in her sights but made the mistake of shooting

Noya first. If it had been the other way around -- had she shot me first -- I'd be dead, too. But Sofia wanted me to see Noya die."

"What happened?"

"After Sofia shot Noya -- I thought she'd killed her, and we were fighting for possession of the gun -- I decided to crash the car into the side of a building and kill us both. I didn't care about me. All I cared about was killing Sofia. Then I heard Noya cough. So I kept fighting Sofia for the gun. I won. She didn't. Unfortunately, in spite of everything, in the end I couldn't save the one person who truly deserved to live."

Directly ahead, a truck was parked in front of a café and a deliveryman was wheeling five crates of wine on a two-wheel dolly. Dressed in gray overalls and a t-shirt, the deliveryman looked to be in his sixties and walked with a limp.

The café was fronted by a patio enclosed by a wrought iron railing decorated with colored lights. Small tables filled the patio. At this early hour, all of the tables were empty save one that was occupied by a young couple. The girl was sitting in the boy's lap and had her arms around his neck. On the table in front of them was a wine bottle, two glasses and a basket of bread.

Approaching a step, the deliveryman turned the dolly and prepared to pull it up the step. When he did, he tripped.

The deliveryman managed to hold the dolly upright although a case of wine slid off and smashed on the sidewalk. The box split open and spilled wine and broken glass. Several unbroken bottles rolled down the walk.

Talanov dashed over to the deliveryman and helped him stand. *"Êtes-vous blessé?"* he asked, inquiring if the deliveryman were hurt. The deliveryman said his ego was hurt more than anything else. He hobbled to a chair and sat.

The owner of the café came rushing out. *"Imbécile! Stupide!"* he cried out, throwing his hands in the air. "Who will clean up this mess?"

"Calm down, Cheval, you are ready to burst like a sausage," the deliveryman said.

"Maladroit! I do not know why I put up with you!" With a string of curses, Cheval stormed back inside.

By now, Zak had gathered up the unbroken bottles and brought them to the table. The deliveryman thanked Zak, who went inside to get a broom.

"The husband of my sister," the deliveryman said of Cheval while Talanov retrieved a metal trashcan near the door and began picking up glass. "I introduced them. He has never forgiven me."

Talanov smiled and kept picking up glass.

"Please, my friend, no more," the deliveryman said, wincing while trying to stand.

Talanov moved quickly to steady the deliveryman and help him back into his chair.

"Thank you," the deliveryman said. "Some coffee and a bite to eat and I will be good as new."

Talanov went back to picking up glass.

"You are not very talkative, *monsieur,*" the deliveryman remarked.

"Long day," replied Talanov in French.

The deliveryman nodded just as Zak emerged from the café with a broom and a dustpan.

"I sweep, you scoop," Zak said in Russian.

The deliveryman raised an eyebrow at the two men while Zak began sweeping up glass.

"Soviet?" the deliveryman asked.

Talanov did not reply.

"Cheval, three *Croque Monsieur,*" the deliveryman shouted, ordering butter-fried sandwiches of ham, gruyere cheese and eggs. To Talanov: "One must eat."

With an appreciative smile, Talanov knelt and allowed Zak to sweep the broken glass into the dustpan.

When they were finished, the deliveryman nodded his thanks.

A few minutes later sandwiches were served and Talanov took out some cash.

"Put that away," the deliveryman said with a wave of his hand. "You have spared me the wrath of Cheval and that deserves a sandwich."

Talanov chuckled and nodded.

"By the way," added the deliveryman, "if ever you pass this way again, I live above the café, up there, on the top floor. Stop by for a glass of wine. You may be interested to know I have a younger sister, Marie-Paule, who is *very* pretty."

Talanov laughed.

The deliveryman shook hands with Talanov and Zak, then handed Talanov one of the bottles of wine Zak had rescued earlier. "Until next time," he said.

Talanov thanked the man.

Before leaving, he paused to read the label. When he did, he almost dropped the bottle.

La Tâche.

CHAPTER 35

With the sun still low in the eastern sky, Talanov and Zak walked slowly along *Chemin du Littoral* eating their sandwiches. Cars sped past them going both directions. Eddies of exhaust mixing with the sounds and smells of the waterfront.

Stuffing the remainder of the *Croque Monsieur* into his mouth, Talanov looked at the wine bottle he had been carrying. "Do you believe in coincidence?" he asked.

"I guess, sometimes," answered Zak.

Talanov kept staring at the bottle. "They tried to kill me, Zak. I gave my life for what I *thought* we stood for and this is how they repay me."

"Did I not warn you about being too good at what you do?"

"Since when is that a sin?"

"When you can't be bought. In a corrupt system -- and ours *is* a corrupt system -- such actions place a target on your back. The question is, what do we do?"

"You may not want to know what I'm thinking."

"If you're thinking what I hope you're thinking, then the question isn't whether or not I'm with you, but what took you so long."

Talanov laughed before turning serious. "What I'm thinking may get us killed, because when a government forgets why it's there -- for the safety and prosperity of its people -- then it's time for that government to go."

"What do we do first, Colonel?" asked Zak.

"I may have a target on my back, but whoever put it there won't try anything right away. We saved Moscow's ass by stopping Sofia from selling that anthrax -- from allowing word to leak out about *Biopreparat* -- so we'll use the protection this affords to bring them down."

Traffic noise along *Chemin du Littoral* made conversation difficult so they cut left down a grassy embankment, across a feeder street and up the opposite embankment toward a bridge spanning several train tracks. It was an ugly corridor of brown rock, wires, rusting electrical poles, signs and posts with colored lights. A few items of trash were blowing like tumbleweeds in the cold ocean winds. On the other side of the tracks, which had been cut into the side of a bluff, was a retaining wall twenty feet high. Beyond the wall were some trees and houses with red tile roofs.

They crossed the bridge and descended into a maze of curving streets that were walled and narrow. The feeling was claustrophobic and shabby, with unimaginative apartment blocks shoved against plastered houses that had been fitted onto the tiniest parcels of land. Stretching to the east was an undulating carpet of more shabbiness.

The street they were on was lined with garage doors, trash cans and cars. Between two of the cars was a phone booth. It was not one of the pretty bright red ones found in London. This one was unpolished metal with large glass windows and graffiti on the door. In a small panel near the top was the word, *téléphone*.

"Got any coins?" asked Talanov.

"You've got to be kidding."

"Black Knife?"

Zak lifted the leg of his fatigues and slid his NR-40 out of its sheath.

Less than two minutes later, one thousand kilometers to the north, a telephone rang. The number was unlisted and was manned twenty-four hours by a rotating team of female CIA operations officers who each sounded like a sweet gray-haired little granny. Advanced software identified the incoming number, which was also recorded. If the caller did not present a current password or ask for the right individual, the caller would be told that he or she had reached a wrong number.

"Hello?" the on-duty granny answered in a shaky voice.

Talanov asked for La Tâche.

Granny asked who was calling.

Talanov identified himself as a friend.

"One moment," Granny said, patching the call through to CIA Chief of Station, Bill Wilcox, who was having his morning coffee two miles away. When Wilcox answered, Granny told him an incoming call to their unlisted number had been made from a public phone box in Marseille. When Wilcox asked who it was, Granny said the caller had identified himself simply as a friend.

"Is the recorder on?" asked Wilcox.

"As we speak," Granny replied.

Wilcox punched a button. "This is La Tâche," he said.

Talanov started to mention Irene but didn't. If Irene was a coded reference to Gorev's defection or the Marbella safe house, then his use of the name could be traced specifically back to him through Agent Pilgrim. He liked Pilgrim and felt he could trust her, but until he knew for certain where this was all going, he was not about to reveal anything that could be linked back to him.

He said, "You have a Collection Management Officer there in your embassy named Carl Ryan. Harvard graduate, five-nine, curly brown hair. He has a blonde wife named Monica who loves using his credit cards. The couple has a daughter on drugs at Harvard. That's a quick summary and here's something extra: Carl's a Soviet agent. I know because I recruited him. Feel free to handle Carl the way we've been handling your agents for years: feed him just what you want him to report."

"I'm afraid you've got the wrong number."

"If this is La Tâche, then I've got the right number. Look into my story about the daughter on drugs. She's in a rehabilitation facility in upstate New York. It's the reason Carl needs cash. So far, we've paid him forty-five thousand dollars, with our next brown-bag drop happening next Tuesday morning, 7:45, in that little café near the embassy. Carl enjoys a nice Banbury cake to go with his morning espresso. Like I said, look into it. One final point: I'm phoning because I want to help eradicate a disease. It's the same disease you've been fighting since the end of World War II and I am sick of being part of that problem. So from now on, with or without you, I'm committed to being part of the solution. I'll phone you one more time, on Wednesday, to see if I've still got the wrong number."

"No need. You've got my attention."

"Look into my story, La Tâche. Because I want more than just your attention."

"Meaning what, exactly?"

"I'll let you know on Wednesday."

"Do you by chance know Irene?" asked Wilcox. Donna Pilgrim had phoned to tell him about a Soviet KGB colonel named Aleksandr Talanov, who may be calling. If this was Talanov, he could become a major asset.

"Am I supposed to?" asked Talanov in return.

"Not really. Just asking."

"Then I'll speak to you again on Wednesday."

"Who is this? What's your name?"

Talanov thought briefly about what had brought him to this point. Or, more specifically, who. Like the girl whose name he never knew so many years ago, Noya had changed his life. He was not able to save her but she had saved him.

And he would forever be in her debt.

"Are you still there?" Wilcox asked.

Talanov refocused. "I'm here."

"Your name?"

"November Echo," he said. "Call me November Echo."

CHAPTER 36

Winter in Moscow can be magical, especially when it is snowing and tonight it was snowing heavily. The flakes were large and blew silently from left to right as Talanov walked along the quiet street in a full length woolen coat, his shoulders bent against the wind, his hands in his pockets, his boots squeaking on the fresh powder. On his head was a sable Ushanka and his breath came out in steamy puffs.

He had spent the day doing paperwork alone in his cramped little office until long after most of the Lubyanka building was empty. It was the festive season in the lead up to New Years Eve and most people had left work early. By six o'clock it was completely dark outside, and by eight his stomach was growling.

In a restaurant a few blocks away Talanov was given his usual table: a round corner booth. He normally ordered something different each visit -- an old habit to mix up his routine -- but tonight he ordered what he had ordered last night -- soup -- which was thick with onions, leaks, potatoes, peas, carrots and large chunks of ham. As always, it was served free of charge and with extra slices of dense homemade brown bread and butter. Anything to honor the esteemed hero.

Talanov was regarded as a local hero around Moscow because official news reports said a Chinese agent named Xin Li had infiltrated the KGB and been caught in Spain attempting to sell state secrets. American agents were also involved and Talanov had been credited with stopping them.

Sitting alone in the booth eating his soup, Talanov was interrupted by a group of Muscovites stopping by to wish him *S Novym Godom . . . s novym schast'yem!* -- To the New Year . . . to the new happiness.

Talanov smiled and returned the greeting.

After the group had departed, he looked across the busy restaurant to the New Year Tree, a broad fir tree cut from the forest, which had been decorated with ornaments and tinsel and colored lights. Between him and the tree were more than twenty tables filled with families and groups of young people. There was laughter, the clinking of glasses and animated conversation. The sight of them made Talanov frown, not because he was against people enjoying themselves, but because Noya should be alive enjoying it, too. She should be singing Christmas carols and eating turkey and tearing open presents with her friends.

So the smiles he gave people stopping by his table were not genuine, not that anyone cared. For one thing, people did not stick around long enough to notice it was a façade. And he knew the reason. In spite of his popularity, he was still KGB.

In the wake of Noya's death -- which was over six months ago -- he'd become even more cynical and bitter toward the KGB and what it represented. And it took everything within him not to let his feelings be known.

But he hadn't, and during these months, working undercover as November Echo, he had supplied La Tâche with the names of numerous Soviet moles operating within the United States government and related private sectors. He also supplied him with information on Soviet weapons programs and ongoing intelligence operations. He remembered La Tâche asking him once how he could betray his country. He replied that he wasn't betraying his country, only the disease infecting it.

"People should not have to live in fear of their government," Talanov said. "That's why I'm doing what I'm doing.

This isn't about Russia. This isn't about America. It's about the Noyas of the world. And don't for a second think I won't hold you every bit as accountable as I hold myself and those I'm taking down. Does this answer your question?"

Talanov remembered how loud the silence was on the phone.

"Then we understand one another," Talanov said, hanging up.

Talanov's reverie was broken when a noticeable hush fell over the restaurant. Looking up, he saw everyone staring at the powerful man filling the doorway of the restaurant. Dressed in a thick black parka and Ushanka, Zak glared around the room and watched everyone avert their eyes. He then made his way across the floor.

"You really enjoy that, don't you?" said Talanov when Zak approached, "scowling at everybody as if one of them were about to become your dinner."

With a grin, Zak flagged down the waiter and ordered a big bowl of beef Estouffade, which would arrive as fist-sized chunks of casseroled beef in a coating of thick gravy.

"This came for you," he said, taking a postcard from his pocket and sliding it in front of Talanov. "It was laying on your desk when I came up to see if you wanted to join me for dinner. When I didn't find you, I guessed you'd be here."

Talanov looked at the card. It had been addressed in Cyrillic to Colonel Aleksandr Talanov. No address. No postage. Just Talanov's name, a simple message and a signature, "Love, Irene."

With a forkful of food poised near his mouth, Talanov stared at the name.

Irene.

Donna Pilgrim.

"He then read what Pilgrim had written. *Remembering our song. Are you going to Scarborough Fair? Parsley, sage, Melissa and thyme.*

"We don't get a lot of American music but even we got this one," said Zak. In his deep, gruff voice, he sang the familiar Simon and Garfunkel stanza: "Parsley, sage, rosemary and thyme." He paused. "Odd that Irene would make such a mistake, substituting Melissa for rosemary."

Talanov still had the forkful of food poised near his mouth while he listened.

Zak continued, "We had studied those medicinal herbs years ago, so I looked through your library and found your copy of the botanical book we were given in survival training. And guess what I read on the way over." He opened the book to the page he had dog-eared and slid it in front of Talanov. Shown beneath the heading was a photo of a plant that looked like mint. Below the photo was the following description: *Known widely as lemon balm,* Melissa officinalis *is a spasmolytic herb possessing powerful anti-bacterial/antiviral properties that fight infection and reduce inflammation and fever. Administer with twelve or more drops of thyme* (thymus vulgaris CT thymol).

Talanov stared in shock at what he had just read.

Zak said, "Melissa wasn't the name of a woman, but the name of an herb."

"And because Gorev was talking to an American student," said Talanov, "he used the English word, Melissa, so that the student would understand him. Otherwise, he would have used one of our Russian terms, *Medovka* or *Limonnaya myata.*" He read again from the book. "Administer with twelve or more drops of thyme." He looked at Zak, who smiled and nodded.

Zak said, "Gorev wasn't telling the student to find Melissa *in time,* but to mix lemon balm -- Melissa -- *in thyme.*"

Talanov sank back and closed his eyes. He knew herbs. Had learned about them in survival training. Yes, he had remembered enough to give Noya the lemon balm, which did indeed stop her coughing, but he just hadn't connected lemon balm with Melissa. Didn't know they were one and the same. If only he had given her more. Even without the thyme, the lemon balm -- the Melissa -- would have kept her alive until the doctors could take over. *He had been so close.* If only ---

His thoughts were interrupted by Zak's hand on his arm. Opening his eyes, he saw Zak nod toward the card.

"Turn it over," Zak said.

Talanov stared at him for a moment then flipped over the postcard. Pictured on the front was a sleek white twin-turboshaft S-76A Sikorsky helicopter with two wide vertical red stripes painted across the fuselage.

Greetings from the Sikorsky Aircraft Corporation, the printed message said. Beneath it was a handwritten message in cursive.

For my hero. Aim for the sky.

With his mouth hanging open in utter astonishment, Talanov looked over at Zak.

Zak removed a bottle vodka from his coat pocket and placed it on the table. "To Melissa," he said, unscrewing the cap.

He offered the bottle to Talanov.

And both men broke into huge smiles.

END NOTE

First Deputy Director Kanatzhan Alibekov -- now Ken Alibek -- was the first *Biopreparat* defector to successfully reach the West. He did so in 1992. Since then, he has testified numerous times before Congress and given comprehensive accounts of the former Soviet Union's biological weapons program, including the Sverdlovsk anthrax leak. He is the author of many articles and books, one of which being his landmark volume (co-written with Steven Handelmann), *Biohazard: The Chilling True Story of the Largest Covert Biological Weapons Program in the World - Told from Inside by the Man Who Ran It.*